"Luke Schrock has arrived at Windmill Farms because he has nowhere else to go. He's dispirited, broke, but not quite ready to give up. And yet he couldn't be more ill-prepared for the girl he finds at this Amish farm. A funny, heartwarming story of friendship, love, and the possibility of happily ever after."

Amy Clipston, bestselling author
of *Seat by the Hearth*

"There's just something unique and fresh about every Suzanne Woods Fisher book. Maybe it's the characters that are both flawed and endearing. Maybe it's the unexpected bursts of humor that make me smile just as I start to tear up. Whatever the reason, I'm a fan. *Mending Fences* features Luke Schrock, an Amish hero like no other. It's a wonderful contemporary Amish romance full of hope, love, and fresh starts. It's also, well, it's also just a really good book."

Shelley Shepard Gray, *New York Times*
and *USA Today* bestselling author

"Suzanne Woods Fisher has written a sweet and poignant story you won't want to put down. As the title suggests, *Mending Fences* is a journey of healing and redemption, a reminder of God's grace and mercy. Definitely a must-read!"

Kathleen Fuller, bestselling author
of the Amish of Birch Creek series

D0171194

Books by Suzanne Woods Fisher

Amish Peace: Simple Wisdom for a Complicated World
Amish Values for Your Family: What We Can Learn from the Simple Life
The Heart of the Amish

LANCASTER COUNTY SECRETS

The Choice
The Waiting
The Search

SEASONS OF STONEY RIDGE

The Keeper
The Haven
The Lesson

THE INN AT EAGLE HILL

The Letters
The Calling
The Revealing

THE BISHOP'S FAMILY

The Imposter
The Quieting
The Devoted

AMISH BEGINNINGS

Anna's Crossing
The Newcomer
The Return

NANTUCKET LEGACY

Phoebe's Light
Minding the Light
The Light Before Day

THE DEACON'S FAMILY

Mending Fences

MENDING FENCES

SUZANNE WOODS FISHER

Revell

a division of Baker Publishing Group
Grand Rapids, Michigan

© 2019 by Suzanne Woods Fisher

Published by Revell
a division of Baker Publishing Group
PO Box 6287, Grand Rapids, MI 49516-6287
www.revellbooks.com

Printed in the United States of America

Library of Congress Cataloging-in-Publication Data
Names: Fisher, Suzanne Woods, author.
Title: Mending fences / Suzanne Woods Fisher.
Description: Grand Rapids, MI : Revell, a division of Baker Publishing Group,
    [2019] | Series: The deacon's family ; 1
Identifiers: LCCN 2018028204 | ISBN 9780800727512 (paper : alk. paper)
Subjects: LCSH: Domestic fiction. | GSAFD: Christian fiction.
Classification: LCC PS3606.I78 M46 2019 | DDC 813/.6—dc23
LC record available at https://lccn.loc.gov/2018028204

Published in association with Joyce Hart of the Hartline Literary Agency, LLC

19 20 21 22 23 24 25   7 6 5 4 3 2 1

Cast of Characters

Luke Schrock—recently returned to Stoney Ridge after a stint in rehab (or two. Or three). Originally introduced in The Inn at Eagle Hill series. His story continued in The Bishop's Family series.

Amos Lapp—deacon of Stoney Ridge, husband to Fern, owns Windmill Farm. Originally introduced in the Stoney Ridge Seasons series.

Fern Lapp—wife of Amos Lapp. Originally introduced in the Stoney Ridge Seasons series.

David Stoltzfus—bishop of Stoney Ridge. Originally introduced in *The Revealing*, book 3 of The Inn at Eagle Hill series. Main character in The Bishop's Family series.

Isabella "Izzy" Miller—new to Stoney Ridge. Boarding at Windmill Farm.

Hank Lapp—uncle of Amos Lapp. Originally introduced in the Stoney Ridge Seasons series.

Jesse Stoltzfus—son of David Stoltzfus. Introduced in *The Revealing*, book 3 of The Inn at Eagle Hill series. His story continued throughout The Bishop's Family series.

Jenny Yoder—girlfriend of Jesse Stoltzfus. Introduced in *The Lesson*, book 3 of the Stoney Ridge Seasons series.

Alice Smucker—victim of Luke's mischief, which triggered agoraphobia and ophidiophobia. Introduced in *The Haven* and *The Lesson*, books 2 and 3 of the Stoney Ridge Seasons series.

Teddy Zook—Amish carpenter.

Ruthie Stoltzfus—daughter of David Stoltzfus. Former girlfriend of Luke Schrock. Main character in *The Devoted*, book 3 of The Bishop's Family series.

Patrick Kelly—convert to the Amish. Love interest of Ruthie Stoltzfus. Main character in *The Devoted*, book 3 of The Bishop's Family series.

*O*NE

A year had passed since Luke Schrock's exile from
Stoney Ridge began. A very long year. He'd been
in and out of rehab twice. Wait. Hold on. Make
that three times. He'd forgotten the three-day holiday weekend he'd checked himself out and went on a bender.

The bus swerved and bumped on the country roads, stirring his stomach and ratcheting up his anxiety. The bus was
stuffy and hot; it made him long for fresh air and cold, all
at once. He was on his way back home.

Home. Luke had a feeling he couldn't name exactly, but
one he'd never had in relation to home before. It used to
mean security, belonging, unconditional acceptance. What
he felt now contained that, all that, but to today was added
a hint of desperation.

This was a bad idea. A terrible idea. He'd never intended
to return to Stoney Ridge. The counselor had strongly rec-
ommended that Luke find sober, supportive living arrange-
ments. What could be more sober than an Amish farm? he
asked Luke.

Uh, well, that depends. Luke had been living among the Amish as he developed a dependency on alcohol.

But then David Stoltzfus, his bishop, agreed with the counselor. He had told him to stop running away from his problems, that coming home again was the only road to manhood.

He recognized the fork in the road that would lead the bus straight into Stoney Ridge. Pulling the cord to hop off the bus seemed like a very appealing option. He could head right toward Lancaster, rather than left to Stoney Ridge. He could do it. He should do it.

But he didn't. The bus zoomed left.

David had promised he'd be waiting at the bus stop. Luke held out a sliver of hope that his mother might be there too, and maybe his younger brother Sammy. There was no chance that Galen King, his mother's husband, would be there. No chance. Not after what had happened to Galen's prized horse. Nope. No chance.

When Luke had asked David what he would do with himself once he was back in town, the bishop was vague. "One thing at a time, Luke. Let's get you home first."

Luke had wanted to ask him if home meant the Inn at Eagle Hill, where his mother and brother and stepfather lived, or if he was using "home" as a metaphor. But something inside held him back from asking, partly because he had a feeling David didn't know the answer.

David Stoltzfus had gone above and beyond the call of duty for Luke this last year. He'd come to visit him regularly, even when Luke told him not to bother. But David did bother, over and over again. He brought books to read, for he knew Luke loved to read. He read them too, and then they would discuss them. Conversation grew easier between them. Those visits, they meant a lot to Luke, and he hoped David had some idea how much. The reason David had never given up on Luke was, he said, because God never gave up on people.

The bus hit a pothole and jolted Luke against the window. He recognized the passing farm as Windmill Farm, belonging to Amos and Fern Lapp, and took note of the new mailbox. Not so long ago, he'd put a cherry bomb in their old one and blown it to smithereens.

Why had he done that? It was a circling discussion in group therapy—what were triggers that caused destructive behavior? The counselor encouraged everyone to identify those triggers, so they'd know to recognize them. And then, to redirect thoughts and feelings and behaviors toward something beneficial.

Luke had tried to identify his triggers, tried and failed. Why had he hurt people, like the Lapps, who had been so good to him? He couldn't find an answer.

For a short while, before blowing up the Lapps' mailbox, he'd even apprenticed for Jesse Stoltzfus's buggy shop at Windmill Farm. Like so many opportunities Luke had been given, it hadn't gone well. The counselor suggested that if anyone got too close to Luke, he would do something to push them away. Translation: self-sabotage. If anything went too well, he would find a way to ruin it. He saw that in himself. What he didn't know was *why*.

That was another reason the counselor had consistently encouraged Luke to return to Stoney Ridge. "Find out *why*," he'd told Luke. "You'll never move forward until you find out why."

"Moving forward." Translation for counseling code: *after-care*. Luke had grown savvy to counselor code. The first time he was released from rehab, he was adamant that he would not return to Stoney Ridge. Moving forward, he was convinced, meant moving on. Make a fresh start.

He tried. He failed. Back he went to rehab.

This time, rehab lasted a little longer. Instead of sixty days, it was ninety days. "Better chance for long-term success," the counselor said. Not so for Luke. As soon as he was released, he went on that three-day bender. David bailed him out of jail and took him back to the clinic. This time, it lasted more than six months. Now *that* should give him a much, much better chance not to relapse. Added to that was the warning from David that this was the last rescue. If he relapsed, if he ended up in jail, he'd stay there. Three strikes was the limit, even for David, the most tolerant man in the world.

Luke had to agree with the counselor on one thing: he didn't seem to be able to move forward. "Why not go back and face your past?" the counselor said. "What do you have to lose?"

Nothing. Absolutely nothing. Absolutely no one. Grudgingly, Luke agreed to return to Stoney Ridge. It was one thing to say no to your counselor, but nearly impossible to say no to your bishop, especially one like David.

After making that decision, he'd had the first good night's sleep in . . . well, maybe in the entire last year. But that didn't mean he wasn't anxious about his homecoming. He was. These Amish, they had long, long memories.

At the turnoff to Windmill Farm, he noticed a woman standing behind a beat-up farm stand. Amos had fine orchards, old trees that had been lovingly tended. Luke remembered that very farm stand, topped with baskets of tree ripened fruit, jugs of cider, and an honest jar. He also thought of how often he used to dip into that jar when he was low on cash.

Ouch. Another stinging memory.

David called those stinging memories one of the greatest gifts given by the Holy Spirit. Convicting memories, David called them. Conviction was meant to turn us to confession. And confession brought us back to God.

Luke doubted David ever had much of anything to confess. If he did, he would know the sick feeling that came along with the stinging memories. The disgust and self-loathing.

The bus jolted again. He squinted, wondering if Fern Lapp was the woman at the farm stand, but quickly dismissed that thought. Fern was thin, wiry—small but mighty. A force to be reckoned with.

This woman looked young. She was tall and held herself erect, like a queen. She wore a Plain lavender dress with a black apron. A blue kerchief kept the hair out of her eyes. Luke leaned closer to the window to peer at the woman as the bus passed by. Who was she? Just then, she looked up and waved at the passing bus, and Luke felt a shock run through him. *Izzy Miller.* She'd been a patient at the rehab center during his first attempt to get clean and sober. He'd been in a group session with her once or twice. She hadn't talked much, but he did notice her. Oh yeah, he noticed her all right. She wasn't the sort of person you'd easily forget. He remembered thinking she was the prettiest girl he'd ever seen. High, wide cheekbones; snapping dark brown eyes; luxurious brunette hair. He also remembered her as being frustratingly aloof; he had tried, without success, to get her attention a few times. Why in the world was she at Windmill Farm, of all places? And why was she dressed Plain?

Well, well. Luke's grim spirits lifted considerably. Stoney Ridge was looking better already.

Izzy Miller rearranged the freshly picked red cherries in the bowl so they'd look irresistible, which they were. Plump to the touch, bright red in color, juicy in taste. Too luscious, she thought, to end up in jam or pies. Not these cherries. They were meant to be eaten the way nature intended. Freshly picked, still warmed from the sun, bursting with juice.

She took pride in how her displays looked, improving their appearance from Fern's practical, no-nonsense style. Even the weathered old farm stand was small and rickety, easy to overlook. She couldn't do anything about its condition, but she could definitely present Amos's orchard fruits in an eye-catching way.

Amos harvested bushels of fruit from his orchards—old trees that produced bumper crops of delicious fruits. Wie der aum, so die Frucht, he had taught her. *Such as the tree is, such is the fruit.* He treasured his old varieties. Heirlooms or antiquities, they were now considered. Amos said they were just the varieties his wise grandfather knew to grow.

The season started with early flowering cherries in late May and early June, peaches and plums in July, pears in August, and ended with apples in the fall. Fern had a huge garden—bigger than most anyone's backyard, at least the yards Izzy'd seen—and harvested a wide variety of vegetables and flowers. Thanks to her greenhouse, Fern was the first in

Stoney Ridge to bring a vine-ripened tomato to the dinner table. Amos said that Fern didn't just have a green thumb, she could grow anything out of nothing.

Growing fruits and vegetables, even flowers, was Amos and Fern's expertise. Izzy was the one who'd arranged the displays with an artistic flair, so much so that they drew attention and became a feast to the eyes as well as the stomach. Like the bus driver who just passed by—he used to zoom past the farm stand without any acknowledgment. Last year, Izzy had set up bouquets of flowers in galvanized buckets, and the driver stopped the bus and jumped out. It was his wife's birthday, he told Izzy, and he hadn't remembered until he saw those bright, bold peonies in the buckets. His wife's favorite flower. Last year, he'd forgotten her birthday and he didn't want to face her wrath again, so he bought two bundles. One for this year and one to make up for last year. He thanked Izzy profusely and told her she might have saved his marriage.

Since then, that bus driver would stop the bus to let everyone out to buy produce. He must have told others too, because Amos and Fern's farm stand had been included on the route of summertime tourist buses swirling through Amish country from Lancaster. By last October, as they were closing up for the year, Amos announced that Izzy had quadrupled the profits from the farm stand. Four times! Fern joked they could soon retire and let Izzy manage the farm.

It was astounding to Izzy. It really was. She'd never been told she had any natural talent, had never thought she could be good at anything. She knew Fern was just teasing, but her words sparked a deep yearning in her, struck a chord in her heart. What Izzy hoped Fern had meant was that she could remain on indefinitely at Windmill Farm. *Ein Platz am Tisch.*

It was a Plain expression that meant a person had a place at the table. That they had a family they belonged to. Izzy loved repeating the phrase to herself, trying hard as she was to master the Penn Dutch language. For the first time in her life, she was wanted. First time.

Look at me, she thought. *I'm living the life I've wanted for as long as I can remember.* She had a roof over her head, she had a true friend—Jenny Yoder—and she had Amos and Fern Lapp. She had everything she'd ever dreamed for. Almost everything. There was still one more piece of her dream—to find her mother. To bring her to Windmill Farm.

The counselor at the rehab clinic had warned her about holding on to such a dream. "I'm all for tying up loose ends," he said, "but I'm worried you're setting yourself up for disappointment. You can't control other people, Izzy. You can only control yourself. A dream like that—it's closer to a miracle."

But, oh my soul, "miracles do happen," Izzy had told her counselor. "Just look at me."

As promised, David Stoltzfus was waiting for Luke at the bus stop on Main Street in the heart of Stoney Ridge. He thrust his hand out to shake Luke's and clasped him warmly on the shoulder. "Welcome home," he said, and Luke felt tears sting his eyes. No one else was here but David. No mother, no brother. And yet . . . David was here.

Luke followed him to the buggy, tossed his backpack in, and climbed up. David handed him the reins, but he shook his head. "I'm a little rusty." There was truth to that, but more important, he felt disoriented, as if he'd never been in a buggy before.

David slapped the reins and clucked to the horse to set it trotting; it lurched forward before settling into a steady walk. "Luke, there's been a few changes in Stoney Ridge."

"Like what?"

"Well, for one, Amos Lapp is now the deacon. Abraham moved to Florida to be with his daughter."

"And the ministers? Have they changed?"

"Just one. Gideon Smucker."

"Sadie's husband?" Luke squinted. "I always thought he was afraid of his own shadow."

David glanced at Luke. "He's a fine minister. Wise and humble." He handed Luke a sealed envelope.

It was from Luke's mother, Rose. He made no effort to open it. "Let me guess. She wishes she could've been here today, she really, really does. But Galen isn't quite ready to welcome me home."

"Maybe you should just read it."

Luke sighed and broke the seal.

Dearest Luke,

I'm sorry, so very sorry, that I'm not in Stoney Ridge to welcome you home. I'll let David explain our circumstances. Please believe me when I say that the timing of this opportunity had nothing to do with your homecoming. I am so proud of you, Luke. You've fought a great battle, as I knew you could. And I believe that a bright and wonderful future is ahead for you.

Love,
Mom

Luke wasn't surprised. He looked up. "So what are these oh-so-special and ill-timed circumstances?"

"Galen was needed in Kentucky. His cousin breeds Thoroughbred horses down there and had some kind of accident. Broke his leg in two places, needed surgery and pins." David shuddered. "Anyway, he asked Galen to help him get through the next few months. Busy months for horse breeding. Galen's stable was empty—he hadn't purchased any horses to train for the summer, so he said yes to his cousin. It's just short-term. They left ten days ago."

Luke ran through the scenario in his mind. He knew of that particular cousin. Each spring, Galen would travel to Kentucky to buy two-year-old Thoroughbreds, retired right from the races, to train them for buggy work. He always stayed with that cousin of his. They loved horses more than people, Luke always thought. "She didn't even say goodbye." He cringed. Had he said that out loud?

"Your mother wanted to. She did. But your counselor advised against it."

Luke snorted. "Because I might decide not to return to Stoney Ridge, had I known?"

"Because you need to make your own decisions, based on what's best for you. Your mother wants you to come visit in Kentucky, as soon as you're ready."

Ready. What did that mean?

As they reached the turnoff to the Inn at Eagle Hill, David drove the buggy right on by. "Uh, David, I'd like to go home."

"Well, that's another one of the changes. The Inn is being run by someone else."

"Who?"

"Ruthie." He glanced at Luke. "Patrick's helping her."

18

Ah, the second blow to Luke's gut. Ruthie, David's daughter, had been Luke's childhood sweetheart, the one person who understood him, whom he counted on, up until that messy time when everything fell apart. Ruthie met Patrick and Luke ended up in rehab.

"So where are you taking me?"

"Windmill Farm."

Luke let out an indignant huff. "Oh, David, come on. Your own son used to call it Fern's Home for Wayward Boys. I think I've gotten past that stage."

"Amos needs help with his orchards this summer, and . . ."

"And *what*?" What was it that David didn't want to say? That Amos was a kind man, and probably the only one who would be willing to host Luke.

"Amos is willing to provide room and board for you, in exchange for working his orchards." The horse had slowed to a crawl, so David flicked the reins to urge it back into a trot. "Birdy and I would have welcomed you into our home, but there's not an inch of space to be spared, not with the babies. And there's no work to be done. I'm no farmer."

"I could work at Bent N' Dent. I could sleep in the back room. I could stock shelves. Make deliveries."

David was quiet for so long that Luke wondered what was running through his mind. Probably . . . that Luke might be bad for business. But then David surprised him. "Let's try this first. If it doesn't work out, then you can work at the store. But I think you might enjoy working for Amos. He's a wealth of knowledge about farming. About all kinds of things. And he truly needs help this summer."

Luke was silent for the rest of the trip, eyes fixed on the rhythmic clip-clops of the horse's shoes on the pavement.

So, all these changes told him a great deal. His family had left town, he wasn't trusted to run the Inn, or to work at the store, and no one in Stoney Ridge seemed to want him here. Why had he even come home at all? He had no home, no one to welcome him back. Where did that leave him? Without his old life and not quite coming up with a new one. In between, floating, nowhere.

He still couldn't answer why he'd come back to Stoney Ridge, even when the counselor had tried to get him to put feelings into words. For some inexplicable reason, Luke knew that David was right. The only path to manhood was to be here, to face his past and make amends. After that, he could leave.

He would leave.

Two

Amos Lapp tried not to let a smile slip out when he informed Luke Schrock that he'd be sleeping out in the barn. Luke looked stunned, and for a brief second, his mask dropped to reveal the face of a disappointed boy. Just as quickly, it disappeared, and the mask returned. That bright blaze of resentment.

"I thought Jesse moved the buggy shop to the back of the Bent N' Dent."

"Yup, that's right. So?"

"When David told me I'd be staying at Windmill Farm, I thought he meant I'd be living in that little room off the buggy shop. It's not so bad at all."

"Not so bad at all. But I'm using it to store equipment. So for now, the only available place for you is the tack room."

"But, Amos . . . a barn?"

Amos lifted a hand to end the conversation. "Don't look so woebegone. Fern's fixed it up real nice."

Head hung low, Luke followed him out to the barn. Amos didn't think the tack room was such a bad place to be, not after Fern had worked her magic. There was a cot made

21

up with clean cotton sheets, a goose-down pillow—Amos's favorite—a flashlight, and a pitcher of fresh water to wash up. Luke would bathe and take his meals in the house, along with the family.

Such a small family it was now. There was only Amos, Fern, and Izzy. And Izzy Miller was another reason Luke Schrock needed to be staying far away in the barn. Amos had raised three daughters, and he understood the way a boy's mind worked. He was taking no chances. He felt a responsibility to Izzy. She was another stray David had brought to them, and it had taken a long time for her to settle in and trust them. When David asked him to consider taking Luke in, Amos's first reaction was a sound *no!* "I don't want Luke setting Izzy back. You know how careless he's been with girls."

"I do know," David had said. His Ruthie was one of those girls.

Fern kept insisting that they agree to offer Luke a place to live, a chance to start again. "Who are we to say someone is beyond saving?" On top of that poignant remark, she had a healthy respect for the bishop. To his wife's way of thinking, one didn't say no to a bishop. Amos had no trouble saying no to David, nor to any bishop. He'd had good bishops and not-so-good bishops, and he knew they were just ordinary men, trying to do the best they could. When a church felt they couldn't say no to a bishop, it had become an unhealthy church.

Now that Amos was a deacon and privy to much, he believed that truth all the more. But Stoney Ridge was a healthy church, and David was a fine leader. Fern was probably right. Who was he to say the boy was beyond saving?

He corrected his thinking. Luke was no longer a boy. He must be twenty by now, maybe twenty-one. He'd always been a tough one for Rose to manage on her own. Amos had never known Dean Schrock, Rose's husband, for he'd died before they moved to the Inn at Eagle Hill. But even Fern admitted that Luke must take after his father. She'd always said Luke was more good-looking than any fellow should be, and Dean Schrock was supposed to have been a looker too. Doors opened too easily, Fern thought, when a person was assessed on God-given good looks and not on character earned. It was a danger, not a gift, she believed, to be unusually attractive. A person didn't develop substance and resources to help them in life. Like a hothouse plant that couldn't survive in the outdoors.

She was probably right. Fern was usually right.

Whatever it was that made Luke Schrock such a reckless boy, it had turned him into a holy terror by his late teens. Amos had to credit David Stoltzfus for not giving up on the boy. He knew why David sent him their way—no one else would have him! Who had forgotten the mischief that boy caused? The blown-up mailboxes, Patrick's dead mynah bird, the road games of chicken. And there were plenty of other stunts he'd pulled on unsuspecting people.

As he closed the barn door and headed back up to the house, he thought that if he were a betting man, which he wasn't, but if he *were* . . . he figured Luke wouldn't last a week.

Luke flopped on the squeaky cot and looked up at the barn rafters. *A barn. I am living in a barn.* How low can a man go? Living among stinking cows and horses and mice and barn swallows. Sleeping in a tack room, along with blankets and bridles and reins, and shelves stacked with spare horseshoes and jars of liniment. There wasn't even a proper ceiling to this cubby. Thick hand-hewn beams crossed above his head. Sunlight streamed through loose shingles on the steeply pitched roof.

He lifted his head off the pillow. Why, there wasn't even a door to the tack room. No door. No privacy. This was *ridiculous*. There had to be a better option than sleeping in a barn.

He'd tried to press Amos to let him stay in the house, or better still, the empty buggy shop, but there was no uncertainty in his answer, no question or lingering pause. The only place for Luke on Windmill Farm was the barn. A *barn*. He thought of how often he'd gathered with friends in somebody's barn to drink and dance and generally disturb the peace.

His glance shifted to the hooks on the wall. There hung clothing for a Plain man, straw hat included. He sighed, thinking of Amos's parting words to him. *"Don't forget. Church is tomorrow."*

Luke squeezed his eyes shut. *Church*. It wasn't that he didn't want to go. He'd always liked church, especially when David preached. Seeing his friends prior to church was fun, the fellowship meal at the end tasted especially good after sitting for three hours on a hard bench.

Would there be any friends left for him tomorrow? Would anyone be glad he'd come? He wondered.

He opened his eyes and looked at the clothes hanging on the hook. He pulled off his T-shirt and took the blue shirt off the hook. He caught a whiff of it and buried his face in the fabric, just for a moment, soaking up the clean smell of sunshine. That scent of clothes dried on a line, how he'd forgotten that sweet smell and all it represented. Someone cared.

He heard a woman's soft voice, singing to herself, and peered out the window. Coming up the field was Izzy Miller, shivvying some stray lambs to join the ewes at the top of the hill. Luke tucked his new blue shirt into his pants, grabbed his flat-brimmed straw hat, and ran out the door.

Fern had told Izzy that a new farmhand was arriving today to help Amos with the harvest, and that he'd be living in the barn's workroom. But she neglected to mention that he had come straight from Mountain Vista Rehabilitation Clinic in Lancaster.

What was his name again? She couldn't remember. He ran over to greet her like they were long-lost friends, then seemed shocked—absolutely floored—that she had no memory of him. But she had none. None whatsoever.

She had just stooped over to rub noses with a black-faced lamb when she heard him call out her name. She straightened up and gave a curt response to his enthusiastic greeting, effectively ending the conversation as she squared her shoulders and continued moving the woollies up the hill. She loved this time of year, when the grass turned emerald green and the air turned warm and when she woke in the morning, there'd be another lamb or two born in the night, already part of the flock. Like magic.

Izzy smiled as a mother ewe nudged her lamb to get it moving up the hill and, startled, it jumped in the air, butting another lamb. Both bleated loudly and unhappily, spooking the whole flock. It had taken months for her to grow accustomed to the skittish tendencies of sheep. At first, she kept thinking she was doing something wrong. After a while, she decided that sheep lived in perpetual panic. In a strange way, she got it. She got them, their panic. They reminded her of herself—she just kept her perpetual panic hidden a little better.

Take that new farmhand. When he introduced himself to her, she felt a shiver of precognition, as if something was going to happen, as if he was going to *cause* something to happen—and it made her hackles rise. She could tell from the way his eyes lit up that he thought she was worth his attention, and she knew enough of his type—too handsome for his own good, *that* type—to know he considered himself something special. Izzy had more on her mind than dallying with a guy fresh out of rehab.

When she reached the top of the hill, she turned around to see the farmhand weaving his way through a clump of woollies. The sheep lifted their heads to stare curiously at him, though he didn't seem to notice. She watched him hop over the fence and head toward the barn. The bottom of the barn had low brick walls, as high as a man's shoulder. She hadn't noticed before, not until she saw the farmhand walking beside it.

Below the big red barn was a fast-running stream bordered by cattails. She could see redwing blackbirds fly in and land near the stream, then swoop away again. Fern had taught her the names of the birds that frequented Windmill Farm. So many varieties! All colors and shapes and sizes. And just when she thought she knew them all, they'd fly north or south, depending on the time of year, and another new one would appear at the feeders. She could identify some of them, but not all. Not yet.

A breeze came up, blowing soft and sweet against her face, ruffling her capstrings. Summer. It was coming. With it, endless chores. The garden needed constant tending, berries needed to be picked, fruits and vegetables canned. She lifted her eyes to gaze around the farm, at the snug house that sat at the top of the hill, at the squeaky red windmill, at the trees in the orchards behind the house that were starting to bloom. All in stages, all in their proper order of time, and Izzy felt intoxicated by her sense of longing. This. All this. A home, a family. She wanted *this*.

The Rhode Island Red hens moved away from Luke as he crossed the yard and closer to one another, clucking nervously, looking behind them to make sure he was not following.

It made him unhappy to see those hens scurry away from him. It reminded him of how he had felt at church this morning, how the women—and a lot of men—had treated him. Why were hens let loose in a yard, anyway? Especially on a morning when church was being hosted. They were a nuisance, noisy and messy.

David had told Luke that he would need to make a public confession to the church, to make things right between him and other church members, between him and God. Luke had expected to sit on the sinner's bench. It wasn't a new spot for him. He'd sat there plenty of times, bent at the knee to express sorrow for veering off the straight and narrow path.

This time, it was a little different. First off, he felt some genuine sorrow. That was new.

And the response of others was different. Normally, all is forgiven and forgotten after confession. Not so today.

Luke was prepared for people to look him up and down at church. As he bent down on the sinner's bench, he felt all eyes—blue eyes, brown eyes, green eyes, scolding eyes, frowning and mocking eyes—were on him. What he hadn't expected was such a cold shoulder from . . . nearly everyone. All but Birdy and David, and one curly haired boy who followed him everywhere from a safe distance.

Edith Lapp wondered if he'd stolen any cars lately. Jesse Stoltzfus asked if he'd improved his pickpocketing skills. Big Teddy Zook, whom he had considered a friend of sorts, wouldn't even shake his hand. Strange, that.

But Hank Lapp might have been the worst of all. A tall man with a bushy white beard and wild white hair and eyes as bright as a hawk's, he spoke in a shout. "WELL, WELL, WELL. SKIN ME FOR A POLECAT IF IT ISN'T LUKE SCHROCK," he said. It was his regular talking voice. "BATTEN DOWN THE HATCHES, FOLKS. LOCK YOUR VALUABLES. KEEP YOUR LITTLE ONES INSIDE. THE GUNSLINGER'S BACK IN STONEY RIDGE."

Luke sighed. His reputation had grown bigger than the truth.

Naturally, everyone heard Hank. Children darted behind their mother's skirt and around their father's legs as if he were packing sidearms. A group of boys hid behind the bench wagon, peeking out to get a look at him as if he'd suddenly grown two heads. That was when he decided to cross the yard and sit by himself in the shade of the henhouse.

"Psst. Do you really carry a pistol in your boot?"

Luke turned around to see the curly haired boy staring at his boots. Behind him were three more boys. "Where'd you hear that?"

"Him." The boy pointed to Hank Lapp, napping under a tree.

Luke had seen a clump of boys hanging around Hank, probably pestering him. He frowned. This was Hank's way of shooing the boys away to get some peace and quiet. Luke looked each boy right in the eyes, then slowly, carefully, he lowered one hand down to his boot top. The boys yelped and ran off.

Then there was Ruthie. His Ruthie. She never even bothered to glance at Luke, rarely left the side of Patrick Kelly except for during church when she had no choice but to sit with the women. Luke tried to catch a moment with her, just to say hello, but she kept slipping away from him, staying close to groups of older women. She knew he wouldn't come near her. Few things were as intimidating as a knot of Amish mothers.

Ruthie had never once come to see Luke while he was in rehab. Not a single time. Not a letter, not a phone call. Not even a word passed to him through her own father, David. Once or twice he posed a question to David about her. Casually, because he didn't like to betray his chaotic feelings.

David's answer was always the same. "Ruthie's doing just fine, Luke. She's moving on."

Everyone was moving on. Everyone except for Luke. He wasn't good at being left behind.

Later that afternoon, back at Windmill Farm, as he helped lead two milk cows to their stanchions, he felt particularly tetchy. The barn seemed large and empty, full of long shadows. He emptied a fresh scoop of feed in front of each cow, sprayed the udders with iodine solution, and wiped them dry. He moved the pail beneath one cow to start the slow process of milking. Painfully slow. The milk made a pinging sound as it hit the empty bottom of the container. The barn door opened, casting sunlight on Luke, and he looked up to see Amos carrying in a stainless steel milk can.

"Here's a clean one," he said, placing it near Luke.

"Amos, I know you only have two cows, but I can't believe you still hand milk them. Even for the Amish, it seems old-fashioned." Yesterday afternoon, Amos showed him how he kept the milk cans in a tank of cold, cold water until the milk truck came to pick them up. The windmill pumped cold water to the tank. It wasn't just old-fashioned; it was archaic.

"That's how my father did it, and his father before him."

That kind of thinking frustrated Luke. Windmill Farm was just standing still, not growing, not improving, not adapting. "I can guarantee that you're the only one in *that church* who still milks by hand." He heard his voice take on a harsh sound. He couldn't help it.

"What's eating you?" Amos said, gently stroking the side of the cow's belly, then scratching her behind her ears.

Surely, Amos must be kidding. If not, he was blind. "Did you not see how cold people were to me? I sat alone for lunch like I had the bubonic plague. No one greeted me, unless it was to give me some kind of warning."

"Oh, it couldn't have been that bad."

"It was worse than bad. Hank Lapp told me that I inspired him to start a new business. Highly lucrative, he expects, since I'm back in town. Mailboxes that double as bomb bunkers."

The laughter in Amos's eyes was both teasing and knowing. "That's just Hank's way. He likes to tweak."

"And of course he likes to shout out his lame jokes to the entire world." He glanced crossly at Amos. "He's your uncle. Did he ever talk in a normal tone or did he always shout?"

"Always shouts."

Luke turned back to the cow. "What happened to the Amish being known as kind people? Where'd that go?"

"Did you expect a red carpet to be rolled out? You can't have expected it to be easy, coming back. You're going to have to put on a little thicker shell to avoid getting so easily offended by Hank Lapp's bad jokes."

"I didn't expect a red carpet. But I didn't think I'd be cold-shouldered, not like I was. What happened to forgiveness?"

"Oh, I don't think that's the problem, Luke. I think people can forgive. They probably all do forgive you." Amos went to the far end of the barn, where the water tank sat, and brought back another container for the second cow. She was shifting uncomfortably from hoof to hoof and making lowing noises. Luke knew that meant she'd be bellowing if he didn't hurry up with the first cow.

When he looked up, Luke noticed how red Amos's face was from the exertion, though the empty container wasn't all that heavy. A weariness came into his eyes. "Let me do it, Amos." He reached out for the container, but Amos jerked it away.

"I'm not a feeble old man."

"Of course not. I didn't mean that." *Wow.* That reaction seemed prickly. Luke was only trying to help him.

"Make it snappy with Sage. Lemon Thyme's getting impatient."

Oh yeah, Sage and Lemon Thyme. Luke kept forgetting their names. Amos had told him that his youngest daughter, M.K., had dubbed each farm animal with an herb name.

Amos set the container down. "I'm not sure David's ever told you this, but I think you ought to know. Those people in *that church*—the very ones who gave you a cold shoulder— they're also the ones who've been paying for your stints in rehab. Each time. Three, if I'm not mistaken."

Luke hadn't known. That information sent a jolt through him. He hadn't known, he hadn't known. He should've, though. He knew the real heart of these people. They had each other's back, even if it didn't always feel that way.

"Like I said, forgiveness, that comes naturally for us. It's trust that's hard to restore. Trust is a fragile thing. There's no such thing as a little violation of trust, especially if you're the one who was betrayed. These people, they don't trust you."

Luke sat down on the milking stool and leaned his forehead against Sage's big, soft stomach. He should have considered that the church had taken up a collection to pay for his costs at rehab. Why hadn't it occurred to him to ask David who was paying for it? Not once did it cross his mind. Sighing, he lifted his head and looked up at Amos. "So what do I do about that? I mean . . . how can I stick around when no one is willing to trust me?"

"Well, Luke, the way I see it, if you don't stick around, you'll never find out the answer to that question." Amos walked over to the barn door and turned back. "And it seems like a pretty important thing to figure out." With that final comment, he shut the barn door behind him.

Izzy learned quickly. It hadn't taken her long to realize that Plain people put more stock in what a person did than in what they said. That system worked well for her, since she didn't like to talk much and she did like to keep busy. She helped Fern without being asked and didn't pester her with conversation. She just watched how Fern went about her day and copied everything she did.

When Izzy first arrived at Windmill Farm, she thought Fern made enough food each meal to feed the whole Amish community. Dinner, which was actually lunch, consisted of dishes like chicken potpie and a beef roast swimming in gravy. Not either/or . . . both! There were relishes and breads and stewed peaches and applesauce. Bowl after bowl kept coming. In the center of the table Fern would place a full pitcher of fresh cold milk. Then she would clang the dinner bell and in came Amos from the barn or the orchards. Not much later, only empty dishes remained, waiting to be washed. It would start all over again at suppertime, which was actually dinner. Maybe only one meat dish instead of two, but afterward it seemed there were just as many dishes to wash.

Nearly a year had passed and Izzy still hadn't grown accustomed to seeing such bounty, day after day. It had never been part of her life to have all she wanted. It often worried her that she was too happy, that one day—*poof*—it would all disappear and she'd find herself back on the streets, scrounging leftovers from garbage bins.

Tonight, Luke Schrock sank down into the chair across from her at the kitchen table. As usual, she didn't look directly at him, she stole a glance. Over the years Izzy had developed the habit of avoiding eye contact. She actually loved to observe people's faces, especially their eyes. But though she liked looking, she did not like being looked at.

Izzy knew her looks received attention, whether she wanted it or not. Boys in school gawked at her. Girls were instantly envious of her, without even bothering to get to know her. Grown men stared at her for a few seconds too long. The strange thing was that how she felt on the inside was nothing like how she must look to others.

It was easier here, among the Plain people, without any makeup, wearing modest clothes that made Izzy blend in. She appeared like any other woman in the church. She liked being invisible. And that big black *bonnet*. Oh my soul, she loved it. It shielded her face, made her entirely indistinguishable, all while giving her the opportunity to study the world around her.

It was one of the things Izzy loved most about being in church on Sunday. She got to look and look while nobody looked at her. Everybody's eyes were fixed on the preacher. She liked to sit in the back row, so she could take it all in.

It had taken some getting used to, the long long long church service. It wasn't easy to sit on a backless wooden bench for three hours, but she had grown accustomed to it. She'd lived in bustling towns or cities most of her eighteen years, so the deliberate quiet of this church community was something she had come to savor.

Whenever Izzy was in church, which was only twice a month, she was able to measure how much progress she'd made in learning Plain ways: the dialect, then the high German, the tunes of the woeful hymns. So filled with woe. Teddy

Zook would stand and sing in a slow, measured baritone—such a big man, belting out such big deep notes!—and others would pick up on his lead. One hymn, the *Loblied*, lasted thirty minutes. Izzy had timed it.

She remembered how shocked she'd felt that very first Sunday. She'd attended only one church, when she was living with a foster family that attended church regularly. What was their name? She couldn't remember. But she had liked them, had felt safe with them, and she remembered that she had liked that church. But *that* service hadn't lasted three hours. In fact, now that she thought about it, the family was always late to church, and whooshed away right after because the father liked to watch football games on Sundays. They'd probably only gone to church for forty-five minutes.

And now, barely a year later, this long Amish church service felt familiar, if not normal. In fact, the entire Plain life felt pretty normal to her.

These last twelve months at Windmill Farm—they were the longest Izzy'd ever lived in one place. She remembered how strange the house had seemed when David Stoltzfus first delivered her to Windmill Farm. She had looked around the small downstairs, shell-shocked. Floor-to-ceiling book-shelves lined the walls, mostly filled with religious titles that she definitely had no interest in. None whatsoever. There was no television, no phone, no radio, no computers, no music. The house smelled of Clorox bleach and lemon wax and was warm to the point of suffocation.

She remembered that Fern had led her upstairs to her bedroom, a large room with two windows. That part, she liked. An easy getaway, if necessary. There was a strip of wood with pegs on the wall. A dress the color of eggplant hung on one peg. One tall dresser but no closet. Two twin beds were covered with cheerful quilts, providing the only bit of color in the room. She put her duffel bag next to the bed by the window. "Not that one," Fern had said. "That's Jenny's. The other bed is yours."

Izzy's heart began to pound. She was sharing a room with someone? Who? What had she gotten herself into?

Into the room walked Jenny, a small young woman. Not particularly pretty or remarkable, not in the way Izzy's world took notice of a female. Easy to overlook, easy to underestimate. She changed Izzy's life.

THREE

The moment Izzy had first met Jenny Yoder, she felt an instant connection, something she couldn't explain even if she tried, which she wouldn't.

On her second day at Windmill Farm, Fern had taken Izzy and Jenny to a comfort quilt gathering. On the way to the gathering, Fern explained to her that each woman was given the task of piecing together a block that would be sewn together and sent to a group home in Lancaster for foster children who were waiting for homes. And didn't Izzy know all about *those*. She sat in the back seat, listening to Fern and Jenny chatter away in Penn Dutch, feeling her stomach twist and turn with every bump and jolt of the buggy.

But when they arrived at the farmhouse where the quilting was to be held, Izzy learned that the pattern to be sewn was the basic nine-patch, and her whole self uncoiled with relief. One of her foster mothers had liked to quilt and had taught her how to make this simple pattern. One thing Izzy knew about herself: if someone took the time to teach her how to do something, she could take off and run with it.

But she'd always needed to be shown how first. This nine-patch quilt block, this she could do. She wouldn't need to ask anyone for help.

Fern's friends had welcomed Izzy warmly, even speaking mostly in English for her benefit. They couldn't have been any nicer, but she still felt like a fish out of water. They had a certain way between them that was beyond her. She was included, but she was alone.

And then something happened, a small thing, but momentous. When everyone had finished their nine-patch, they placed their blocks on the table to arrange and sew into a larger quilt. Izzy and Jenny laid their squares next to each other, then looked up in surprise. Their blocks were identical, down to the specific choices of fabric for each square. Every single square, it all lined up, color for color. Izzy felt a moment of panic—would Jenny be angry? Would she think she had copied her? She hadn't! They had sat in different circles, on opposite sides of the room.

A slow grin spread across Jenny's delicate face, not stopping until her eyes were dancing with amusement. "Well, no wonder I like you so much. You have wonderful taste."

Jenny laughed, and then Izzy smiled, relieved. Their friendship had grown quickly. Jenny shared her story with Izzy, that she and her brother Chris had converted to the Amish in their teens, helped along by the Stoney Ridge Amish. Fern, mostly.

It wasn't much later that Jenny asked her if she'd considered going Amish. Izzy was intrigued by the Plain lifestyle. She always had been. But join them? She hadn't known it was even possible, not until Jenny brought it up to consider. In a way, Jenny had forged a path for Izzy.

Jenny took it upon herself to mentor Izzy in all ways Amish—language, customs and traditions, and the everydayness of the Plain farm life. Clothing and hair were the first change Izzy made, and the best. When Izzy first put on a simple blue dress, and pinned her thick hair up into a bun to be covered with an organza prayer cap, it seemed as if she had walked through a door into another world. She belonged to something bigger than herself. Something better. And in a strange way, she also felt beautiful, truly beautiful, for the first time in her life. First time. Plain and beautiful.

She owed this transformation to Jenny. Izzy had never had a best friend before. She'd moved too often for friendships to have the time they needed to take root. In a perfect world, Izzy and Jenny would stay at Windmill Farm for the rest of their natural lives. But Jenny's life seemed set toward a different path.

David Stoltzfus's only son, Jesse, had run a buggy shop out of Windmill Farm. From the moment she had arrived, Izzy had observed something brewing between Jenny and Jesse. Izzy had seen the whole thing, could have predicted it. The way Jesse's voice sounded shaky when he was around Jenny. The way Jenny's cheeks went bright red at any mention of Jesse Stoltzfus.

Then the new year came and went. Jenny confided that she and Jesse were making plans for their future. Izzy went a little numb, preparing herself for the inevitable. She knew this drill oh so well. "Wonderful" wouldn't, couldn't last.

Soon after, Jesse moved the buggy shop to the back of his father's Bent N' Dent store, where there was plenty of room to expand it. And Jenny left Windmill Farm to take a well-paying job as a live-in nanny to an English family. Izzy missed her terribly, painfully, a hole-in-her-heart kind of feeling, though she never revealed that to Jenny. "Wonderful" wouldn't, couldn't last. But it *was* wonderful while it lasted.

Luke sat in the phone shanty, waiting for his counselor to call. Same time, each week. He picked up the phone after the first ring.

"So Luke, how's the first week gone?"

"It's been okay. Pretty much what I expected it to be."

"How did you expect it to be?"

Luke hesitated. "Awkward."

"How so? Anything happen that you didn't expect?"

Plenty of things. Sleeping in a barn's tack room, for one. Getting the silent treatment from most everyone at church, for another. But if Luke said aloud what was running through his mind, he knew it would sound ungrateful, and the rest of the conversation with the counselor would be focused on changing his attitude. Instead, he shifted topics. "There's a girl staying here, at the same farm. I remember her from rehab. Izzy Miller. Do you remember her?"

Silence. A beat too long. Luke's ears pricked.

"Have you interacted much?"

"No. I've tried, but she's pretty frosty to me." It was almost as if she didn't like Luke, but . . . that was impossible. Everybody liked him. Girls, especially.

"Maybe her feelings have nothing to do with you, Luke. Maybe she's trying to figure things out for herself."

What he meant was, *It's not all about you.* Luke had gotten pretty good at interpreting counselor code.

"I guess you're right. I was just . . . hoping to have someone to talk to. You know, someone who could relate."

"Who else could you talk to? Besides a cute girl?"

Ah, point taken. Luke sighed. He ran through a few people in his mind. David and Amos, bishop and deacon, but they were busy men. The two ministers weren't the talking type, unless they happened to be preaching. Then, they talked plenty. Hank Lapp was the only one who seemed to have time to spare, and that was a frightening thought.

"Luke, you have to reach out to others. Be willing to be vulnerable. Remember, you have an uphill climb ahead."

He snorted. "You got that right." He swallowed. "They don't want me here." His voice sounded wobbly and he cringed. Such a giveaway, that wobble.

"Maybe so. Maybe not. It's up to you to make them see you differently."

After they hung up, Luke stayed in the phone shanty for a long time, head bent. He saw a string of weekly phone calls like this one, stretching out for months, leaving him depressed and discouraged. It was how he always felt after therapy sessions. Wrung out.

A swirl of emotions ran through him, including a strong desire for a drink. Triggers that caused a craving for alcohol, that much he had figured out. Triggers of disappointments, one after the other. The only way he knew to cope with disappointment was to pretend it didn't matter . . . and that took him right to self-anesthetizing.

The problem was, even if he recognized triggers for what they were, he didn't know how to stop the disappointments from coming at him. He didn't fit in anywhere—not here among the Amish, not in the world beyond. Maybe *this* was as much as he could ever hope for; *this* was as good as it would ever get for him.

Argh. No wonder he was depressed.

⌒

Amos scraped his chair back to sit in it, folded his hands in his lap, and tipped his head down in silent prayer. Izzy followed suit, her heart overflowing with gratitude for having a place in this home. She wished she could tell Amos and Fern how much she appreciated being here, how much she cared for them, but expressive words were hard for her to voice. She hoped they knew. She thought they did.

Amos and Fern spoke English at the table for Izzy's benefit. She understood more of Penn Dutch than they realized she did, but she didn't mind keeping it that way, especially now that Luke Schrock was a live-in barn guest. Mostly, though, she did her best to avoid him. It wasn't easy. As big as Windmill Farm was, they seemed to bump into each other several times a day. Everything about him annoyed her. Every single thing he said or did.

Before supper tonight, she'd been out in the pasture, calling to the sheep to herd them into the pen for the evening, as Luke walked up the driveway from the phone shanty.

He stopped to watch her, leaning his elbows against the pasture fence. "Do you mean to tell me you've named those sheep?"

"Each one. Same with my hens. They all have a unique personality."

His mouth curved into a cynical smile. "Oh, I think you're gonna regret that."

She frowned at him. "Why's that?"

"When it's time for Amos to send them off to slaughter, it'll feel like you're sending pets to the butcher."

Spinning around, she pointed a finger at him. "You're wrong. Amos doesn't send his sheep to slaughter."

"Oh no? Then what does he do with them? He's sure not raising them for their wool." He pushed himself off the fence and walked up to the house for supper.

A couple of ewes suddenly butted heads and started a lot of blatting. "Lucy, Ethel! Stop that fighting." Those two! They were always causing trouble.

Could Luke be right? No. Certainly not. His words felt like a cloud fleeting across the sky, blocking the sun. A chill went down her spine.

After supper, before evening devotions, Izzy was in the kitchen alongside Fern to wash and dry dishes. "What does Amos do with the sheep?"

Fern handed her a rinsed dinner plate to dry. "Do with them?"

Izzy wiped it dry with a dish towel. "They don't . . . he doesn't . . ." She set the dinner plate in the cupboard and started all over again. "Does he raise them for their meat?"

"Of course. Each fall, he sells off the lambs that are under one. The younger the better for the price. Flavor too. Over twelve months, they're sold as mutton." She looked up at the ceiling. "How does the saying go? My father used to repeat it all the time. Es nemmt en schlecht schof as sei eegni Woll net draage kann." She glanced at Izzy. "Can you translate?"

"Something about a sheep . . . and wool?"

"It's a poor sheep that can't carry its own wool." Fern swished hot soapy water into a large bowl and stirred. "Each year, Amos sells off the oldest ones for mutton. Don't you remember? Same thing happened last year."

No, Izzy didn't remember. Last year, she was overwhelmed with all she had to learn about farm living. Amos's sheep had no names, no personalities. This year, she knew each one.

The oldest ewes? But . . . that meant Lucy and Ethel. Izzy couldn't hide the shock she felt. She hadn't expected this, the heartlessness. They were living creatures! "Isn't there some other way?"

"Another way?" Fern handed her the clean bowl to dry. "I know you've got a soft spot in your heart for animals, Izzy, but this is a working farm. The flock needs to be culled each year so it stays strong and healthy."

Later that night, Izzy came downstairs to get a glass of water and there was Luke, awful Luke, seated at the kitchen table, reading a book. He glanced up at her, then did a double take, and she realized that she hadn't worn a cap and her hair was down, unpinned. It was only a few inches below her shoulders, not nearly as long as the Plain girls who'd never cut their hair. She frowned at him and went to the cupboard to get a glass.

"I can only read by flashlight in the tack room because Amos won't let me use a lantern," he said, sounding embarrassed. "Fire risk, he says. The flashlight's batteries went dead and Fern was all out of new ones. So she said just to stay here."

Izzy filled the glass with water. "You don't need an excuse for my sake." She glanced at the book, wondering what he was reading.

He noticed. Lifting the book, he said, "*The Gift of Good*

Land. Wendell Berry is a poet and a farmer, committed to family farms. He lives in Kentucky. He's sympathetic to the Amish. In fact, there's a chapter in this book about Amish farming. That's what I'm reading."

She turned toward him. "Like I said, you don't need an excuse for my sake."

"I guess . . . you just seemed surprised to find me reading."

"Actually," she said as she hurried up the stairs, "I was surprised to find that you *could* read."

If there was one thing in the Amish life that most delighted Izzy, it was horse-and-buggy travel. A horse moved along at a steady but slow pace—slow enough that she was able to count the number of horses and foals grazing in fields, to notice the bright yellow mustard along the sides of the road, to see birds in overhead trees. She found herself watching in wonder as the countryside rolled on by.

Amos gave her driving lessons whenever he had some free time, which wasn't often. So far, this spring, she'd had only three lessons, and last time she had actually held the reins to steer the horse up the long driveway. A victory! She'd learned a lot about horses this last year, and Bob the buggy horse was as calm and reliable as a horse could be, but that didn't mean she trusted him on a public road. No sir! The first time she'd been in a buggy, a truck went barreling past, and the buggy shook so much she was sure it would blow apart. She wasn't ready to do much more than sit in the driver's seat and hold the reins, but she was working at it. Today, Amos had said she could try driving to the Bent N' Dent. She'd hardly slept, she was that excited.

As they finished the noon meal, Amos told her to be ready to go at three o'clock, so she waited in the shade of the barn for him, dancing with excitement. To her surprise, Luke was the one who led Bob out of the barn. "Where's Amos?" she said flatly.

"Something came up, he said. He told me to take you to the store. Or rather, to have you take me to the store."

She frowned. She'd been doing her best to avoid Luke, to answer his abundance of nosy questions in a way that curtailed conversations, to decline his constant offers to help her with her chores. "I'll wait until Amos has time."

"Don't be silly. I've been driving buggies since I was eight years old. Let me give you a few tips."

Izzy recoiled. *Let me give you a few tips* . . . That was just the kind of remark from a man that made the hair stand up on the back of her neck. "I'd rather wait for Amos."

He turned away from her and began backing the horse between the shafts of the buggy. "I still have to go to the store for Fern." He finished fastening the last buckle and looked up. "Why not come along? Keep me company?"

She shook her head and started back to the house when she heard him call out, "Izzy, why're you so mean to me?"

She racked her brain for a solid excuse. Things being the way they were, she was naturally suspicious of him. In her position, who wouldn't be? Still walking, she turned around for a few steps and lifted her palms in a helpless shrug. "Just can't find any reason to be nice."

~

Well, this was going to take some work.

As insulting as Izzy's last response to Luke was, he registered that her voice could actually be quite sweet. Normally, she spoke to him in a deadpan voice. He noted again how attractive she was, but today it struck him more forcefully. Even when she scowled at him, she was *stunning*. The problem, he heard a little voice tell him, was that even though he barely knew her, he'd seen enough to conclude that she did not play games. It was clear that she did not care a whit about him. Less than a whit.

He had pulled out every trick he knew to charm her. He left fresh-picked flowers in her watering bucket. He'd noticed how early she had to get up to get the sheep out of the pen and into the pasture to graze, so he woke extra early to let them out for her. He overheard her rave to Fern about a cinnamon roll from the Sweet Tooth Bakery. It was the best thing she'd ever eaten, he heard her say. So he borrowed Amos's scooter early the next morning and rode into town to buy a cinnamon roll for her before they sold out. He left it on the farm stand for her to find when she opened up for the day. She thanked him for these gestures, in that flat tone she reserved for him, but it made no difference in how she viewed him. Like he was just . . . some guy. Not *the* guy. How could that be? No girl had ever been immune to his charms before, not even Ruthie.

That girl, that Izzy. She was a challenge. He grinned. He liked a challenge.

Later that day, Izzy brought Sage and Lemon Thyme up to the barn. Usually Luke milked the cows, but he wasn't back from the trip to the Bent N' Dent, Fern and Amos weren't back yet, and the two cows were bawling with misery.

Amos and Fern had a strict policy at Windmill Farm. The welfare of animals came before people. If it was time to milk or feed livestock, whoever was home was responsible for the animals. They were treated with respect and kindness. Izzy grasped onto and adhered to that principle. She'd seen plenty of situations where animals were nothing but punching bags for angry, frustrated people.

She walked behind both cows as they slowly sauntered into their stanchions to find the mixed feed waiting for them. She sat on the stool, wiped each cow down, and settled into the rhythm of milking. It was hot in the barn, especially so today, but she didn't mind that much. She enjoyed being alone at Windmill Farm, and the peace that filled the farm at day's end. Even the barn swallows that rushed in and around the rafters were quiet now. She finished milking the cows and took the heavy milk container back to the tank. As she walked back down the barn aisle, she froze when she heard the familiar snap of a bottle cap—*hiss*. There, leaning against Bob the buggy horse's stall, was Luke Schrock, with two open bottles of beer in his hands.

She frowned at him. "What are you doing?"

"You said you have no reason to be nice to me." He lifted the beers. "I thought I'd give you a reason. I brought you a gift."

Izzy thought it over, watching him, thinking how good that cold, fizzy beer would taste on a warm afternoon. Cold and bitter . . . and then there were those last few foamy drips. She thought about how many beers she'd had in the last few years, and what they'd brought her. Temporary dulling of permanent pain. She thought about that, all that and much more in that long heavy moment before she made a choice.

Slowly, so slowly, she walked over to Luke and took the bottle from him.

$\mathcal{F}$OUR

A pleased look covered Luke's handsome face, until Izzy turned the bottle upside down and poured it out on his boots.

"Hey!" He hopped like a grasshopper to get away from the spilled beer. "What's that for?"

What was that *for*? How could he ever understand what that was for? In the last year, she had undergone a sea change, inside and out, everything from how she dressed and looked to how she thought and acted. She wasn't going to let a guy like Luke Schrock take anything away from her. Everything came too easy for him. Nothing had ever come easy for Izzy. If she was going to have a future, a good life, she had to be the one to make it happen. That awareness fired up her determination to stay the course she was on.

"Look," she said, trying but not succeeding to keep a handle on her fury. "Look, Luke Schrock, you can do what you want with your life. It's your stupid life to waste. But for me, I have one shot." She held up one finger close to his face. "This is my *one* shot to get it right. Can you even understand that? I have plans. There's something I want. If you think I would jeopardize all that I'm working toward by drinking a bottle of beer, with *you*, think again."

"But I'm sure—"

"You're sure of nothing." The words, she practically spat them. She stomped toward the door, then thought of something else she wanted to say, so she turned to face him. He had an odd look on his face, shock and pain and disappointment, all swirled together. "Do you ever, *ever* think past tomorrow?"

She left him with that, a little surprised that he didn't try to defend himself. As she slammed the barn door, she licked her lips. That cold beer sounded so good, its familiar yeasty scent even smelled so good, but she had said no. She'd said no!

For a moment, everything stood still. Even a barn swallow stopped swooping in and out of the roof vent, disappearing into its nests in the rafters. Izzy felt herself suddenly cloaked in the satisfaction of doing something perfectly right.

It was the first time she'd been offered a drink since she left rehab. First time. And she'd turned it down. She smiled. Turned it upside down! Right on that jerk's boots.

Luke sat on his cot, holding the beer in his hands, looking at it. Booze—it had always made him feel loose and limber, made him feel better about himself. It covered up his growing disgust with himself. Right now, a sick sensation hit him in the pit of his stomach as he turned the bottle around and around in his hands. *What kind of* fool *am I? What kind of fool?*

What *kind* of a man would offer a drink to a recovering

alcoholic? A terrible, terrible man, that's who. What was the matter with him? Why did he think *that* would be a way to connect to Izzy?

He'd done his errand for Fern at the Bent N' Dent and drove the horse past a gas station with a convenience store. He saw a guy walk out of the store with a six-pack, and that was when the idea came to him. At the time, he thought it was such a good idea.

He sickened himself.

"Do you ever, ever *think past tomorrow?"* That was Izzy's parting shot, and it hit him like a blow to the jugular. He'd heard it plenty of times before. He'd always had trouble seeing "down the road." It was like his brain just stayed in the present, looking for fun, for kicks. Did he ever think past tomorrow?

The counselor had tried and tried to impress it on him. Why did it strike him so forcefully today?

Everything Izzy said, even the way she emphasized her words to him, seemed to hint at some stupidity on Luke's part. And she was right.

If he were smart about women, which he had just proved he wasn't, he would wise up and write her off as a lost cause. Instead—evidence of his lack of common sense—he felt even more intrigued by her. She had a coldness about her, a lack of emotion that fascinated him. He couldn't even charm a smile out of her. He had tried to amuse her, tried to make her laugh and notice him. Nothing worked. She was like the Sphinx.

He rolled the bottle back and forth between his hands. Izzy said she wanted something. What was it? And what did it have to do with the Amish? A girl who looked like her could be modeling, or TV acting, or hooking a rich boyfriend. Something like that. He could not figure that girl out.

There was only one thing he knew for sure about Izzy Miller—she hated him. He had tried to be friendly, flirty, complimentary, helpful . . . nothing worked. He glanced again at the bottle in his hands. *This* was a stupid overture. He had just set back their friendship from zero to negative ten.

What made him think *this* would create a friendship? It occurred to him that this was just what she meant—think past tomorrow. He laughed scornfully. Drinking together would've created one night of kinship—and ruined both of them.

The barn door opened and he heard Amos's heavy footfalls. He jumped off the cot, jostling the beer so that he got a strong whiff. *Man, it smelled good.* Luke walked out to find Amos in front of his workbench, looking at a pair of shears. Luke saw him pick up one screwdriver after the other, trying to undo the bolt that held the shears together.

"Amos," Luke said. "I'll help you fix those. First, turn around, please."

Amos set down the shears and turned to face him.

Luke held up the bottle of beer and Amos's eyebrows shot up. "I want you to see that I bought this, I opened it, I offered it to Izzy—she turned it down, by the way—and I haven't had a sip." He turned it upside down so it spilled onto the barn floor. Cats came out of nowhere to lick it up. "I can understand if you want me to pack up and go."

Amos watched the cats on the ground for at least a full minute. Finally, he lifted his head to glare at Luke, eyes narrowed. "Is that what you want? To leave?"

"No. I want to stay. I . . ." He swallowed. "I made a stupid mistake. But I didn't drink the beer. I promise, Amos. I didn't drink it. Not a sip."

Another full minute passed. Amos's eyes softened, ever so slightly. Then he did something completely unexpected. He dismissed Luke's confession with a wave of his hand. "So, then, help me get the bolt out of these shears. They need sharpening."

Luke's eyes went wide with shock. "That's it? You're not kicking me out?"

"Not tonight. I will, if you ever do it again. Or if you try to drag Izzy down. She's worked hard to make a new life for herself. I'm not going to let you undo all her progress. Try a stunt like that with her again and you'll be out of here before you know what hit you. You just used up your one blunder."

"Blunder?"

"David told me to allow you one slip-up. Just one."

Blunder. That was a kind word. Luke might have called it something else. "Amos, can you tell me what Izzy's story is?"

"Nope. It's hers to tell." He took off his hat and ruffled his thinning hair. "So why'd you do it? Why would you bring beer on my farm? Why would you offer it to her?"

"I guess . . . I wanted to get Izzy to notice me. She hates me, I think."

"Hate is a strong word, but she might. Especially after what you just did. You can't ask something of people they don't want to give. If she doesn't think much of you, that's her choice. She has a choice whether to like you or not, you know."

"Well, sure, I know that." But he didn't. Luke had never

had trouble with girls not liking him. Even Ruthie, who had grown tired of his drinking and mischief, she had *liked* him. Everyone liked him, even when they were mad at him. It was part of his charm, which, the counselor pointed out, was also part of his problem. He'd been given too many free passes by others.

"I spoke to David. He had a suggestion about how to get people to trust you again."

"What is it?"

"I'll let him give you the details. Tomorrow, if we have time to see him."

"Tomorrow?" *Do you ever look past tomorrow?* Izzy's words kept echoing in Luke's head.

"Tomorrow. Maybe the next day. We have cherries ripening, fast. And then it's time to start thinning out the peach blossoms. By tomorrow night, after a full day of cherry picking, you'll be plenty sore and not so interested in talking to the bishop." He turned back to his workbench. "So, what about these shears?"

Luke walked to the bench and took them out of Amos's hands. "Thank you."

Amos eyed him. "You telling me the truth about not drinking that beer?"

"Smelled it. Came close to drinking it. But I'm telling you the truth. I didn't touch a drop."

"Then, after you fix this, we'll go in and tell Fern we need something good to eat to help us celebrate."

"Celebrate? Celebrate what?"

"Have you ever turned down a cold beer on a hot day before?"

"Huh." Awareness spilled in slowly, like a shaft of sunlight hitting a window. A thoughtful grin spread over Luke's face. "Come to think of it, I don't believe I ever have."

⁘

Amos left the shears with Luke to repair and walked back up to the house. David had warned him to expect something like this, to not overreact if it happened. He said it would probably happen when something frustrating occurred, because that's when the recovering alcoholic had to dig deep and use different skills to handle a difficult situation. Their first go-to would be their old go-to. "The first step in learning is unlearning," David had told him. "It's the casting off of old habits."

Izzy had never had a relapse, but then, she had a focused mind. Luke Shrock had nothing on his mind.

Amos stopped to catch his breath. That's it! That's the trouble with Luke. He didn't have any goal, anything to shoot for. But what? He'd have to ask Fern. She was good about that kind of thing. He started back up the hill and heard the door open. Fern was heading down to meet him. For once, she hadn't startled him by appearing without warning.

"It's happening too often."

"What?"

"Halting halfway up the hill to catch your breath."

Did she see everything?

"Izzy told me what happened."

He grunted. "Is she upset?"

"Yes. No. Both, I suppose."

"Does she want us to make Luke leave? Because I warned you, that day David asked us to let Luke board here. I told you that if he created any problem for Izzy, he was out."

Amos felt fiercely protective of Izzy, just as he had of his own three daughters.

"Izzy can handle herself. She showed us that tonight."

"I told Luke I won't let him undo her progress."

"She's stronger now."

Amos hoped Fern was right. "Luke told me about the beer. He didn't drink it. Not sure if that's because I came in—"

"You're not sure if he would have drank it?"

"Not that part. I'm pretty sure he'd decided he wasn't going to drink it. It was the telling me part. That's what I'm not sure of."

"Hmmm," Fern said, in that way she had that made him know she had something else to say. Her gaze shifted down toward the barn. "But he did tell you."

"He did. He poured out the beer on the ground. Your cats might be acting a little funny tonight."

"Amos, I've been giving some thought to Luke."

Good. Fern was just the one to figure out how to help Luke. She had a tolerance for troubled people that Amos found astonishing, as if she could see a diamond deep inside. He saw no such diamond. His only thought about Luke was to tire him out with hard labor. "What's the plan?"

"A fix-it shop."

"For Luke?"

She glanced up the hill. "In the buggy shop. If we get it cleaned out, there's plenty of room to make a shop."

Amos mulled that over. Luke was a surprisingly capable fellow. So far, he'd fixed an old plow, a loose part on Bob's buggy, and tonight, his favorite shears. No one had been able to bring that plow back to life, but somehow Luke jerry-rigged it to work. Fixing things—that was a pretty important skill to have in life.

"I can't spare him until the harvest is in. September, probably October." By then, Amos was confident Luke would be long gone. He looked up at his wife and saw that she was quite serious about this. "Think anyone would trust him with their things?"

"There's no one else in Stoney Ridge who can fix things, now that Hank is retired and Jesse has no time for buggy repairs since he started at the Bent N' Dent."

That was a generous assessment. Hank never really fixed anything, anyway. Hank was Amos's uncle, his favorite, a one-of-a-kind character. Hank thought about doing a lot, and even started quite a bit, but rarely got around to finishing anything. Fern might just have the right idea for Luke. He smiled at her. She was a gem, a true jewel.

She smiled back, as if she knew what he was thinking. "I made an appointment for you to see Dok tomorrow morning. Get your heart checked. Nine o'clock. Don't be late, she said. She's squeezing you in." She pivoted on her heels and walked toward the house.

Blast! *That* woman. She was a tireless dictator.

In the morning, Luke was relieved that Amos and Fern were away from Windmill Farm when David dropped by, and Izzy had gone to visit Jenny Yoder. It was humiliating enough to have this kind of a talk with David. The bishop sat at the kitchen table and put a yellow pad of paper in front of Luke, along with a pen. He sat back and folded his hands together. "Luke, it's going to take work to build a good reputation."

"Der alt Bull blarrt als noch." *The old bull keeps on bellowing.* Another way of saying scandals never die. It was one of those bromides Fern spouted all the time.

David looked up at Luke. "Es is ken Laschst so gross as die as mer sich selwert macht." *There is no burden so great as that which is self-made.*

Luke lifted his palms in surrender. "Touché."

"I had a long talk with your counselor yesterday. He said that he's been working through the Twelve Steps with you."

"That's true. We've gone over all of them. They're helpful, especially step 1. I think about that one a lot." *We admitted we were powerless over alcohol—that our lives had become unmanageable.* He had memorized all of them. Everyone did. It was part of the program.

"Your counselor suggested going over them each and every day. As part of your time in prayer."

"Yup. I've been doing that."

"What about steps 8, 9, and 10?"

Luke's stomach twisted. He rubbed his forehead. *Step 8. Make a list of all persons we had harmed, and become willing to make amends to them all.* "I've made a list." The counselor had asked him to make a list, and so he did. He just hadn't done anything about it.

"Excellent. Where is it?"

"I'm not sure. Probably down with my stuff in the tack room. Want me to go look for it?"

"No." David's eyes flashed to the paper pad. "Start again."

"You mean, now?" Oh gag. He suddenly had a flashback to the rehab clinic, sitting in group therapy, feeling just as uncomfortable.

"Now."

Luke sighed. He picked up the pen and wrote down three names. Then he set the pen down and looked up at David. He had the same look on his face that his counselor had.

"Just three names?"

"Just three. Don't look at me like that! Everyone blames me for anything that went wrong in Stoney Ridge." David lowered his eyes at that, in a way that made Luke feel ashamed. He suddenly thought of how he sounded, like a spoiled child. "No, not everyone."

David lifted his eyes. "Tell me about these three."

"I put a cherry bomb in Amos's mailbox. I killed Patrick's mynah bird. And I hurt Galen's sorrel bay—but that was an accident."

David reached inside his coat and took out a thick envelope. He handed it to Luke. It was a list of offenses Luke had made. One after the other, page after page.

Luke skimmed each page. "You have got to be kidding. You're saying I need to make amends for something I did when I was . . . what . . . thirteen years old? Or something as minor as cutting down a rope swing at Mattie and Sol's house?"

"Isn't that what steps 8 and 9 are all about? Make a list of all persons harmed. Become willing to make amends to them. And then step 9. Make direct amends wherever possible."

Luke couldn't argue with that. He just hadn't realized that so many people held grudges in this town. What about forgiveness? What about second chances? "So let me get this straight. You want me to go to every single person on this list—every single person—and apologize to them? For things that happened years ago?"

David nodded. "There's power in apology, son. So yes, I want you to offer each person a sincere, heartfelt apology. But there's something else I want you to do. I also want you to ask each one how your behavior affected them. And you don't leave until they tell you."

Luke jumped up from his chair. "You can't be serious. What good would that do?"

"Quite a bit. For you, to understand consequences of choices. For those you harmed, it will give them an opportunity to express their hurt. There's a cost to our actions . . . and someone is paying for that cost. You need to see what you've cost people, Luke. Up close."

"Why not just put me in the village stocks? Or whip me publicly?" He slapped his forehead. "Why not just brand me as a sinner?"

David smiled. "Trust me, Luke. This exercise—it's in your best interest. It will promote healing, full and complete healing, for you. For others too."

"I couldn't disagree more. It might be nice for people to have a chance to yell at me, but I have no doubt this 'exercise' will set me back. How am I supposed to forgive myself when I keep getting reminders of what a jerk I've been? This whole idea—it'll send me right to the bottle."

"About that. Sit down and cool off."

Luke made a show of sitting down, scraping the chair legs against the floor.

"Now, can you explain what happened yesterday afternoon?"

Luke crossed his arms against his chest, shrugged, and looked away. "If Amos told you, then you already know what happened."

"Sounds to me like it was something the old Luke might have done. A way to get attention from a pretty girl."

Luke felt that same sharp poke at his gut that he'd gotten when Izzy had asked him if he ever thought past tomorrow. He changed the subject. "If I understood a little more about Izzy, then maybe I wouldn't have to try so hard."

David's face remained impassive.

"Can't you tell me something about her? Anything?"

"Like what?"

"I remember her, David. She was at rehab when I first arrived. Why is she here?"

"Amos and Fern invited her to live with them."

"I figured that. But why does she want to live here?"

"She has an interest in the Plain life."

"Lots of people are interested. That doesn't mean they drop everything and convert."

"Izzy's interest is . . . well, very intentional. She knows what she wants. A little bit like Patrick Kelly. He felt a calling to the Plain life."

"And didn't that just turn out swimmingly? He's marrying my girl." Luke knew this was not a mature attitude. But he also knew he could be real with David because he didn't go away. Nothing, *nothing* seemed to push him away from Luke. He wanted Luke to feel comfortable saying anything to him, as long as he spoke with respect. That wasn't hard— Luke had profound respect for David, more than for anyone else he knew.

He waited for David to say more, but he had nothing more to volunteer. "Here's the way I figure it. She came here because she had no place else to go."

"Like you?"

Ouch. *Yes, like me.*

David pointed to the thick stack of papers. "It'll take you a while to get through the entire list. Remember, it's not a race. This is meant to be a therapeutic process, and healing takes time. I'd start from the top and proceed from there. I'd recommend you get to Alice Smucker as soon as you can."

Alice Smucker? He couldn't remember doing anything to bother her. Oh wait. Hold on. Now he remembered. He threw a snake into her buggy.

Luke read the first name. *Amos Lapp. Blew up mailbox.*

FIVE

Luke waited nervously until Amos and Fern returned from wherever they'd been all morning. When he heard the faint jingle of tack and traces, he went outside to take Bob out of his harness and lead him to his stall. He waited until Fern and Amos got out of the buggy, but they didn't. They remained inside for the longest while. Luke stood a few feet away and froze when he realized that they were having some kind of important conversation. The window flap was open and he could see that Fern was crying. Fern Lapp. Crying! Not in a weepy way, but quietly. Dabbing the corners of her eyes with tissue sort of way.

Amos tipped his forehead against his wife's and whispered something to her. Luke ducked to offer them privacy. He backed up, hoping to slip away unnoticed, but didn't realize there was a large water bucket in his path. Over he went, head over feet, landing in the bucket with a splat and a yelp. Startled, Amos and Fern peered out the buggy window at

_ _ as Izzy came out of the house. All three stared at ʟuke, sitting like a fool in a water bucket.

He scrambled out of the bucket, face burning red. "I wasn't listening in, Amos. I wanted to ask if I could talk to you privately for a minute . . . but then I realized you . . . Fern . . . needed some alone time . . . so I—"

Amos opened the buggy door and climbed out. "First let me get the horse into the barn."

Luke brushed water off his pants. He could feel drips rolling down his legs into his socks. "I'll do it." Amos looked tired. Gray with exhaustion. "You go inside and take a break."

Amos frowned. "I'm not dead yet." He started unfastening the horse's harness buckle.

"Oh Amos, let him help." Fern put her hand on her husband's arm. "Let's go in and get some lemonade. I made a pitcher before we left. Should be cold by now."

He stopped and tucked his chin against his chest. "Fine."

Luke watched them head toward the house. Something didn't seem quite right, and he could tell Izzy had the same response. She was watching them too, arms crossed, with a puzzled look on her face.

After the door closed behind them, Izzy didn't move. She just stared at the closed door. Suddenly, she remembered Luke, spun around to frown at him, then went into the house.

Why did everybody frown at him so much? He didn't know. He unfastened the rest of the buckles, grabbed Bob's harness to lead him forward, and watched the buggy slip down, its shafts sticking up in the ground like two huge chopsticks. He scratched the horse's nose and was rewarded with a gentle nudge. He settled the horse into his stall and made sure he had fresh cool water and a handful of oats for his trouble. It was a warm day, one of the hottest so far. He was fiddling with the latch on the horse's stall door as Amos came into the barn.

"What are you doing?"

"I found Bob out of his stall this morning, helping himself to breakfast. I thought I'd tighten up the screws on the latch."

He walked over to Luke. "Hmm. Sure you didn't leave the latch undone?"

Luke looked up. "I might have. Still, when I checked it, the screws seemed a little loose."

Amos looked a little better. Some color had returned to his face. He seemed older to Luke than he had this morning, which was a weird thought, but it was true. His skin was more lined and creased. Luke wasn't sure it was the right time to have a serious talk. Then again, there probably never was a good time for these kinds of talks.

"Good lemonade?"

"Hit the spot. 'Timeless in labor and wisdom and love, the wife of a farmer was sent from above.' Remember that, when you get married."

Getting married couldn't be further from Luke's thoughts. He plopped down on a bale of hay. Amos was peering into Bob's stall, probably to check and see if Luke had taken proper care of him. Satisfied, he turned around. "So, what's on your mind?"

"I want to apologize for blowing up your mailbox."

Amos nodded.

This wasn't so bad. Maybe, it didn't have to be so serious.

Maybe David was right. All that he needed to do was offer a heartfelt apology.

But Amos was waiting for more.

"And uh, I wondered if that admittedly juvenile act had any adverse effect on you?"

Amos stood across the aisle, facing Luke, elbows raised up high, leaning his back against the stall. The horse lifted his head to watch them, a curious onlooker. "I had a sister, eldest in the family. Our mother died when she was young, so this sister . . . she raised me and my brothers."

Luke had forgotten how slow, how measured and deliberate Amos could be when he told a story. He wasn't quite sure where this story was going, but he hoped it didn't have something to do with the cherry bomb blowing up the mailbox. He made himself calm down as he listened to Amos unwind the story about his sister.

"Her name was Julianne. I named my firstborn, Julia, after her. We tried to get my sister to come visit us here at Windmill Farm. Tried and tried, but she didn't like to travel. Finally, at long last, she agreed to come. She sent a letter with details about when she was coming. But we never got the letter."

Ah. Here it came. "Because I blew up the mailbox."

Amos nodded. "Since we didn't answer the letter, Julianne assumed we'd changed our mind. That we didn't want her to come."

Oh, come on. That seemed a little oversensitive. "Amos, couldn't you call her and explain? I'll call her for you. I'll make an apology."

"Turns out she was coming to say goodbye. She had a cancer that went fast through her, just like that." He snapped his fingers. "She was gone just a few weeks later. I've been sorry I never had a chance to say a proper goodbye to her. To tell her how much she meant to me. How much she did for me."

Oh . . . man. That shed a different light on the situation. "I'm sorry, Amos. I didn't realize. I'd never considered something like . . . well, that a letter like that would be the casualty to a prank."

"A prank." Steepling his fingers in front of him, Amos cleared his throat. "Who was it who said that every action has an equal and opposite reaction?"

"Um, I think it was Isaac Newton."

"I think that's what David wants you to learn through this healing time. Your actions—your *pranks*—have caused equal and opposite reactions." He raised his head and looked at Luke with his frank brown eyes. "It wasn't just a prank. You stole something from me with that cherry bomb. You robbed me of a chance to let my sister know how much I loved her before she died." Amos pushed the door open, and for a moment, a ray of piercing sunlight streamed through, illuminating the barn. Then he closed the door behind him and the barn turned shadowy again.

Luke had robbed Amos. Robbed him. It was a disarmingly honest choice of a word. He never would have thought of using that precise word, but it captured Amos's feelings. He stood, sighed, took off his hat and raked a hand through his hair. He felt that odd disoriented feeling again, a little bewildered, like he'd lost his bearings. It reminded him of a time as a boy when he had peered into his house from a back window, then went around to the side of the house to look through another window. And then yet another window. Each time, he discovered an entirely different perspective on the interior of the house. Same house, new views.

Oh boy, he thought with a sinking heart. Oh boy. This fence mending was going to take some work.

Six

I zzy's cold treatment of Luke made no apparent impact. She still woke each morning to find that her sheep had been fed and watered, and led out into the grazing pasture for the day. The clumsy folding wooden window to the farm stand—something that was a daily aggravation for her—had been opened and pulled back into its hooks. The two cows were milked and turned out for the day. She'd hardly milked those cows since he'd arrived at Windmill Farm, and her aching hands thanked him for it. But if Luke thought he was winning her over, he was sadly mistaken.

"Maybe Amos needs to give Luke more to do," she grumbled to Fern one afternoon. "I can take care of my own chores."

"Don't judge Luke too harshly," Fern said. "He's just trying to help."

Izzy wondered.

She closed up the farm stand and picked up the mail in the mailbox before heading up the driveway. There was another letter to Luke from his mother. The third one since he'd been at Windmill Farm. From the way Luke handled the envelopes—stuffing them in his pocket with a puckered brow—she had a funny feeling that he never even bothered to read them. Outrageous! She'd never received a handwritten letter in her life.

Izzy set the envelope at Luke's place setting for supper. When he came into the kitchen and saw it waiting for him, a cross look came over his face. Here and then gone. He reached out and grabbed it and jammed it in his pocket, just like always.

Izzy planned not to say a word about it. It wasn't her business what Luke Schrock did. But there was something about the way he handled those letters from his mother that made her mad. *Stay out of it, Izzy,* she told herself. *It's his letter, and you don't want anything to do with him, anyway.* But out it burst, anyway, full of shaky fury. "You don't deserve a mother at all."

The words fell like a stone into the quiet room, stilling Luke, who had been tinkering with a dented cap on a hurricane lantern—something Fern had left on his chair for him to fix. Slowly, he lifted his head.

She glared at him, could feel sparks flashing from her eyes as her annoyance boiled up and over. "Do you realize that? You're lucky to have a mother who loves you. You're lucky to have a mother at all." She heard the edge of longing in her voice and was embarrassed by it. "You act so sorry for yourself, playing the victim card. You've been given more than most. And what do you do with it?" She crossed her arms against her chest. "Nothing."

He looked at her a little strangely, and for good reason. Izzy wasn't sure if he was shocked because it was the first time she had initiated a conversation with him—and it was—or if it was because she sounded so furious. To her amazement, he actually looked "real" for a moment. The tough-guy façade dropped off and he looked honestly stirred and shaken. It made her anger drop a notch or two. Before he could respond, in walked Amos and Fern, deep in a perplexing conversation about an unwanted insect found in a few peach trees, and supper got under way.

The next morning, Izzy went down to the farm stand to set it up for the day. She half expected it to be closed up tight after the sharp way she'd spoken to Luke last evening. To her surprise, he had still opened it up for her. The sheep had been put in the pasture, the cows had been milked. She thought she had Luke pretty well figured out, had attributed plenty of critical characteristics to him, but she hadn't expected this. She hadn't thought him to be steadfast.

The sound of footsteps approaching made her spin around. Luke was heading toward the farm stand, a large box of fresh-picked cherries in his arms. She moved some things around so he'd have room to set it down. "Put it there." She looked around the farm stand for some plastic bags and found them at the bottom of a box she kept tucked in the corner. She wished she had some shelves, more storage. Before the first bus came through, she would put those fresh-picked cherries into one-pound bundles, tied up with a twine knot, ready to go.

She rummaged through the box to find a small chalkboard and a piece of chalk. It was something new she'd started this season—the day's produce and price per pound were written out in her best handwriting. Calligraphy, Fern called it, and while Izzy didn't think it was all that good, she had found a book to teach her precise lettering. It seemed to make a difference—these bags of red cherries were snatched up by the tourists.

Luke didn't get her hint that she was ignoring him. He had set down the box and leaned a hand on the small counter. "My mother . . . she left for Kentucky with Sammy, my little brother. And Galen, her husband. They're gone for a few months. Maybe longer."

She wondered why he bothered to tell her this, because she already knew.

Luke took off his hat to cuff the sweat off his forehead and raked his hair back out of his eyes with his fingers. It was getting long, Izzy thought. Soon he'd look like any other Plain man. Sort of.

Luke dropped his hat back on his head and cleared his throat in a nervous way. "You see, my father died when I was just a boy. He left a lot of problems for my mother when he died. I'm not sure I understand all of it, but he had a finance company—sort of an investment company—for the Plain people. He made some bad decisions, really bad, and the company went belly up. A lot of good people lost their life savings. Then he died, unexpectedly . . . and my mother had to pick up the pieces. She had a lot on her shoulders. Dealing with the company's bankruptcy, trying to pay people back what she could, taking care of my father's mother, who, believe me"—he rolled his eyes—"was no sweet petunia. My brothers and sister and I, we've all given her a lot of trouble. But my mother, she's a strong woman. Strong and kind. If anything, probably too kind."

It was the first honest conversation Luke had ever had with Izzy, though it was more of a monologue. She took care to show no sign of interest, but she was listening.

"You misspelled cherries. Two *r*'s."

She wiped it with the back of her hand, embarrassed, and fixed it, trying to act nonchalant. Spelling was not her strong suit.

"Galen King was our neighbor. He and my mom, they ended up getting married. I'm glad for her. Galen is good to her. He loves her. I guess it's just that . . . sometimes it seems like she moved on before I did." He scuffed a clump of dirt with the toe of his boot. "I was hoping she'd be here when I got back. I guess that's why I haven't bothered to read the letters." He looked up at Izzy. "Dumb reason, huh."

"Yup. You're trying to punish her. She hasn't done anything wrong. She's living her life, that's all."

Luke blew out a puff of air. "Okay, I told you about my mother. So Izzy, what happened to your mother?"

Something seemed to snap shut inside of Izzy as a feeling of familiar sadness crept in. She stilled her writing but didn't look over at him. "That's none of your business."

"Oh no. No no no. You can't dish out what you gave me last night at dinner, and then act all high and mighty. If I'm lucky to have a mother at all—and you're right, you're absolutely right, I *am* lucky to have a mother—then what's happened to your mother?"

Stalling, Izzy finished the chalkboard and set it on its stand, trying to think of how to answer Luke, if she should answer him at all. Her mother's face suddenly swam into view, at least what she thought she had looked like. Only fuzzy memories remained of her mother. Some bad, but some good—singing a song, baking cookies together. All those recollections ended abruptly one day.

Something had happened, something terrible, and a social

worker arrived at the little house to plunk Izzy into foster care. She was never told where her mother had gone or what had happened to her.

Some foster homes were nice enough, but not all. Her first foster family was the best one, and there were days when she nearly forgot she had a missing mother. Nearly. She lived with them for a few years. But then her foster father lost his job and they had to move to another state to live with their elderly parents. Izzy begged them to take her with them, but they couldn't add another child to the mix. On the day that the social worker drove Izzy away from that family, she felt something harden inside, like the way Fern's caramel could harden over her brownies. There might be something still soft underneath, but it would take a fork and knife—or maybe a chisel—to break through. She made a promise to herself: she would never let herself hurt like that again. Never.

The older she grew, the less interested families were to foster her. One time, a social worker drove her to a new home. The foster mother took one look at her and shook her head. "No way. Not here. I don't want a girl who looks like *that* to be around my man." Izzy was only twelve.

Mostly, she ended up in group homes—depressing, dreary, soulless places. She quizzed the social workers whenever she met with them. Where was her mother? Could Izzy write to her? Could she visit her? Someday, maybe, they would say. But not until she was older.

When Izzy was young, she created stories about her mother, about why she had disappeared so suddenly and so completely. Her favorite was that her mother was living under the Witness Protection Program, hiding because she'd provided valuable information to the Feds about the Mafia.

Another story was that her mother was a famous actress—Nicole Kidman came to mind because she had hair like Izzy's mother—and couldn't dare claim a love child without risk of losing Keith Urban.

As Izzy grew older, those fantasies slipped away, but her determination to find her mother only grew stronger. Finally a social worker admitted that her mother had made her a ward of the state of Ohio, so any communication was impossible. She suggested Izzy try to forget about her mother and just move on. Izzy couldn't accept that then, and she couldn't accept that now.

Those were her secrets. Her burdens. She couldn't share them.

Chin tucked low, she kept on scooping cherries into plastic bags. She had taken so much time thinking that Luke just gave up, assuming she wasn't going to answer him, which she wasn't.

"All right then," he said. "Answer me this. You really think I play the victim card as a way of life?"

She stopped pouring cherries into bags and turned to him. "Absolutely." She put her hands on her hips. "Absolutely I do. It's your comfort zone. Blame others instead of taking responsibility for yourself. Instead of being grateful for a chance to start again. Pity party of one."

He stared at her in that intense way, with those electric blue eyes of his, and she could feel the color building up in her cheeks. "Well, I did ask, didn't I?" He tipped his hat to her, backing away, and pivoted on his heels, walking up the driveway to the barn.

Windmill Farm's orchards in the month of June seemed to Luke to be as close to the Garden of Eden as a man could get. Row after row of carefully tended old, old trees, some over sixty years old. Some even older, Amos said, planted as saplings by his great-grandparents. Many of those were gone now, but a few apple trees remained and bore fruit. Amos said he never sold those late-in-the-season apples. They were meant just for the family. They gave the best cider known on earth, said Amos. He promised him the first sip after the fall harvest and Luke couldn't wait to sample it. He stopped abruptly, surprising himself. Would he still be here this fall? He didn't usually think much beyond a few days at a time. To think past a week felt like it hurt his brain. Mind stretching.

Today the orchards were a kaleidoscope of color: kelly-green leaves, swelling apple blossoms of pink and white, petals carpeting the ground, cherry trees dotted with bright red, and above it all, a sky wide and blue as a robin's egg. He picked a ripe cherry, a perfect one, ate it, and wondered as he swallowed if this was the fruit that had once tempted Eve. Or maybe it was something else entirely, something that had long become extinct. But he could imagine the temptation of a just-picked cherry. Yes, he could.

Right after breakfast, Amos had taken him up to the orchards to start thinning the peach buds. It seemed like a shame to tear a budding fruit away, but Amos explained that doing so was helpful for the fruit. "Believe it or not, I get the same amount of bushels if I thin than if I don't."

"How?"

"Fruit size. Bigger, better flavor, better pest control," Amos explained in his slow, deliberate way. "Thinning, done properly, helps a tree focus its energy. Grow strong roots."

And then he proceeded to teach Luke how to carefully thin the buds. "Start thinning when the fruit is about the size of a quarter. Leave the largest, best-looking fruit per cluster. Use two hands to prevent breaking the entire spur. Two hands!"

Luke rolled his eyes under the shadow of his hat brim. This wasn't exactly rocket science.

"Hold the branch with one hand, pinch the fruit with your thumb and forefinger, and twist. Do it again."

And again and again. By the time Amos was finally satisfied that Luke wouldn't ruin his treasured trees, he'd thinned out an entire peach tree. Oddly enough, Luke had been affected by Amos's attitude, and the trees were starting to become precious to him too.

As he climbed the ladder to thin the next peach tree, Izzy's words replayed in his head. *Comfort zone of self-pity.* It wasn't an entirely new thought. The counselor would say that Luke preferred his "default position." Translation: old habits. He'd tried to help Luke see that he kept returning to a frame of reference that, though familiar and comfortable, had not been successful for him.

"It's almost like wearing a pair of glasses with the wrong prescription," the counselor had said. "You have to be willing to take them off and try on another pair. To see things clearly, distinctly. Instead of fuzzy. Instead of with self-pity."

Pity. There was that word again. Pity party. He was a pity party of one.

Izzy's words had slapped Luke with surprise. Kind of harsh words from someone who had only known him a few weeks. He wondered why in the world he'd tried to get Izzy to talk to him. Whenever she did, she said mean things.

But she was right too. He hadn't bothered to open any

letters from his mother. It was his way—his stupid, immature, stuck way—of feeling in control. Making his mother work for his love. Making her feel bad.

Argh. He hadn't even recognized it in himself, not until Izzy pointed it out to him.

He didn't want to stay stuck. He really didn't.

Tonight, he would read his mother's letters. Maybe he would even write back to her, to let her know he was doing okay. Not great, but okay.

He led the cows to the barn and milked them, then filled Bob's bucket with fresh water and left hay in his manger for him to find when Amos and Fern returned. The clean feeling of resolve continued in his heart. He washed up and went inside for supper. Izzy was chopping carrots on a wooden block and looked up in surprise when he walked into the kitchen.

"Where'd Fern and Amos go?" he asked.

"Amos had some deacon work to do, so Fern went along with him. They said not to wait supper for them." She kept her head down as she cut, but there was a determination in the way she sliced those carrots that made him . . . well, a little nervous. It was a very big knife she held in her hands. She scooped up the carrots on the side of the knife and sprinkled them over the salad. "Supper's ready," she said, setting the bowl on the table.

She slipped into her chair and bowed her head, still averting her eyes from him. He watched her as he settled into his chair, impressed that she was going to even eat with him. But then, Izzy never missed a meal. She liked to eat, and he admired a healthy appetite in a girl. He lowered his head, offering thanks, and by the time he lifted his head, she was already spooning out some green beans onto her plate.

So cool was the air between them, Luke figured they'd spend the entire meal in punishing silence. It was so quiet that he could hear himself chewing. This was ridiculous. He should do something.

"Izzy, I'm sorry that I offered you a beer. It was foolish of me, and I regret it. Hugely. Enormously. But there's a reason I did it. It was because I was trying to get you to talk to me."

A shadow passed over Izzy's face, disappearing as quickly as Luke had marked it.

She didn't respond.

"I'll never put you in a situation like that again. Never. I give you my word."

She glanced at him briefly and shrugged her shoulders. What did that mean? That she didn't believe him? Or more likely, that she didn't care what he did.

"Can we start over? I'm Luke Schrock." When she still didn't answer, he said, "Why can't we be friends? Just friends. Nothing more."

She eyed him. "You don't seem like the type of guy who has friends who are girls. Just girlfriends."

"I don't deny that. But it would be good for me, I know that much. And it might be good for you too. To have a friend who's a guy. No strings attached. No expectations. Just friends."

"Somehow I doubt you'd be a good friend. I've heard stories about you."

There it was again. His reputation kept returning to interfere with his new life. Tricky, that. "Fair enough." Luke steepled his fingers together, the way David would when he was thinking something over. "Have you ever heard Fern use this saying? 'Every saint has a past and every sinner has a future.'"

"No. I've heard plenty of her sayings, but not that one. It doesn't make any sense."

Luke sighed. "Izzy, why not take a chance on me? At least, let me prove to you that I can be a good friend."

Before she could respond, a horse whinnied in the distance, and another answered. It meant a buggy would soon be rolling up the driveway. Luke got up from his chair to meet the buggy and relieve Amos, so he and Fern could come in and get started on supper.

He unhooked Bob and walked him to the barn. Inside, he hooked the horse to cross-ties, checked his hooves for stones, brushed him down, and then led him into his stall for his waiting hay. By the time Luke rejoined everyone at the kitchen table, they were nearly done with supper. Izzy never did give him an answer. Actually, he was getting to know her well enough to realize that silence *was* her no.

SEVEN

Fern took Izzy along to her monthly comfort quilt gathering, held this June at Edith Lapp's house. Today they were making a pinwheel pattern, complex and multicornered. A year ago, that difficult quilt block would have sent Izzy spiraling into a silent panic. Not so, today. It amazed her how much she'd learned in the last year, mostly through oh-so-careful observation. She watched everyone, noticed everything. It pleased her that the women spoke Penn Dutch around her as they worked on their blocks, as if she were one of them. Amazing.

She wished Jenny were here. Ever since she'd started nannying for that English family, she couldn't get away during the day to join in on gatherings. She missed her. Unlike awful Luke Schrock, Jenny didn't probe or pry—she was much like Fern in that way. In many ways, in fact. Amos said Jenny moved to Stoney Ridge when she was young enough that Fern had a strong influence on her. They walked alike, talked alike, cooked and baked alike. Even the way they wore their aprons was similar—doubled around their small waists and pinned in the front, not the back.

As the women finished the blocks, they set them on the Ping-Pong table in the basement for Edith to arrange. This was always Edith's self-appointed job, whether the gathering was held at her home or not. Edith Lapp was a solid-looking woman, with broad shoulders and big, capable hands. There was nothing soft about her, especially not her personality. Yet for all her prickliness, she had an eye for color. She was the one who, last spring, had shown Izzy how to display flowers, fruits, and vegetables in an eye-catching way. That was the very day that the bus driver stopped for peonies for his wife, and the farm stand's sales took a decided upturn.

Edith would inspect the blocks, narrow a few down to the very best, turn them over to examine their backside, then choose the best block as the centerpiece. All others would fan out from that centerpiece. Same thing, every month.

As humble as Amish women could be, and should be, and were expected to be, and mostly were, they all held their breath as Edith flipped through the blocks, one after the other. When Edith finally plucked the best from the rest, the maker of that block would sputter in surprise, blushing furiously as she insisted her block didn't belong in that center spot. Edith paid no mind. Same scenario, every month.

The funny thing was that Izzy had quickly figured out that each woman was vying to get her block chosen for that centerpiece. They competed with each other, they just did so quietly.

As she pondered those thoughts, she realized that the room had grown quiet. Everyone had turned to look at her. Everyone except Edith. She was focused on laying out the quilt top. Izzy's gaze swept the circle of Plain faces, all eyes fixed on her. Her heart started thumping. What happened? What had she done wrong?

Fern tugged her sleeve forward toward the Ping-Pong table to see the chosen center block for the quilt. She pointed to it. "I do believe that one is yours, Izzy."

⸻

It was a moonless night, so dark there were no shadows. Something startled Luke out of a sound sleep. He blinked a few times, slowly emerging out of the fog of sleep, until he realized someone was in the room with him, breathing heavily. He froze, as his mind tried to grasp and sort out the situation. Then he heard a snort, a familiar kind of snort, and got a blast of hay-breath on his face.

"Bob!" Luke jumped off the cot. "Bob, what're you doing? How'd you get out of your stall?"

He grabbed a rope off the pegboard and tossed it over and around Bob's neck, lasso-like. Now what? The tack room was tiny and narrow. "Okay, buddy, you're going to have to back up the way you came in." Slowly, he maneuvered Bob backward until he was out in the aisle of the barn again and could circle around to be led to his stall. The door was slid wide open. Had Luke not fastened the latch? He slid the door shut, fastened the latch, double-checked it to make sure it was tightly latched, then yawned and went back to bed.

Close to dawn, Luke woke with a gasp to find Bob standing over his cot again, breathing down on him. Again, he maneuvered the gentle horse backward, then to his stall, and fastened it shut. This time, he gave up on sleep and dressed for the day. He wiggled the stall's latch a few times to see if it needed tightening, but the screws seemed snug. He milked the cows and led them out to the pasture for the day, opened the holding pen for Izzy's sheep and herded them into the grazing pasture. The sky was full of low-lying gray clouds, so he wanted them to eat up while they could. If lightning and thunder started, the animals would all be herded back to the barn. Not all farmers had that policy, but Amos did. On Luke's way to the house, he got a whiff of bacon sizzling in the frying pan. Best smell in the world, hands down.

Amos was on the porch, sipping coffee.

Luke opened his mouth to tell him about Bob, but Fern called to them to come in and eat while it was hot. His stomach rumbled with hunger. He sat down across from Izzy, who kept her eyes averted from him, as usual, and followed Amos's lead to tuck his chin for a silent prayer. Tiredly, his eyes sagged shut and he basked in the scent of coffee and bacon. Amos often took a long time in those silent prayers; Luke prayed too but more efficiently than Amos. He usually finished and had a few minutes left to think over the day's agenda. This morning, he relaxed in the warmth of the kitchen, the comforting smells of bacon and coffee, and drifted off. He wasn't sure how much time passed, but when he jerked awake, he opened his eyes to find Amos, Fern, and Izzy staring at him, a bit concerned.

Izzy broke the silence. "I figured you swallowed an olive pit or something and needed the Heimlich." If she thought he was in grave danger, she made no effort to help him. Instead, she pointed to the plate beside him. "Pass the toast."

"What's the matter?" Fern said. "You look like you missed a night's sleep."

Luke frowned. "Just about. I woke up to find Bob breathing down on me. Twice."

Amos looked stricken. "Bob? My Bob?"

"That's the one."

"You mean to tell me he was in the tack room? How'd he get out of his stall?"

"I don't know."

"Did you forget to latch his stall? You must've."

"That's what I thought, the first time. I double-checked it after I led him back to his stall. But then it happened again. I woke up to a loud, nose-clearing snort from Bob. Right in my face."

"Poor Bob," Fern said.

Amos nodded in agreement. "I'll go down to the barn after breakfast and make sure he's okay."

"Bob? Bob? What about me?" Luke's gaze jumped from Fern to Amos to Izzy and back again to Fern.

Izzy had been buttering her toast, listening to the conversation. To his outrage, he saw a look of mirth flit through her eyes. Here and then gone. This was *not* funny. "People. I would appreciate a little sympathy. It was a very weird way to wake up. It was like Bob was a doctor standing over a patient. If he could talk, I half expected to hear him say, 'You okay?'"

With that last sentence, Izzy ducked her head down, and her shoulders started shaking. It was so strange that even Fern set her coffee cup down to watch her.

A giggle bubbled up into Izzy's throat, then burst out. She started laughing so hard that she had to clasp her hands tight over her mouth, but still the giggles came. Fern's eyebrows lifted with a smile. Slightly at first, because that was Fern's way, but then her smile grew from ear to ear. She looked at Amos, and their eyes shared some kind of message, and then he, too, started to chuckle.

"Wait just one minute." Luke looked at them, astounded. "Did you all set me up? Is this a prank? Some kind of rite of passage for Fern's Home for Wayward Boys?"

A cackle burst out of Fern, like a rusty hinge opening, and Luke realized she was laughing. Fern Lapp was *laughing*. Amos's belly jiggled with amusement, and Izzy had both hands clasped over her mouth, tears running down her face like a river.

"What is the *matter* with the three of you?"

Fern took in a deep breath, getting herself under control. "Oh Luke, that felt good. I haven't laughed so hard in a long, long time. Not since Jimmy Fisher's eyebrows got blown off and he walked around for a month with a surprised look on his face." She took in one more deep breath. "No, nobody has set you up."

"Is Bob a trick horse?"

That only got everyone laughing again. "Bob's a little long in the tooth for tricks," Amos said, wiping tears off his cheeks. "No, there's got to be some other explanation."

"What?"

Amos shrugged. "Don't know."

"If we don't know why it happened, it'll happen again."

Fern slapped her palms on the table. "Now *that*, Luke Schrock, is the first wise thing that's ever come out of your mouth."

Amos nodded in agreement. "First one I can recall." He gave her a broad smile and reached his coffee cup up for a refill. Fern jumped up to pour it and breakfast picked up where it had been before Luke had nodded off.

Izzy hadn't meant to eavesdrop. As a favor to Fern, she'd taken a basket of ripe peaches from Amos's orchard over to Edith Lapp. Edith's grandparents had helped Amos's grandparents plant those peach saplings, back when they were but children, and in remembrance, he always made sure Edith received the first fruits of the season. Izzy couldn't imagine what it would be like to have lived in one place so long.

So she'd brought the basket over to Edith's and was in the kitchen, emptying Fern's basket into a bowl, trying to avoid Hank Lapp and his yelling, and that was when she heard Luke arrive. So frustrating! He was everywhere she was.

To leave meant she had to go out the way she came in, and that meant bumping into Luke. *No thank you.* She'd wait until he left if it took all day. She tried to remain utterly silent in the kitchen so that Luke wouldn't hear her. Edith and Hank wouldn't. She was pretty sure they'd already forgotten she was here.

She cocked an ear to the open door to find out when Luke would wrap it up and leave—whatever it was that brought him here, of all places. That was really all she wanted to know. Soon, she was engrossed.

"I came to apologize to you," she heard him say. "A few years ago, I played that trick on your sister."

What trick? Whose sister? Izzy crept closer to the door.

"It was a shocking thing," Edith said.

"SHOCKING," Hank echoed.

"Every day that summer," Edith said. "Same time each day."

"WHY WOULD YOU DO SUCH A FOOL THING?"

Izzy leaned closer to the door. What had Luke done?

"That summer, you see," Luke said, "I was conditioning Galen King's Thoroughbreds for traffic. I went past your house each afternoon, and saw an older woman sitting on the porch."

"My sister, her health was poor," Edith said. "She came to spend the summer with us. My brothers and I, we each took a turn having her live in our homes. She liked being with me in the summer. Every afternoon, she'd sit on the front porch and watch the world go by."

"Yes, well, I noticed her. And then I thought it would be amusing if she were to see me gallop past on Galen's horse, riding backwards."

"AMUSING? YOU COULD HAVE KILLED YOURSELF."

"At the time, it seemed more funny than dangerous." Silence fell. Luke cleared his throat and said, "So I wondered how that—well, hoax—might have seemed to your sister? Guessing it wasn't so amusing to her."

More silence. Awkward, awkward silence. Then Edith said, "My sister had Alzheimer's disease. You galloping a horse while sitting backwards provoked great confusion and distress to her."

"NO ONE BELIEVED HER."

"Not at first."

"NOT FOR A LONG WHILE, EDITH. We thought she was just plain CUCKOO. That made her even MORE distressed."

"Then one day we saw it for ourselves," Edith said. "The horse went flying by, with you hanging on backwards. But us seeing it too, that only made it worse for her."

"Why?" Luke said.

"Gave her NIGHTMARES," Hank said.

"Terrible nightmares. She feared it to be a premonition of her death."

"SHE THOUGHT THE ANGEL OF DEATH WAS A-COMING FOR HER."

"And she stopped sitting out front on the porch in the afternoons. Something she'd loved to do."

Izzy heard Luke let out a discouraged sigh. Strange, how a sigh could say so much. "Could I speak to her?" she heard him say, his voice surprisingly tender. "To apologize."

"She's not here," Edith said crisply.

"Maybe I could write to her. Try to explain."

"SON, SHE'S GONE TO HER GLORY."

Edith sucked in a deep breath. "Not long after."

"You don't think . . . I mean, that backwards riding, surely it couldn't have . . . it didn't scare her to death." Luke's voice rose an octave. "Did it?"

No one answered. Not even Hank.

$\mathcal{E}$IGHT

In the middle of the night, a loud crashing sound burst through the air. Woken from a deep sleep, Luke thought it was thunder and lightning at first, until he heard the sound of screeching tire wheels. He jumped out of bed, grabbed his pants, and put them on as he ran outside to see what in the world had happened. He noticed a light go on up in the house, first one, then another. Everyone was awake, including every animal on the property. The horses were nickering, the cows were restless, the sheep were mewing.

Luke ran down the driveway, barefoot. He was almost to the bottom of the hill when he stopped in his tracks. He could see that a car had driven straight into the farm stand, then drove off. The stand was shattered, split into two pieces, right down the middle.

Amos joined him and let out a deep, defeated sigh.

"Who do you think did it?"

"Not sure. There's a group of boys, one church over, who have a car hidden. Could've been them. They've been causing a lot of trouble this spring." Pieces of splintered wood were scattered everywhere. Standing in the moonlight, with the shadows around him, Amos suddenly seemed utterly worn out. "Maggie, my first wife, she and I built that stand over thirty years ago. Later, my daughters used to sell fruit and vegetables there. Each one. I think of each one of them whenever I see it. Sweet, sweet memories. Gone, now." He closed his eyes, looking tired and hurt.

Luke didn't know what to do, what to say. He just wanted to make it all better. "I'll get this taken care of tomorrow, Amos. I'll clean everything up once it's daylight."

Fern and Izzy had walked down the driveway to join them. Fern said nothing, but tucked her arm through Amos's elbow.

"Why'd they do it?" Izzy asked.

"For kicks," Luke said. He knew, because he was once just like them.

Luke couldn't get back to sleep for the rest of that night. A barn cat yowled, over and over, and as soon as the sky started to lighten with the coming of dawn, he got up and dressed, found his gloves and tools, and went down the hill. He walked around the farm stand, surveying the damage with the flashlight. It was thoroughly demolished, like it had been constructed of balsa wood. He yanked pieces of splintered wood from the wreck and tossed them into a wheelbarrow. Each time the wheelbarrow was full, he pushed it over to the far side of the barn, out of sight, and dumped it out in a pile. Later, he'd pull nails out of the wood and salvage those pieces that could be reused.

He worked harder and harder, faster and faster, almost as if he were trying to outrun what was happening to his head, or maybe his heart. Finally, he stopped and dropped down to his knees, head hung low, eyes squeezed shut. The silence of the early morning felt almost overwhelming to him. Even the birds weren't singing yet.

He'd never been on the other side of this kind of damage. He'd never had to clean up a mess. He'd never had to see the look on someone's face whose property had been carelessly damaged, for no good reason. He'd never had to hear their memories, like he did when Amos told him about building the farm stand with his first wife, Maggie. He'd only been on the "for kicks" side. To be perfectly honest, he enjoyed knowing he'd caused distress to others. It made him feel powerful.

The thought revolted him.

For the first time in years, Amos lay in bed long after Fern got up to start the day. He hadn't been able to fall asleep until nearly dawn. His mind kept replaying images of his Maggie, of building that farm stand together when they were newly married. And then of his children, working the stand each summer.

Amos had three daughters and one son from his first marriage with Maggie: Julia, Sadie, M.K., and Menno, who was a special child. Menno's thoughts had circled slower than most people's did, but his heart had responded more quickly than others. Amos put his hand over his heart, feeling the scars beneath his pajama top. Menno had a fine heart. He knew that for a truth.

They were a happy family, living at Windmill Farm, tending the orchards the way his father and grandfather and great-grandfather had done. Amos and Maggie had been grateful for what God had given them, and did their best

93

to teach their children to love God, and love being Plain. In that order.

And then Maggie died an untimely death. Amos knew that God was sovereign in all things—all things—but losing his Maggie broke his heart to pieces. She was so young, so full of life, and she didn't deserve what had happened to her. She'd gone to help an English neighbor with her children, and she never came home. Something had gone terribly wrong.

It seemed as if the world lost its color for Amos after Maggie's death, like it was all in black and white. It took him a long time to surrender his anger with God over allowing Maggie's passing. A long, long time.

And then, one day, Fern Graber appeared as the new house-keeper at Windmill Farm, thanks to an advertisement in the *Budget* that his uncle Hank had placed. She soon became indispensable to them all. Shades of color started coming back. Not quite as brilliantly as when Maggie was still alive, but there was color, nonetheless. One by one, his children left the nest to marry and start families of their own. Somehow, Fern brought more in. Motherless children who needed them. Jenny Yoder. Jesse Stoltzfus. Izzy Miller, his favorite. Luke Schrock, his least favorite.

And in the midst of caring for these young people, Amos was learning the greatest lesson a man could ever learn—love wasn't finite. Just the opposite. It was limitless. There was always more love left in this world to give, and to receive.

Fern had always known that truth. She opened her heart to those in need, reminding Amos of David Stoltzfus in that way. The two of them never gave up on anyone, and over time Amos had learned to trust their instincts. Izzy was a different girl than when she first arrived here. It took her six

Suzanne Woods Fisher

months to look Amos in the eyes, as if she automatically didn't trust him and thought he might try to hurt her. He took care never to touch her, not even brushing shoulders past her in a doorjamb. He wondered about the men in her life, and it made him ashamed for his gender.

He still had reservations about Luke's boarding at Windmill Farm, even if he was stuck in the barn. He wasn't going to let Luke Schrock throw any kind of glitch into this important time of healing for Izzy. He often reminded Fern as much, and she would give him a look. *The* look. "Luke is in a healing time too. They both need us, Amos Lapp. You just watch and see what the Lord can do."

Amos hoped she was right. He might be the head of this family, but he knew that Fern made all the decisions.

Still, if Luke caused any trouble that set Izzy back, he would feel he was to blame. And with the doctor wanting to run more tests on his heart, he felt troubled that he might have allowed Fern to open the door to something bigger than they could handle. Even Fern had her limits.

Out of the corner of his eye he saw the time on the alarm clock. Good grief. It was already past seven in the morning. He threw off the covers and rolled out of bed to get the day started.

Izzy put the stamped envelope into the mailbox and gazed up at Windmill Farm, at the squeaky red windmill, the woollies that dotted the green pasture, the marten houses with birds zooming in and out like it was an airport. Oh my soul, how she loved it here.

This morning, nosy Luke Schrock had asked her what

brought her to Windmill Farm and she had hedged, avoiding a response. The answer was no business of his. That, and it was a complicated answer. She'd been thinking of it all day long.

It was a strange path that brought her to this Amish farm. It had to do with alcohol, a graveyard, and an old woman.

An older girl had smuggled booze into the group home, right under the housemother's nose, and taught Izzy the benefits of a buzz. By fifteen, Izzy never went a day without a drink or two. Or three.

This girl talked Izzy into running away to move in with her cousin in Lancaster, Pennsylvania. After plotting and planning their escape, the two slipped out of school during lunch period one day to hitchhike all the way to Pennsylvania. The cousin looked Izzy up and down and invited the girls in. That very night she found out why he was so welcoming. She ran from him, ran from the apartment, walking the city streets until dawn, and ended up wandering through a graveyard. She followed the smell of wood smoke to find an old woman living in a makeshift tent. Over a little campfire, the woman was stirring a pot of hot water. Izzy watched her open a package of Quaker Oats oatmeal and pour it in. Izzy was so hungry, her stomach practically twisted inside out. The woman noticed Izzy, lifted another package of oatmeal, and waved her over to the fire.

That old woman, her name was Sheila, offered Izzy more than food. She took her under her wing and taught her how to live on the streets. "Sleep in a graveyard, darlin'," Sheila said in her raspy voice, "and no one'll ever bother you."

She told Izzy to disguise her looks so that she didn't attract attention. She cut Izzy's hair short, gave her a Philadelphia

Phillies baseball cap to wear, showed her how to keep her head down, chin to her chest, and to never look anyone in the eye. She taught her how to identify likely candidates for handouts and which garbage cans near the public market were the best ones to scrounge food for the day.

A few months later, Izzy went back to the graveyard at day's end to discover that Sheila had packed up and moved on, without a word of warning. She'd left the tent behind for Izzy but nothing else. It was another abandonment for Izzy, another moment of realizing she couldn't, shouldn't, depend on anyone.

One afternoon, near the Lancaster Public Market—a good place Izzy had discovered for easy pickpocketing among distracted crowds—she noticed a horse and buggy parked at a hitch.

Seeing the buggy evoked a long-forgotten memory. An Amish family had lived near the house where she and her mother had been staying. When her mother left her at home alone, which was often, Izzy would wander over to that Amish family. There were children there, all ages, all varying shades of redheads—she remembered that vividly—and they waved Izzy into their circle to play with them. The older ones spoke English to her. One time, they even took her for a buggy ride. It was her favorite childhood memory.

She longed to be one of them. Their home was so peaceful. The family sat around the table for meals, three times a day. The father, that kind, kind father, he was *home*. Sometimes, she remembered, when the father mowed his lawn, he would slip across the street and mow theirs too.

She walked over to the buggy and circled it. On the front seat sat a wool scarf and a pair of gloves. Too trusting, she thought. She reached in and snatched the scarf and gloves, pocketing them. Emboldened, she slid open the buggy door wider to look for loose change or anything else that might be valuable. She found a few dollars tucked under the floor mat and stuffed them in her coat. She slipped out of the buggy and walked up to the horse to stroke its velvet nose.

"My horse likes you."

Izzy whipped around, startled. Her heart started to pound as she realized this Amish man had probably seen her rifle through his buggy. She backed away, but there was something about this bearded man's eyes that made her stop. She dipped her head, but not before she'd given him a quick once-over. Those eyes, she thought. They were gentle. She'd expected accusing eyes.

"His name is Bob," the Amish man said. "He's been my buggy horse for eight years now. He's a fine Thoroughbred. Bought him off my neighbor Galen King when he was only two years old. Right off the tracks. We think of him as one of the family."

Izzy glanced at the horse. Bob. Bob the buggy horse. Like one of the family. She found herself envying Bob.

"Say, are you hungry? You look a little hungry. There's a food truck right over there. Let me buy you a burger."

She shifted from one foot to the other. "I didn't think you people were that type."

With the lift of an eyebrow, he said, "The hungry type? We're always hungry for a good hot meal. You stay here, I'll be right back."

She watched him cross the street and stand in line at a food truck. *Run, Izzy*, she told herself. *Get out of here while you can. He saw you steal his things. He* must *have seen you.*

But she couldn't make herself go. Or rather, her empty stomach couldn't make her go. She hadn't had a hamburger that wasn't fished out of cold garbage in a long, long time. Still, she watched the Amish man carefully, making sure he wasn't calling the cops. She was ready to bolt, if she needed to.

She always had a plan to bolt, wherever she was. Sheila had taught her that particular strategy for living on the streets, and it had proved useful many times. Have a getaway plan figured out for every situation. Each one.

She continued to watch the Amish man as he patiently made his way up the line of the food truck to order a hamburger. He returned with a white bag and held it out to her. "My name is Amos Lapp. I'm Amish, in case you're wondering."

Cautiously, she took the bag from him. Inside was a burger and fries, smelling so good her tummy rumbled. Still, she wondered what he wanted from her.

But Amos Lapp only smiled. "Better eat them while they're hot. French fries taste like cardboard when they're cold." He got into the buggy, gave the horse a clucking sound, and drove off, giving her a wave as he passed.

She watched him go, wondering how he knew what cardboard tasted like. The smell of the hamburger and fries overcame her and she sat on a bench to dig into the bag. Hot, crisp, salty French fries had never tasted so good.

A week later, she saw Bob the buggy horse at the Lancaster Public Market again. Same time, same place. She scratched the horse's big nose and smoothed his forelock, when the Amish man appeared out of nowhere and offered to buy her a hamburger and fries. He never asked her name, or anything else from her. Or of her.

On the third week, she made a point to be there, waiting for Bob the buggy horse and the Amish man to drive in to the hitching post. She hid behind the food truck, watching for them. Like clockwork, the horse and buggy appeared. A young woman hopped out of the buggy and the Amish man followed, after he tied the reins to the hitching post. She must be his daughter, Izzy realized, and the feeling of envy was so strong it nearly made her choke.

This time, as she patted Bob, the man said he had something for Izzy. He reached into the buggy and pulled out a large brown paper bag. "I thought you might like a change of menu. My wife, Fern, she put this together for you."

So he had a wife. A daughter and a wife. And a horse.

Inside the bag was food. A container of beef stew, a loaf of bread, and a small blueberry pie. All homemade. Izzy made herself eat it all slowly, savoring every bite. She washed out the containers as best she could and hid them in the bushes. The next week, she put the bag of containers on the buggy seat while Amos Lapp was inside the public market. And she added the scarf and gloves. The dollars, she'd spent on beer.

From a distance, she watched Amos walk over to the buggy and notice what was inside. She saw him look around for her, then smile when he spotted her. He waved, motioning her to come to the buggy. There was another bag in the back seat. He handed it to her. "From my wife. Fern loves to cook."

"You don't have to do this." *Please don't stop.* "I . . . I can take care of myself." *No I can't.*

"We like helping. I have three daughters, and lots of grand-children."

Out of Izzy burst a long-buried question. "Do you happen to know a family named Stoltzfus?"

Amos paused a beat, then tipped his head. "It's a common name among the Plain people. But our bishop is named David Stoltzfus. He has a big family. One boy and a bunch of girls. He's a fine man."

He waited for her to explain more, but she didn't. He seemed to sense that she didn't want any questions.

"If you ever need some help, you can call." He reached inside his coat and gave her a card. "You'll have to leave a message on the phone shanty's machine. But I'll get the message. I'll do what I can to help you. David will too."

Izzy hesitated, then reached out to take the paper. Her hand was shaking, she hadn't had a beer since yesterday, and he noticed.

"There's lots of ways our church can help you. Just . . . call and let me know you want the help."

Izzy pocketed the paper. "Why? Why would you want to help someone like me?"

He blinked as if her words had startled him, but his voice remained kind and steady. So kind. "What does that mean . . . someone like you?"

She kept her eyes cast down. "Just a girl on the streets."

"But you're not just a girl on the streets. You're a child of God. You're of great value to the Lord, a pearl of great price."

The kind look in his eyes was what undid her. Had anyone *ever* looked at her like that? Like she was worth something. Amos Lapp reached inside his pocket and pulled out a few quarters. "Just in case you want to call. There's a public phone inside the market." He put them in her hand. "Call anytime. There's a better life you're meant to live. If my wife and I can help you find that life, we'd like to."

She felt a shiver of something—hope maybe, longing, or relief. She didn't know. She just knew she couldn't turn away from it. Whatever it was this man had, she wanted it.

She could have spent the quarters he'd given her on booze. She should have, because by that night, she was feeling sick from not drinking. Nauseous, headachey, shaky. She hated being so dependent on booze. Hated it! But couldn't help it. In the middle of the night, unable to sleep, she left her tent in the graveyard and went to the public market to leave a message before she lost her nerve. She remembered feeling as if she might throw up, but her fingers kept pushing those buttons, and she waited, listening for the Amish man's familiar voice. She should hang up. *Hang up, Izzy, hang up.* But she didn't. It was like something bigger than herself was pushing her along, to that life she was meant to live, like the Amish man had said. In a shaky voice she hardly recognized as belonging to herself, she said she'd be at the public market at the same time tomorrow afternoon. That she needed some help. When she hung up, she promised herself that she wouldn't drink until tomorrow afternoon, no matter how sick she felt. If that bearded Amish man didn't show up, *then* she could drink. Not until then.

But there he was, waiting for her, along with Bishop David Stoltzfus.

ℕINE

One of the reasons Izzy liked spending much of her day down by Windmill Farm's farm stand was that she could be the first to get the mail each day, and the postal delivery guy was quite inconsistent. You never knew when he was going to be driving by. She never missed him, though. Even if she wasn't down at the farm stand, she recognized the sound of his squeaky truck wheels as they rounded the bend, and she would stop whatever she was doing to hurry to the mailbox. Before she opened it, she would say a prayer. *Please, please, please! Let today be the day.*

Izzy had a ten-page list of addresses for women named Grace Miller who lived in the state of Ohio. The entire state. A very nice librarian at the public library had printed off the information for her. For the last six months, once or twice a week, she wrote a letter and mailed it, hoping one of the letters would find the Grace Miller she was looking for. Her mother. In each letter, Izzy explained who she was, where she was currently living, and that she wanted to establish contact with her. So far, most of the letters had come back, stamped *Return to Sender*, unopened. The rest were never answered. She kept track.

Today, she held her breath and repeated the prayer as she opened the mailbox. In the bunch was the usual stuff. A bill from the Hay & Grain, this week's copy of the *Budget*, which would bring hours of delight to Fern. She would spend the evening poring over it at the kitchen table, hemming and hawing over each district's stories, as if she knew every person in every church throughout all of North America.

As Izzy closed the box, she noticed one more envelope, a small yellow one, addressed to her. Her heart started to race. The return address said Grace Miller. First time. This was *it*. This was from her! She opened it as quickly as she could, tearing the envelope to get to the letter.

Dear Isabella,
 First things first. I am not the Grace Miller you are looking for. You can trust me on that. I am a 95-year-old woman who had three sons, and I've outlived them all.

Izzy dropped her hand holding the letter, disappointed. She sighed and finished reading it.

Second thing. It sounds to me like your mother has done a pretty good job staying out of sight. If she don't want to bother herself to find you, what are you doing, wasting your time trying to find her? My advice is to let her go, honey. She'll bring you nothing but heartache.

> *Yours truly,*
> *Grace Miller*

She tucked the letter back in the envelope and bundled everything together to take to the house. Why was this so hard? Or more importantly, why did she feel this compulsion to find her mother? Maybe she should just let it go. Stop looking. She tried that thought on for size as she went up the steep driveway. By the time she reached the top, she knew it didn't fit. She had to keep trying. She had a question to ask her mother. She just had to keep at it. Her mother was out there, somewhere. She had to find her. She *would* find her.

Inside the house, she put the *Budget* on the table so Fern would see it when she arrived home. The other letters she set at Amos's place setting. He always sat at the same seat. They all did. Fern said it was the Plain way of letting each person know they belonged somewhere, that they had a place at the table. *Ein Platz am Tisch.* Izzy liked that feeling. She liked that there was a Plain way of doing everything. After growing up with no structure at all, the Plain structure gave her great comfort.

She flipped through the pile left on Amos's chair for her yellow envelope to take up to her room and add to the pile of returned letters. And to cross this particular Grace Miller off the address on her list. Izzy had created a very orderly system with these letters. She was two-thirds of the way through the Ohio Grace Millers. Somehow, making it an orderly project helped her detach from the disappointment she felt when letters were returned. Worse still was the fear she kept suppressed of those letters that were not returned. A fear that her mother might have received one of those letters and didn't want to be found.

No. She wasn't going to allow herself to think that. She needed to think on something else, something upbeat, something lighthearted. As soon as she logged this letter into her spreadsheet, then she would go outside and feed the chickens. Those fat red hens always lifted her spirits.

She picked up the newspaper, looked through Amos's bills, swept the floor with her eyes to find today's letter. Where'd it go?

The kitchen door opened and in walked Luke Schrock. "You dropped this halfway up the driveway," he said, handing her the torn yellow envelope.

She snatched it out of his hands and eyed him carefully. Had he opened her letter? Had he read it? She couldn't tell. Oh my soul, she hoped not. Before she could think to ask, he was already out the door and off to the barn.

Luke had often been puzzled about Izzy's fascination with the day's mail. He'd seen her put letters in the mailbox, and each day she rushed to be the first to get the mail. Several times, he had noticed the way her countenance changed after she got the day's mail. She would hurry to the mailbox, a skip in her step, riffle through the letters and junk mail and newspapers, then slowly close the mailbox door. Chin tucked, her shoulders slumped as she walked up the driveway. It was tangible, her discouragement. It was palpable.

Those were the times, he had figured out, when she didn't receive what she was looking for. On the very few times when she did receive a letter, like today, she wasn't fit to keep company with a grizzly bear.

He thought of asking her to whom she was writing, but knew better than to ask Izzy anything of a private matter.

He could practically hear her snap back: "That's no business of yours, Luke Schrock."

Luke hadn't meant to read this letter, he truly hadn't. But the letter had fallen out of the envelope on the driveway. As he bent to pick up the letter and envelope, he saw that it was addressed to Izzy. Then a few words in the letter jumped out. *Grace Miller . . . out of sight . . . heartache.* He couldn't help himself—he scanned it quickly, reread it, glanced up when he heard the squeaky hinges on the kitchen door open and shut and knew Izzy had gone inside. He stuffed the letter into the envelope and started back up the hill.

Should he tell her? Should he not? He kicked around the thought of confessing that he had read the letter, but Izzy barely gave him the time of day as it was. If he admitted he'd poked his nose into her private letter, she might not ever speak to him again. She could be tetchy like that.

He felt a little ashamed of himself, but it was balanced out by the satisfaction he felt in knowing something about her. Inside the house, he handed her the letter and took off to the barn before she could grill him. He knew he would crack. Surprisingly, he'd never been a good liar.

As he went into the barn to the tack room, his mind rolled over with this information. So, Izzy was on a quest to find her mother. Luke gathered the facts he'd just discovered: her name was Grace Miller, she lived in Ohio, and obviously, she wasn't easy to find.

Then a new thought roared through as he considered again the letter in the yellow envelope. He would try to find this Grace Miller for Izzy. He could find her, he knew he could. How he'd go about it—that, he had no idea.

Amos and Fern sat in Dok's office, waiting for her to finish with a patient so she could tell them the results of Amos's recent tests that he'd undergone at the hospital. Stress tests, Dok called them. And they did stress Amos. They were awful.

One of the tests had him hooked up to all kinds of electrical currents while he walked and walked and walked on a treadmill. Another one had monitors taped to his chest that he had to wear for seventy-two hours. He buttoned his top shirt button and kept his coat on during lunch after church, despite a hotter-than-Hades kind of day, hoping no one would notice.

Amos resented wasting time and money on these tests, because he knew what they would tell him. He knew. His transplanted heart—this magnificent organ given to him by one he loved so dearly—was failing.

As summer deepened its hold, the weather turned hotter than hinges. Luke's work changed almost daily, from picking the ripe stone fruit—apricots, peaches, and nectarines—to mowing the first cutting of hay, raking it, and putting it up in the barn. The cut hay would feed Bob, the two milk cows, and Izzy's sheep through the winter when there was no grass left to graze.

Luke didn't mind farm labor as much as he thought he would. He could see the progress he made each day, and working in the open fields was peaceful work. He had a little breather now before the first variety of apples started to ripen, followed soon after by pears. The second mowing of hay wouldn't start until August. Somehow Amos knew, just by touch, when to cut so that the hay had the most milk in it.

On a hot July day, as Luke walked down the hill from the orchards to the barn, his gaze took in Windmill Farm. It was a beautiful piece of property, but it seemed like everything, every piece of it, needed fixing. The farm had always been pristine. Now, there was a blade missing off the red windmill, equipment was rusty, and everything squeaked. Everything. Hinges, floorboards, stair steps.

He tossed his sweaty shirt in a pile on the floor and looked around the small room for another shirt. On the workbench, he noticed the rather extensive fence-mending list that David had given to him. He had planned to get through this list before the end of June. Give it one month. Get all those humbling conversations behind him as quickly as possible. But here it was, July, and he had stalled on it. He picked it up and looked at the next name David had written.

Alice Smucker. Snake in buggy.

Oh boy. Here we go.

He found an old red scooter in the barn and rode it over to Alice Smucker's. When he knocked on the door, he saw a curtain corner open and drop again, and the sound of scampering inside. He rapped on the door again. "Alice, it's Luke Schrock. I'd like to talk to you for a minute." He knocked again. "I'll stay outside."

"Go away!"

Encouraged that she was at least admitting she was home, he persevered. "Alice, could we just talk? Through the door, maybe?"

A long moment of silence. Then, "What do you want?"

He took off his straw hat and adjusted the brim. "I came to apologize to you. To make amends. I know I scared you, that day I threw a snake in your buggy. It was a stupid thing for me to do. I'm sorry I did it, Alice. I hope you can forgive me."

"I forgive you. Now go away."

He put his hat back on. "Alice, there's one more thing."

"Go away. I said I forgave you."

This was weird, talking through a door. "Alice, I need to ask you if that snake, well, I wondered if it has affected you in some adverse way?"

Silence.

He started to ramble, then, something he did whenever he was nervous. Pressure talking, the counselor had called it, and it usually gave him cause for regret. He recalled a time when he talked nonstop during his first group therapy session, until finally someone in the group took off his shoe, threw it at him, and told him to shut up. "David told me to ask you specifically, Alice, if there's been any lasting effect. Maybe a nightmare? I can understand that. It would be frightening to have a snake in a buggy, and then to have the horse take off down the road like it did."

It was a harmless Eastern garter snake, he did remember that much. A common snake in Pennsylvania, kind of a pretty one with a cream belly. Alice had screamed like she was on fire, which scared the horse too. She hadn't been hurt, just badly shaken. And the horse was fine. He galloped for a while—a jerky canter might be a better description, for he was an old horse and quickly lost interest in the excitement.

At the time, it had seemed so funny to Luke—watching

plump Alice bounce along the buggy's front seat as the horse took off down the road.

"I think it'd be good for me to hear how you felt, Alice. Scared, I'm sure. And maybe it'd be good for you to say whatever you want to say to me too. Maybe it would make you feel better."

The door cracked open. He saw an eye peer out at him. One big worried eye. "I haven't left the house. Not since that terrible, terrifying day." And the door slammed shut.

Luke let out a soft moan. "Ohhh."

$\mathcal{T}$EN

A stillness, deep down in his soul, came over Amos. He stood at the top of the hill and turned slowly in a circle. His gaze wandered from the orchards on one side, to the house and farm on the other. Beyond the weathered fencing of the green pastures, beyond the red barn lined by a creek, beyond the road lined by trees, beyond the distant ridges that surged against the blue sky, filled with white puffy clouds. Something in that "beyond" was beckoning to him.

But in the pasture below, the cows bellowed a mournful wail. Milking time. Where was Luke?

By the time Amos had led both cows to their stanchions in the barn and brought hay in for them to munch on, Luke slid open the barn door. "Where you been? The cows need milking." He knew he sounded testy, but he didn't like his animals to be kept waiting.

"Sorry, Amos. I meant to be back by now. I had a little bit of spare time this afternoon, so I went over to Alice Smucker's." Luke ran to the back of the barn to get clean milking pails.

Amos took off his hat and wiped his brow with his handkerchief.

As Luke passed him to reach the cows, he said, "Why don't you go to the house? You look a little beat. I'll take care of the stock."

"Never mind me." Amos stuffed the handkerchief back in his pocket. "So how'd it go with Alice?" His gaze met Luke's and he saw him swallow hard, as if a pinecone were stuck halfway down his throat.

Luke sat on the stool in front of Lemon Thyme and wiped her down. "She said she hasn't left the house, not since the day I tossed a snake into her buggy." He glanced up at Amos, then down again. "That was a long time ago."

Amos nodded. "She's pretty bad off."

Luke's head jerked up. "All because of a snake in a buggy? Don't get me wrong. I'm not saying it wasn't a foolish thing to do. It was, it truly was, and I'm ashamed I thought it was funny. But we do live in the country. Snakes in cornfields and gardens are part of everyone's life. What if a car had backfired? Or if there were thunder and lightning? I mean, there's all kinds of unpredictable things that happen in life. I remember the tricks Galen had to try to socialize a buggy horse in training. One of them was with snakes. He knew a horse had to be conditioned for just about anything out of the ordinary."

Amos took in a deep breath, held it, then let it go. "Alice . . . she's always been the nervous type. Always imagined the worst kind of scenario. Something about that day, with the snake—well, the worst-case scenario came true for her. It set off something in her, something else, on top of her fear of snakes. She has agoraphobia. She's afraid to leave her house. David's tried everything—even brought doctors to her house. Nothing's helped. She won't step outside her house on the odd chance that she will encounter a snake."

"Well, if David and the doctors can't help, what can I do about it?"

Amos lifted his shoulders in a shrug. "I don't have the answer for that. But I do know she's been suffering." He went to the door, then turned back. "It's sure no way to live."

A weird feeling came over Luke. His heart started racing and his chest felt tight, like an anvil had dropped on it and he couldn't fill his lungs with air. He wondered if he might be having a heart attack. One thought kept circling through his head: *I did this to Alice. I might not have meant to, but I caused her to go off the deep end.*

He had to get away from the sour reek of the barn. As soon as he finished milking the cows, he bolted outside for fresh air and blinked against the sudden wash of sunlight. He stumbled to the side of the barn to get away from the glare and leaned against the barn's foundation to take in great gulps of air. Then his eyes lifted and he froze. On this side yard was the pile of wood from the destroyed farm stand. He'd planned to go through the pile to salvage wood and reclaim nails. Amos's apricots and peaches and nectarines, they'd taken priority. He'd forgotten all about this pile of wood.

As he gazed at the jumble of broken, splintered lumber, into his mind came a bright flash of insight. *This, this is what*

I've done to Alice Smucker. To others on the list. He'd left them in a broken heap. He let out a moan as he dropped to his knees in front of the pile.

What had he done to these innocent people? What had he done? Why had he done it? Tears started, one after the other until they were streaming down his face. His chin dropped on his chest. "I am a mess. A complete and total mess."

"If you ask me, I've always thought God does his best work with messes."

Luke's head jerked up. Amos stood a few feet away from him. How long had he been there? Still on his knees, he brushed tears off his face with his shirtsleeve. "Amos, I've done this kind of thing to plenty of people. I've never cared about what damage I'd left behind."

"Until now."

Luke gave a slow nod.

"Maybe this is just the place God wants you to be, Luke. Humble. Contrite. On your knees."

The clouds that had filled the afternoon sky were breaking up, limned from the setting sun behind them. Amos watched the moving clouds for a long moment. "A man can never tire of watching the changes in the sky. It fills me with wonder." He took a step closer and reached out to grab Luke's arms to lift him to his feet. "The movement of God's Spirit is always accompanied by a deep sense of awe."

"Is that in the Bible?"

"Nope. That's a David Stoltzfus quote from last Sunday's sermon."

Duly noted. Luke hadn't been paying attention.

Together, Amos and Luke finished caring for the animals

for day's end. Normally, Amos gave Luke instructions about what to do and left him to it. This time, they worked side by side, and Luke noticed how slowly Amos moved, how often he had to rest. He'd always seen Amos take a lot of pills at meals, part and parcel of the heart transplant he'd had years ago, but this seemed different.

Over these last two months that he'd been working directly for Amos, Luke had developed a strong admiration for the man. He'd learned a great deal from him—not just about caring for orchards, but other things too. Like just now, when Amos found him wrung out from emotions, on his knees and crying. He didn't let him off the hook, never minced words, but he also gave him a hand to help him stand up. There were times when it even occurred to Luke that Amos was the kind of father he'd wished he'd had. Caring, calm, wise. Firm but kind.

Concern for Amos's health filled Luke with a brand-new feeling. A sense of purpose. He was needed here, and he couldn't remember a time in his life when he had ever felt needed. The tightness in his chest loosened up, leaving Luke some breathing room for good intentions.

Purpose number one: cure Alice Smucker.

It was a scorching Saturday in July. A perfect afternoon to head to the library and bask in the air conditioning.

At the public library, Luke saw two librarians behind the desk and waited in line for the friendly one. He recognized the other one and wanted to stay clear of her. He'd had a run-in with her before. When it was his turn, he asked the friendly librarian if she knew of any books that helped people overcome their fear of snakes.

She peered at him over her bifocals. "Ophidiophobia?"

"Uh, no. I'm trying to help a woman with an abnormal fear of snakes."

She tried to swallow a smile. "That's what it is called. Ophidiophobia. Fear of snakes." She went to her computer and tapped furiously—it was impressive, for she never looked down at the keyboard—and then she wrote some numbers down for him. "Here's a few books that might give you the information you're looking for." She put a star beside one title. "This one, in particular, would be my choice."

"Thank you," Luke said, meaning it. As he hunted among the bookshelves, he thought of how he enjoyed reading so much that he'd wondered if he might like to work in a library. That was when he'd he'd never go back to the Amish. He'd even filled out a job application and handed it to that crabby librarian. She'd read through his application and pointed out that an eighth-grade education wouldn't even get him a job flipping burgers at McDonald's.

She had handed him back his application with a sneer. "Come back after you finish high school, college, and have completed graduate work in library science."

Science for libraries? What was *that*? He just knew he liked to read, and he liked being around people who liked to read.

He found the title that the friendly librarian had placed a star beside and sat down to read it. Within a few pages, he knew he'd found some valuable information. He needed paper and pencil to jot down notes and went back to the main desk to ask the librarian for them.

The crotchety librarian spoke first. "No."

The friendly librarian rolled her eyes. "Oh goodness, Betty. It's just paper."

"If we give paper to one patron, we have to give it to all."

The nice librarian sighed and handed Luke a pad of paper and a pen. He read and wrote and read and wrote. He hadn't even realized it was quitting time until the lights started going off. He scrambled, gathered his papers, and went to the main desk to check out the book.

Librarian Betty stood by the door with her large arms crossed against her generous chest. She had a beaklike nose and black button eyes that scowled at him as if she suspected him of trying to steal books.

He handed her the book. "I'd like to check it out. There's more information in it that I need."

"Where's your library card?"

"I don't have one."

"We close early on Saturdays. I'm not staying late to get you a library card." She lifted one eyebrow. "No doubt you don't even have proper identification."

"What kind of identification do I need for a library card?"

"Something with a picture." Those thin lips of hers pulled even thinner. "Driver's license is preferred."

Very funny. "I could bring my police record. It has my mug shot on it."

Her beady eyes went wide for a second, then narrowed. She thought he was tweaking her, but he actually wasn't.

"If you don't have a photo ID, bring some kind of proof of residence. An electric bill, for example."

Was she being serious? The sneer he'd sensed under her words certainly seemed snarky. "I'll come back tomorrow with something that proves residency."

"No, you won't."

"I will. I'll be back." There must be something at Windmill Farm he could use to prove residency.

"Not tomorrow. We're closed on Sundays. I read Amish fiction. You people are supposed to obey the Sabbath."

You people. Those kinds of sweeping remarks irked Luke. If he were a more mature person, like Amos or David, he'd respond in silence. Alas, he wasn't. "Say, did you hear the story about the Quaker farmer? A fellow broke into this farmer's house to look for cash. He figured that since Quakers were pacifists, he'd get away unharmed. But the Quaker farmer caught him in the act and pointed a shotgun right at him. 'Son,' he said, 'I would never do thee any harm yet thee is standing where I am just about to shoot.'" Luke chuckled. "I love that story."

The librarian glared at him. "I suppose you think you're funny."

"Actually, what I think is that many folks have ignorant perceptions about others. Even if they happen to work in a library." So maybe he shouldn't have added that last remark.

Her eyes narrowed again. "And I think you people ought to pick up after your horse and buggies."

Oh *that.* It was a longtime festering debate in Lancaster County that he had no interest in discussing. Some people liked the signs of rural life that were part of the horse and buggy world. Others thought it was a public nuisance. He could see what side this librarian fell on the debate.

The friendly librarian walked over to them, took the book out of Luke's hands, went back to the main desk, took out her own card, swiped it against a machine that beeped, and handed the book back to Luke. "It's due back in three weeks."

"Thank you."

"You shouldn't do that," Betty said. "If you do it for one—"

"I know, Betty. I have to do it for all." She smiled at Luke. "Please remember to bring it back within three weeks."

"I promise. You can take that to the bank." He tipped his hat at scowling Betty as he sailed through the door.

A tour bus had come by the makeshift farm stand this afternoon and bought Izzy out of the day's peaches in less than five minutes. Five minutes! She thought she might see if Luke could pick more peaches for Monday. Amos wouldn't let a single peach get picked before it was fully tree ripened, but she hoped that Sunday's Sabbath pause would mean double Monday's harvest. She could be selling twice the amount, if she could only get more produce to sell. She thought about asking Amos to consider buying additional fruit from a neighboring farm, maybe strawberries and blackberries and raspberries, but she suspected he would tell her that enough was enough. They didn't need more.

But they did! There was always a need for more.

And where was that new farm stand, anyway? All talk, that Luke Schrock. No action.

She swooshed the last little lamb into the pen behind its mother and closed the gate. She turned around to see Luke walking toward the garden with a bucket in one hand. He waited for her at the path intersection. "Izzy, are you afraid of snakes?"

"No."

"Would you help me catch some? Preferably harmless."

"Why do you need snakes?"

"I'm trying to help a woman overcome her fear of snakes."

"That sounds like stirring up bees. No good can come from it."

"Some good might. I'm trying to help her. She needs help."

She caught eyes with Luke and could see something strange in his face. To her surprise, he seemed genuinely concerned about this woman. "Who is she?"

"Alice Smucker."

"I don't know her."

"That's because she won't leave her house. Not since I scared her with a snake in her buggy."

"What'd you do a fool thing like that for?"

"I don't know." He let out a deep sigh. "Haven't you ever done something stupid in your life?" He rolled his eyes. "Probably not. Anyway. I did plenty of stupid things. This happened more than two years ago, and Alice hasn't left her house since. I need to make this right." He strode past her.

"There's a bunch of garter snakes that live under a big rock in the garden," Izzy called after him. "But you can only take one. Fern says they keep the gophers away from the tomatoes."

Luke pivoted. "Mind showing me where the rock is?"

She walked up to him. "Are you sure this is a good idea? Seems like it might scare this lady all the more."

"I haven't had time to finish the chapter in a book, but it talked about conditioning a patient to fears. Exposing the snake to her, little by little. I thought I'd get started."

Izzy squinted up at him. She was tall, but he was taller. "Don't you think you should finish the book?"

"I thought I should, you know, strike while the iron is hot."

Izzy wondered at that logic. But she could tell he was sincere, and so she helped him find the rock with the snakes underneath. He lifted the rock, she picked one up and put it in a sack.

"Most girls are afraid of snakes," he said.

"I was. But not after I realized they're more afraid of me than I am of them."

"Kind of a metaphor, I'd say."

"How so?"

He didn't elaborate. "Izzy, aren't you afraid of anything?"

That question, she chose not to answer. "So where is the new farm stand? That card table is way too small."

Luke tapped his head. "It's in the works."

Right. All talk. No action.

A storm blew through Stoney Ridge on Sunday morning, clearing the air with a cooling breeze. After Luke returned home from church, he drove the buggy over to Alice Smucker's and knocked on her door. "Alice, it's me, Luke. There's something I want to talk to you about."

"Go away."

He sighed. "Alice, I've been reading up about snake phobias. That's what you have. A snake phobia. I'm the one who gave it to you, and I feel I should be the one to help you overcome it too. Would you be willing to try?"

"No."

"Alice, there's a better way to live. I think I can help."

Silence.

He dropped his shoulders and started to walk away. Then he heard the door open, just a crack, and he slowly turned around to face the eye that was peering out at him. "How?"

He walked back to the door. "I've been reading about a man who first helped people with phobias. His method guarantees success. He's considered to be a genius."

The door opened just a tiny bit more. "How? How does he do it?"

"First, he helps people become educated about their fear. That takes away a lot of the power of the phobia. Little by little, he helps them face their fear, until they're no longer afraid."

The door opened a little bit wider. She was interested! That told Luke a great deal.

"Alice, if you'd like to try to face your phobia, I have some snakes in a sack in my buggy."

The door slammed shut.

Luke left Alice alone for a few days, but he couldn't stop thinking about her. He had to try again. The book he'd been reading had much to say about the success of conditioning patients. He knew he could help Alice, but he also knew he needed a good reason to stop by her house. A rock-solid one so that she'd actually open up the door to him.

The opportunity came the following day, after he'd dropped Amos and Fern off at Dok's office for an appointment. He stopped in the Bent N' Dent just as Jesse received a call from Alice Smucker for some groceries to be delivered.

It seemed fortuitous! Like a sign from above. "I'll deliver them."

Jesse looked at him suspiciously. "Why?"

"I'm trying to do you a favor."

Jesse hemmed and hawed, and finally relented. "I'm only saying yes because I'm the only one in the store this afternoon and Alice wants her stuff pronto." He pointed to Luke. "No funny business."

A truly humble person is not easily offended. It was a saying Fern oft quoted, aimed like an arrow at Luke. He was proud of his efforts to be humble. "I'll be back in an hour or so and let you know how it went. I have to pick up Amos and Fern at Dok's by three."

Luke picked up the boxes of groceries, one in each arm, and hurried out the door before Jesse changed his mind. Man, when did he turn into such a straight-and-narrow guy?

At Alice's door, he knocked and knocked and knocked. "Alice! I've brought your groceries from the Bent N' Dent." He knocked again. He knew she was in there.

"Leave them on the stoop. I'll get them later."

He went back to the buggy and picked up one box of groceries. He turned, then stopped when he saw the sack with the snake wiggle. He'd brought it along with him, only one little harmless garter snake, just in case. He thought he might see if Alice would at least look into the sack. Step one in the conditioning process. He grabbed it and put it on top of the groceries, set the box down on the stoop, and went back for the second box. He heard the front door shut and whirled around. *Oh no, oh no . . . Don't tell me!* She'd taken the box inside.

He bolted to the house, but before he could reach the door,

he heard Alice let out a bloodcurdling, ear-piercing scream. When he opened the door, she was up on a chair, screeching to high heavens. Luke bent down to snatch up the sack with the snake, only to discover the sack was empty.

Oh no. No, no, no, no, no.

ELEVEN

By the time Luke had captured the garter snake, apologized profusely to Alice, and stopped at the Bent N' Dent to explain the situation to Jesse, word had traveled ahead of him.

As Luke walked into the store, Hank Lapp spotted him and shouted, "THERE HE IS! STONEY RIDGE'S JUVENILE DELINQUENT IS BACK IN BUSINESS." He roared with laughter. "THE SNAKE BUSINESS."

Luke wasn't sure how Alice was able to get a message out to people when she wouldn't leave her house, but somehow, she did it. And if Hank Lapp knew, then the entire town would know by nightfall.

Jesse glared at him and pointed a thumb toward the back room. "Dad wants to see you."

Luke's heart sank. He was hoping David hadn't yet returned to the store.

In the back room of the store, David sat at his desk. He glanced up at Luke, put down his pencil, and pointed to a chair. "So what happened?"

Now, that was another thing Luke appreciated about David

Stoltzfus. He actually asked him what happened first, instead of assuming he knew all, like Hank Lapp.

"I was trying to help Alice get over her fear of snakes. I went to the library and read up on it. Did you know there's an actual name for it? Ophidiophobia. Fear of snakes. I found a garter snake, a harmless, tiny garter, and I was just going to show it to Alice. But that's when things went terribly wrong." He explained the sequence of events.

David listened carefully. "Luke, Alice is a woman full of fears. Not just snakes, but all kinds of phobias. They hobble her life. You're not qualified to cure her. Amos and I, we just wanted you to realize how you'd added to her fearfulness."

"Oh, trust me. I get it." Luke took off his hat and ran a hand through his hair. "I wanted to help her, David. I still do. No one should live like that. Her house . . . it smelled like stale air. Like she hadn't opened the windows in years."

David leaned back in his chair. "You did what we asked you to do. Now, I'd suggest you move on to the next person on your fence-mending list."

Luke should've felt relieved, but instead he was disappointed. "But I do want to help Alice."

"I appreciate your intent, Luke, and I believe your sincerity. Birdy has a saying she's fond of: 'There's a vast difference between putting your nose in other people's business and putting your heart in other people's problems.' Your heart is in the right place." He put a palm on his desk. "But I still want you to move on down the list."

"Tell me something. How did Hank Lapp hear about this?"

"Edith Lapp. She dropped by Alice's while you were hunting

for the snake. She came right to the store to tell me what had happened. Hank was already sitting by the stove."

"I suppose the whole town has heard it by now."

"Probably."

"Fern has a saying too. 'When once a dog has killed a sheep, it will be blamed for the death of every sheep.'"

David smiled. "Maybe so. But it does seem to me that you have an opportunity here."

"How so?"

David leaned forward on his desk and fixed those sharp brown eyes on him like he was pinning him to his chair. "Prove them wrong, Luke. Prove them wrong."

Izzy walked through the garden rows, inspecting the tiny shoots of onions she'd planted last week. She picked a few forgotten raspberries and popped them in her mouth as she walked around the beds. Pole beans wound their way up, twirling around the cornstalks. She bent down to see how the pumpkins were setting. Three Sisters, Fern had called this trio. Cornstalks provided support for beans, beans provided nutrients to the dirt, and pumpkins provided shade for the plants' roots. Fern said Three Sisters was a practice passed to the first Amish settlers from local Native Americans, and if it worked for them, there was no reason to change anything.

Why indeed? Izzy had to swallow back a smile when Fern told her that. Didn't that sound just like the Amish?

She picked more zucchini—*so* many zucchini, when would it end?—and carried them to the house in her apron. She noticed the library book that Luke had left on the kitchen table and spent some time skimming through it. When she saw Luke drive the buggy up the lane, she went outside to take it to him. "You left it inside." The weight of the universe looked to be resting on his shoulders. "I heard about the snake in the groceries."

"You too? Good grief. Gossip runs faster in this town than downhill water."

"Sounds like it didn't go well with Alice."

"It was a disaster."

She barely swallowed back a smile when she heard Luke's version of what had gone wrong, especially when he did a perfect imitation of Hank Lapp's overly loud voice in the Bent N' Dent. She tried not to laugh, covered her mouth tightly with her hand, but the thought of poor Alice Smucker screaming like a banshee, of Edith Lapp rushing inside to rescue her, and then the story spreading like wildfire through Stoney Ridge—she couldn't help herself. Soon, she was doubled over, laughing.

Luke watched her with a curious look on his face. "Do you mean to tell me that all I've needed to get you to talk to me is to show myself as a buffoon?"

That got her giggles starting all over again. "Oh, no. You've already done that plenty of times."

"Then what's so funny about this time?"

She dabbed tears from the corners of her eyes and took a deep breath. "I suppose . . ." She took another deep breath to stop herself from another laughing bout. "I suppose it's because you were trying so hard to do the right thing. And it was *so* the wrong thing to do. You'd better finish reading the book. To the end, this time." She tossed him the book and hurried up the porch steps before she started laughing again.

As Luke read through the book, he realized his mistake with how he handled Alice and her fear of snakes. He had introduced the object of fear much too soon. He would have to start the process of conditioning her to snakes all over again, assuming she would even open the door to him. In the book, the treatment involved conditioning the patient slowly and cautiously. That made a lot of sense to Luke. It was how Galen conditioned his horses to traffic. Slow and steady.

The next day he went to the public library with the paperwork he needed to get a library card—a bill for his continued once-a-week-phone-call counseling session. Might be odd, but it proved his residency. He got his card. He checked out a children's picture book of snakes. On the way back to the house, he stopped at Alice's house and knocked on the door. He saw her peek under a curtain corner at him.

"Alice, I see you there."

"Why do you keep terrorizing me? Why me? Go bother someone else!"

"I'm not trying to scare you. I'm really not. I don't have any snakes with me. I promise. I just want to talk."

"I don't want to talk to *you*."

Fair enough. "Could you listen, then?"

Silence, which he took as a yes. "Alice, I went to the library and found some books that might help you get over your fear of snakes. It's a common thing, apparently, this fear of snakes. Lots of people are afraid of snakes. It's nothing to feel bad about, Alice. But it's something that can be cured."

An eye peeked back around the curtain.

Encouraged, he continued, a little louder. "I read about a

doctor who has a method for curing people. Little by little, you get accustomed to snakes."

The curtain closed.

"Hold on. Alice, I'm not going to insist on anything. I just want to help you if I can. So I brought a book for you."

The curtain twitched.

"It's a children's book about snakes. There's pictures, and some information about snakes. Things you might find interesting, like . . . um, let's see . . . did you know they don't have eyelids? I didn't know that." He turned the pages. "Cobras are very protective of their young. That's interesting, don't you think? That a mother has an instinct to protect her babies. Alice?"

She wasn't talking, but she wasn't shouting at him to go away either. "Alice, it might not be easy at first, looking at these pictures of snakes. But try to go through it a couple of times. Notice different things about them—their colors, their sizes. See if it doesn't make you feel less anxious about them." The psychiatrist-author warned that even a drawing of a snake could elicit a gut-wrenching feeling at first. But with more pictures and photographs, this became less and less upsetting.

He set the book on the doorstep. "I'll just leave it here for you to look at, Alice. When you're done with it, set it back down on the step and I'll come get it. I need to return it in a week or else there's a cranky librarian who might send a hired gun after me." Why did he say that? His humor, it was really off the mark.

"Is her name Betty?"

Luke perked up. "She's the one. She scares me."

Silence. Then, "Me too."

Well, now this was an interesting turn of events. He thought he should stop now, before he said something stupid. He set the book down, said goodbye, and walked to the buggy. By the time he had backed the horse out of the driveway, he happened to glance over at the little house. The book he'd left on the doorstep was gone.

In the cool of the barn, Amos listened to Luke's update on Alice Smucker with interest. He wouldn't have expected her to give an inch for Luke. It gave Amos hope. Alice might actually want to try to get well. Everyone in the church felt worried about Alice and tried to coax her out of her house, but she'd only been getting worse, not better.

Still . . . Luke Schrock? Acting as a counselor? That didn't sit well either. No indeed.

Amos leaned his back against a bale of hay. "Luke, keep moving down your list of fence mending. Don't get stuck on Alice and avoid the rest of the list."

"David told me the same thing. I'll keep going. It's just that . . . I don't want to give up on Alice."

"Who's next on the list?"

"Big Teddy Zook."

"What happened with him?"

"It wasn't that big of a deal. Just something stupid. You know what Fern says. Stupid and teens go together like bread and butter. Salt and pepper."

"There you go again."

"What?"

"Dismissing a regrettable action as nothing more than boys will be boys. I don't buy that thinking. I think each one

132

of us needs to understand we're responsible for our own actions, whatever age we are." Amos leaned back in his chair. "So, what happened with Teddy Zook?"

"He came into the Bent N' Dent one day when I was in the store. He had an egg in his coat pocket, a small egg, and showed it to Ruthie. An egg! I have no idea why. But I went up to him and gave him a huge bear hug. Smashed his egg." He frowned. "I do remember he cried and cried, a big guy like him."

"Did Ruthie have something to do with why you smashed the egg?"

"Probably." Definitely. A way to get her attention.

"You need to go find Teddy Zook. Talk to him. No, better still, listen to him. Find out why that egg was important to him."

"Do you know why? Could you give me a heads-up?"

"I know why. That's why I won't give you a heads-up." He rose. "Keep cleaning up your messes, Luke."

⌒

After supper, Luke scootered over to Big Teddy Zook's. Teddy was a giant of a man, six foot six inches in his stocking feet, and nearly as wide as he was tall.

Luke found Teddy working in his father's carpentry shop. The roar of a diesel engine filled the small shop, providing electricity for the various saws and tools. Teddy stood at a lathe. Luke took in a deep breath of wood scents, sawdust, varnish, and diesel gas. He saw projects in varying stages of production: a header for a bed, a coffee table, a spice cabinet. The room was extremely tidy, well organized, with tools hung against the pegboard. Masking tape outlined the shape for each tool, clearly marking a space for each one.

Luke waited until he had finished his task and the sound of the diesel engine died down. The power of the lathe combined with Big Teddy, gentle giant that he was, made for an intimidating sight. Luke sure didn't want to startle him.

Teddy had been working on shaping a table leg out of a long block of wood. He held it up against an identical one, and Luke, standing by the door, could appreciate the precision of the spooling. Impressive. He didn't realize Big Teddy Zook had that kind of craftsmanship. Come to think of it, he didn't even know Teddy was a carpenter. He'd never thought much about him.

Teddy set down both table legs, took off his safety glasses, and stretched. As he turned, he spotted Luke at the door. "You," he said in a flat voice.

Luke took a step inside. "Yes. Me." He took another step. "What you did there, with that spooling, it looks really good."

Teddy eyed him suspiciously, frowning. "Why are you here?"

So many frowns. "You mean, why am I in Stoney Ridge? Or why am I standing in your carpentry shop?"

"Both."

"Same answer to both questions, I guess. I came to apologize, Teddy. Not sure if you remember or not, but a while ago, we were in the Bent N' Dent, and I purposefully smashed that egg you had."

"Oh, yeah. I remember. I remember like it was yesterday."

Long memories, these Amish. "Well, I hope you can forgive me."

Teddy narrowed his eyes. "That's not hard for you, is it?"

"It is kinda hard, actually. I mean, it's humbling to ask for forgiveness."

"But we all have to give you our forgiveness, don't we? That's part of being Plain."

"Well, I can't insist on it if you don't feel it. But I want you to know that I'm genuinely sorry."

"Why? What makes you sorry about that day?"

Big Teddy wasn't as dumb as he thought. "I'm sorry because I broke something that you felt some kind of attachment to. And I didn't care. I see that now." He took off his hat. "Do you mind telling me why that egg was important to you?"

Big Teddy crossed his arms and appraised Luke for a long moment. So long that it made Luke very uncomfortable. He would've liked to know what Big Teddy was thinking. "Follow me." Big Teddy took two long strides and brushed past Luke at the door. He had to jog to catch up with him. Teddy was on his way down the hill to a grassy marsh area that wove through the Zook property. He stopped and lifted his hand toward the murky-looking water. "There's a Massauga rattlesnake in there."

"Rattlesnake?" Luke gulped.

"It was, anyway. Till you came along."

Ah. "That egg?"

"Yes. I'd found it that very day. I couldn't believe it when I found the egg, intact and recently laid. I'd stopped into the Bent N' Dent to get a box for it, and some newspaper to keep it insulated and protected. I should have left it where I found it, but I saw an eagle circling and was worried about it. So I tucked it in my pocket. I showed Ruthie the egg, because she's interested in that kind of thing."

She was? Luke had no idea.

"And then, you had to do your typical Luke act."

The Luke act. Ouch.

"Be the showoff. Take center stage. You can never let anyone else be the center of attention, can you?"

Luke didn't know how to answer that. He had no defense for it, because . . . it was true. Especially if Ruthie had been anywhere nearby. He'd always been conscious of her whereabouts, and would seek to draw her attention to himself, no matter what.

"It was the last egg I've been able to find. Since then, the Massauga rattler was put on the Pennsylvania endangered species list."

"Because of me?"

"Probably not just because of you, but you sure contributed to it. This was the last known snake in the entire Lancaster area. I keep hoping I'll find another out here. So far, no luck."

"What would you do if you found the snake?"

"Notify the game warden. They would harvest it to protect it. Improve its chances for successful breeding."

"Maybe I could help you look."

Teddy gave him a look as if he didn't think he was capable of tying his own shoelaces, much less hunt for a rattlesnake. "It's no job for a novice."

"You can teach me what to look for." Luke lifted his palms in the air. "Teddy, I'm serious. I'd like to help. If there's a chance that we might be able to find the snake, well, that would be something, wouldn't it?" He could hardly believe his own ears. Was he really offering to help find a rattlesnake? A *rattlesnake*?

"I don't know. They're very tricky, those rattlers. They shy away from people."

Oh, that was a relief to hear. "Work at Windmill Farm comes in fits and starts. When a crop is ready to be harvested, I can't do much else. But when there's a break and I have a little spare time, I'll come over. Most likely, it'd be after supper. Would that be a good time to look for a nest?"

Teddy shrugged. "Good a time as any, I suppose. That's when I usually hunt food for my other snakes."

"Your other snakes?"

Teddy let out a long-suffering sigh, as if he was speaking to someone who was very, very slow-witted. "Follow me."

Luke followed Teddy back up the hill to a small shed behind the carpentry shop. It was lined with cages, each one filled with a snake. Different snakes, all shapes and sizes. Luke's jaw dropped. "Teddy, what're you doing with all these snakes?"

"I raise 'em. Sell 'em to farmers to help cut down the rodent population. Field mice, rats, moles, gophers. It's been a nice little side business. These snakes, they're like pets to me."

Luke put his hands on his hips and walked along the rows of caged snakes. "How'd you ever get interested in raising snakes?" Of all pets, why snakes?

"My mother, actually. She loved snakes, and taught me to love them. Most folks are scared to death of them, but they're much more scared of people." He opened one cage to reach in a hand and pull out an enormous snake.

Luke backed up a foot or two. "Whoa. Isn't that a rattlesnake?"

"No. Looks a little like one, but it's an eastern hognose.

One of the best rodent controls God gave to farmers. It's nonvenomous, obviously."

Luke peered at its diamond-shaped scales. "What's so obvious about it not being venomous?" It looked plenty dangerous to him.

"Don't you know anything about how to identify snakes?"

"Nothing. Not a thing. All I know is that garter snakes are good for the garden." He'd learned that much from Izzy.

"Well, look at the head. How would you describe its shape?"

"Hmmm . . . kind of round."

"Good. Now look at the pupils in its eyes. What do you notice about them?"

"Uh, they're round too."

"Right. Round pupils, like a human's. So look at the snake in the cage next to you. How is its head shaped?"

"It's more like a triangle."

"Yes. What about the eyes?"

"Huh. The pupil is more like a slit."

"Exactly. A vertical pupil. That's one way to tell it's venomous."

Luke jumped a foot in the air. "Is that one a rattlesnake?"

"Copperhead. Northern copperhead. She could kill you in one bite. A beauty, ain't she?"

Beautiful. Huh. Luke had never considered snakes to be beautiful, not once. He would place himself closer on the scale to Alice Smucker's fear of snakes than Teddy Zook's love for them. But he did appreciate that Teddy cared about them. The cages were clean, big, and airy, protected from the elements.

Teddy slipped the Eastern hognose snake back into its cage. "Want to help me feed them?"

"With what?"

"Frozen mice. They only eat one every few days. Then they need time to digest, so you leave 'em alone. They don't like to be bothered while they're digesting."

That wouldn't be a problem.

Teddy waited for an answer. "So, you gonna help?"

Luke gulped. "Uh, sure. Sure. Right. Absolutely. Can't think of anything I'd rather be doing."

TWELVE

L uke hadn't forgotten Alice, but he did think Amos and David might be right about one thing. He was fixating on Alice to avoid the rest of the fence-mending list. It was nearly the end of July, and he was only halfway down the first page. Even worse, new names were added to it. Like . . . Izzy and her farm stand. Even if it wasn't his fault that the first one was destroyed, it was his fault that the new one hadn't gotten built yet. On the way home from helping Teddy feed his snakes—and *that* was not an experience for the squeamish—he thought about ideas for a new and improved farm stand.

Back in the tack room, he sketched a couple of different versions, then decided to show Izzy and see what she thought of them. Amos and Fern were working on a jigsaw puzzle on the front porch and Izzy was inside, baking zucchini bread. There was an abundance of zucchinis from the garden, more than anyone knew what to do with. Lately, they'd been eating zucchini ribbons in place of pasta noodles, shredded zucchini pancakes in place of potato pancakes, zucchini salad in place of cucumbers. Luke was pretty well done with zucchini, but he had to admit the cinnamon scent of this zucchini bread might change his mind.

"Izzy, could you take a minute and look at these?" He set out four sketches on the kitchen table.

She'd just finished washing a bowl, and dried it with a rag as she walked over to the table. "New farm stands?"

"Yes. As long as we're building a new one, I thought it would be good to make it larger, so you could even sell things like your zucchini bread." He pointed to one sketch. "I wondered if you might like some shelves. Or in this one"—he pointed to a different sketch—"I designed it so you'd have more counter space."

"What does Amos think?"

"I haven't shown them to him. I wanted to see what you wanted first."

Izzy gave him a strange look. "The farm stand belongs to Amos and Fern. They should decide what's best."

"I know. But you're the one who's made such a success of the stand. You're the reason the tour buses stop each day. And you plan to be here for a long while, don't you? You should have what you want."

The look on Izzy's face grew stranger still, as if she was caught in between a laugh and a cry. Suddenly she set the bowl on the table, dropped the dish towel beside it, and hurried out of the room, bolting up the stairs.

What had he done? What had he said that was so wrong?

Izzy threw herself on her bed and buried her face in her pillow. What was the matter with her? Why was she so upset? It was sketches of a farm stand, that's all it was!

She could tell how pleased Luke was as he set them on the table. He grinned real big, then lifted his hat a little and peered at her from under it, almost shy. The next minute, he was looking at her and she thought he must have asked her a question, and she wasn't even listening. A well of emotion rose up and she ran from the room like a child. Mortifying!

About ten minutes later, Fern knocked on the bedroom door and came inside. She sat down on Izzy's bed. "Luke says he upset you."

Izzy turned her head to the side to answer. "He did."

"Can you tell me what happened?"

How could she? She didn't know herself. "He was showing me sketches for the new farm stand. He'd put so much time into them, Fern. So detailed, so carefully thought out."

"I noticed. He showed them to us."

"He asked me what I thought, what features I wanted, and I couldn't respond. I just . . . lost it and ran up the stairs." Like a silly, stupid, overly emotional girl. Slowly, Izzy rolled over to sit up. "It's not Luke's fault. He didn't do anything wrong." She wiped her face. "I didn't expect to feel emotional over something as small as whether I'd like counter space or shelves."

Fern rose and went to the window, her arms folded against her. "Do you think it might have something to do with the fact that no one's ever asked you what you wanted before? Sounds to me like you've had very few choices in your life."

Izzy had never considered it that way. "I told Luke to have Amos choose whatever he thought was best."

"It might be a good exercise for you to figure out what

you do want, Izzy. You're the one who spends her days in the farm stand. Amos and I, we think you need some practice making decisions."

"No, no. Fern, what if I make a mistake? It's not like it can be rebuilt."

"But you can make a mistake. That's part of the experience of decision-making. If it isn't right, we'll fix it. Like ripping out a seam on a quilt block and starting again."

Fern made it sound easy, but it wasn't. "Shouldn't Amos be deciding about this farm stand?"

"No. He agreed with Luke. This is your call. I think it might be a good idea to let Luke know that you're new at decision-making."

"He must think I'm crazy."

"No, he thought he'd said something wrong and he feels badly. That boy, he's making some progress. He was never one to feel much empathy for others. I do believe he's finally coming around."

"I wish the first farm stand hadn't gotten wrecked. I know it was meaningful to Amos."

"It was falling apart and in dire need of repair. Those boys did us a favor, in more ways than one." Fern smiled. "So, what do you think, Izzy? Shelves or counters? What are your plans for that stand? Do you want to expand and add baked goods?"

Izzy shook her head. "I'm not a good enough baker. Tonight's batch of zucchini bread sunk in the middle."

"Too much shredded zucchini. Another crop of zucchini and you'll be an expert." She patted Izzy's knee. "When you first got here, you didn't know the difference between adding salt or sugar. Look at all you've learned, from me, from

Jenny. You're a fast study. A real smart girl." She smiled and headed for the door.

Izzy wanted to smile in return, but instead her eyes blurred with tears. She'd never been told that she was smart, not once. Mostly, she'd been told she was stupid, far behind other students—and she was! Changing schools as often as she did had made it hard for her to catch up. She had hated school.

But Fern didn't say things unless she meant them.

The next morning, Izzy apologized to Fern and Amos for being in such an odd mood last evening. They said they understood and not to worry on it. That left only Luke. She found him in the orchards on the top of a ladder, thinning apple buds. She watched him for a while. When he noticed her watching him, he started down the ladder.

"No," she said, lifting her hand. "Stay there. I just came to say one thing."

He peered down at her. "What, then?"

She cleared her throat. It felt as if she had ground glass in there. It wasn't easy for her to be conciliatory to Luke Schrock. It took everything she had to be polite and lady-like and apologetic for acting crazy as a loon last night. "Number four."

"Number four?"

"The sketches. For the new farm stand. That's the one. I liked that one best. So don't mess it up." She pivoted on her heel and hurried down the hillside.

⟨⟶⟩

Izzy and Fern spent all day Saturday over at Mattie Riehl's house with half the women of Stoney Ridge. Today they were piecing together blocks of fabric to make comfort quilts for teenagers in a group home in Lancaster. This quilt wouldn't have pieced blocks like the other quilts. This one would just have big squares of fabric sewed together, then knotted with yarn to keep the filling in place. Not fancy, but useful. And cheerful. As Mattie said, a comfort quilt meant that somebody cared.

As she pinned two pieces of fabric together for Edith Lapp to sew—Edith could be fussy about seams, so she knew to make them line up perfectly—Izzy thought about who might be on the receiving end of this quilt. *It could've been me*, she thought. *Not so long ago, this would've been me.*

Now and then, boxes from well-meaning organizations would arrive at the group home where Izzy had lived. Hand-me-down clothes, books, cereal, and soups. She'd never thought about the people who gave, only the things they gave. It felt strange to be on the giving side. It felt good, like she was filling a hole inside herself with every block of fabric. Stitch by stitch.

And then Fern insisted Izzy drive the buggy home, which shocked her. Amos still hadn't let her take the buggy on any public road. She'd thought it was because he was so protective of Bob. But it occurred to her just now that maybe she was the one he was protecting. Fern was always the one who pushed and prodded Izzy to try more and do more. Not Amos. He treated her as if she was as fragile as spun sugar.

She climbed into the driver's seat and they were off, bouncing down the bumpy road, turning off the main road, rumbling past fields and pastures. She took extra pains to manage the horse well, slowing him to a walk as a truck barreled past them, then flicking the reins to urge Bob to trot again, just like Amos drove him. She glanced at Fern to see if she had noticed how skillfully she handled the big horse. Then she glanced again. Fern had a look on her face like a cat in the cream.

"You feeling all right?" Izzy said.

"I'm right as rain."

"You look a little funny."

"That's because there's a surprise waiting at home."

Izzy didn't like surprises. They were never good. She liked to be prepared for whatever she had to face. "What kind of surprise?"

"Well, now, that takes away the very essence of a surprise, doesn't it?"

Izzy kept casting sideways glances at Fern. She seemed pleased, which helped Izzy relax a little.

As she rounded the last bend in the road that led to Windmill Farm, Fern clasped her hands together and let out a soft, "Well, well, well."

Oh my soul. It was the new farm stand.

Izzy pulled Bob to a stop and handed the reins to Fern. She walked up to the farm stand, breathing in the smell of fresh-cut lumber. Cedar, she thought. Freshly stained. The stand was twice the size of the old one, with a metal corrugated roof to keep the rain and sun off the produce. Shelving along the back, just like she'd wanted. A large, wide counter in front. And an easy-to-open-and-close window.

By now, Fern was out of the buggy and beside her. "Big Teddy Zook helped Luke build it."

"Oh my soul," was all Izzy could manage to say, over and over—an expression she had picked up as a small girl from a kind neighbor lady.

Fern pointed to a painted sign that Izzy hadn't even noticed. "Look at that."

IZZY'S FRUITS AND VEGETABLES
NO SUNDAY SALES

Again she was at a loss for words, this time overwhelmed by the wonder of it all. *Oh my soul.* This farm stand . . . it was perfect.

⌒

Luke jerked awake to whiskers tickling his face.

Bob! Not again.

He stumbled out of bed and grabbed a harness hanging on the wall. Leading the big horse back to his stall was no easy task in the middle of a pitch-dark night, but he was getting used to it, which seemed weird. Back the horse up at a tight angle, then turn him around to lead him to his stall. Once he had him in the stall, he locked the latch and checked it three times before heading back to bed.

The next night, it had been just long enough for Luke to fall deeply asleep and wake up disoriented to find Bob in his tack room. Luke led the horse back to his stall, and this time, he tied a rope around the stall's steel poles, attaching it to the doorjamb.

Over breakfast, Luke brought up the idea of adding a metal lock through the latch.

Amos looked at him as if he'd lost his mind. "No. Absolutely, positively not."

"But why?"

Pouring maple syrup over a tall stack of hotcakes, Amos said, "Plenty of reasons."

"Can you give me one of them?"

"In case of fire. That horse is too valuable."

"Then, could I let Bob stay out in the pasture for a night?"

"Absolutely not. Wolves. Coyotes."

"Just *one* night."

"That horse, he's like a family member to me. I'd never let a family member sleep in the pasture."

And yet Amos didn't mind that Luke slept in a barn. He clasped his hands over his face. He was losing it.

The next night, it happened again. Luke staggered into the kitchen, bleary eyed, sat down at the table, and put his head down on it. "I give up. That horse keeps outfoxing me." He was so tired that the room swam.

Izzy was setting the table. "Have you considered that it might not be the horse's doings?"

Luke lifted his head. "What do you mean?"

"Might be the mischief of another animal."

Luke leaned back in the chair. "The barn's closed up. What could be getting in?"

She shrugged. "Sounds to me like a raccoon."

Fern looked across the room at Amos, who was sitting in a chair reading his Bible. "Amos Lapp, why didn't you think of that?"

"I did." Amos turned the page of his Bible. "I was just waiting to see if Luke could figure it out."

Luke clunked his forehead on the tabletop. He hadn't thought of it. Izzy had.

That evening, Izzy helped Luke bait a trap—a humane trap, she insisted on—with strips of uncooked bacon.

"Skunks can do sneaky things too," Luke said. "What if it's a skunk? The whole barn'll stink to high heaven."

"If it's a skunk," Izzy said, "then I will owe you an apology, right after you take a very long bath in tomato juice. And if I'm right . . ."

Luke looked at her.

"Then you have to clean out the henhouse for me."

"So the best I get is an apology. At worst, I get sprayed by a skunk or I get to clean out the henhouse."

"Exactly." Was there the tiniest suggestion of a smile at the corner of her mouth?

It occurred to him that they were actually having a conversation, getting to know each other, without any need for him to have to apologize for something stupid he had done.

She disappeared briefly to find a flashlight and they walked down to the barn. They set the trap beside Bob's stall.

"Dude," Luke said. "This just might work."

"Dude, this might," she teased him back. They were sitting near each other on the barn floor, and she held his gaze for a full few seconds without looking away like she normally did. He noticed.

Quickly, she stood up. "Maybe you'll get a full night's sleep. I sure hope so. You've been looking terrible lately."

Around three in the morning, Luke woke to hear the sound of clip-clops on the concrete barn floor. He sat up on the cot just as Bob walked into the tack room and stood over Luke, breathing out that musty hay scent. The horse almost seemed pleased with himself at what was becoming a nightly ritual.

"Argh! What is going on here?" Luke jumped off the cot, grabbed a rope, and led Bob back to his stall. With a flashlight in hand, he double-knotted the rope around the stall latch and checked the trap. The trapdoor was wide open. The bacon was gone.

"Blast!" He scanned the barn with the flashlight, hoping to catch sight of . . . whatever *it* was.

$\mathcal{T}$HIRTEEN

For the last few days, Izzy had woken early, dressed fast, and hurried downstairs. She wanted to be in the kitchen, ready for the next installment in the ongoing story of Bob's nightly visits to Luke's tack room. She almost hoped the trap hadn't caught the animal that was opening Bob's stall—the morning updates were *that* amusing. Luke looked even more bleary eyed with exhaustion, thoroughly exasperated, but there was something kind of sweet about how he patiently led Bob back to his stall each night. Throughout the day, her mind would supply funny versions of Bob sniffing and snorting as he stood over Luke's cot.

As she set the kitchen table, Fern came downstairs to fill the coffeepot. "I already filled it, Fern. It's ready to heat up."

Fern looked at her with one sparse eyebrow lifted. "You've certainly turned into an early bird."

Izzy finished folding a cloth napkin and set it at Luke's place. "Oh, well, the morning sun wakes me up."

Fern put her hands on her hips. "Your room faces west."

"Does it?" Izzy felt her cheeks go warm. "It's bright in the morning. I know that much." She glanced out the window to see Luke striding toward the house, passing through the deep shadow cast by the barn. She opened the squeaky kitchen door. "Any luck?"

As he neared the bottom of the steps, he stopped and looked up at her. "None. Absolutely none. But the bacon disappeared."

"It's got to be a raccoon. They're known for their burglary skills."

Fern came outside to join them. "What about Bob . . . did he stay in his stall?"

"Woke me up at two and four. Just as happy as a horse could be, breathing over me with his musty breath."

Izzy tried to smother her giggles with clasped hands over her mouth, but they couldn't be contained. Fern's eyes began to smile; her mouth was soon to follow.

Luke was indignant. "Ladies, it is not at all funny to be woken up by a horse. This is a very alarming matter."

That seemed only funnier still. Even though Izzy felt bad, she was laughing too hard to stop. She wanted to tell Luke she was sorry, but she couldn't get the words out. Finally, she put her hands up in surrender and ran for the stairs.

She was halfway up and slowed when she heard Fern say, "Well, I have to hand it to you, Luke Schrock. Hearing Izzy laugh so wholeheartedly is music to my ears."

"Don't give me any credit," Luke said. "It all belongs to Bob."

"I will. I'll give him an extra carrot today."

"*Fern.* Don't encourage him. I need some sleep. Can't I move into the house?"

"I think you're doing more for all of us just where you are."

Luke groaned. "Well, I'm glad I'm adding some value to Windmill Farm." He yawned loudly, loud enough for Izzy to hear halfway up the stairwell. "Then, where's the coffee? I need double-strength. Triple."

The kitchen door squeaked open. "I HEARD THERE'S NOCTURNAL GOINGS-ON AT WINDMILL FARM. NEVER FEAR. I CAME TO HELP."

Hank Lapp had arrived. To help. *Hank.*

Amusement started bubbling up in Izzy again. This was new to her, this uncontrollable laughter. She'd never had trouble tamping down laughter—not until Luke Schrock arrived at Windmill Farm. She covered her mouth with her hand and hurried up to her room, closing the door before she doubled over with giggles.

———

Amos had a tolerance for his uncle like few others, but Hank Lapp jolted the senses more than Fern's strong coffee. Amos was moving slow this morning, slower than usual. Fern had encouraged him to stay put and rest as long as he could. As he lay in bed, he thought of all the endless chores that needed to be done around the farm—fences to mend, hay to mow, orchards to glean, animals to tend to—and he felt tired down to his bones.

Added to the farm's seasonal work, there was Jenny and Jesse. If they got married this year, and Fern said it sure looked like that would happen, then the wedding would be held at Windmill Farm. How did she know something like that? She'd planted a whole bed of celery a few months back, but he thought she just liked the vegetable, not that she was expecting a wedding.

Jenny was like a daughter to Fern. Like Izzy was becoming. He smiled to himself. Fern and her strays. How she loved those motherless children. You'd never know it to look at her, his Fern, and most folks were a little intimidated by her, but she had the biggest heart in Stoney Ridge.

He couldn't disappoint Fern. Nor Jenny. Somehow, Windmill Farm needed to be spruced up in time for a fall wedding. For the first time, he felt thankful Luke Schrock was boarding here. Amos sure hadn't wanted him, hadn't wanted the extra trouble or the extra help. He still held his suspicions about the boy, but he couldn't deny that he had turned into a surprisingly conscientious worker. He'd even taken on projects Amos hadn't expected of him, like sanding down and repainting the front porch steps. The paint had chipped badly on them after last year's harsh winter. Or was it the year before last?

Amos was just considering getting up when he heard his uncle's booming voice ricochet up the stairs. It wouldn't do to have Hank wonder why he was still in bed at . . . what time was it? He turned to peer at the small alarm clock next to his bed. Nearly half past seven. He eased out of bed, his joints stiff and achy. His body was failing him. He felt its decline a little more each day. He also felt the peace of God growing stronger within him, the sense of Heaven's nearness. Death would win his body, but not his soul.

He dressed as quickly as he could, which was pretty slow, and went down the stairs to see what his uncle had in mind to counterattack the raccoon. They could be cunning, those critters. He thought about an article in a farming journal he'd read recently about raccoons. They had incredible memories, it said, and could retain information even longer than dogs. If he remembered correctly, it also said something about how extensive research couldn't determine the intelligence of raccoons because they were too wily. They kept escaping from the cages.

Downstairs, he slipped into the kitchen and made a beeline to the coffeepot to pour himself a cup, hoping Hank was too absorbed in the raccoon and horse conversation to notice his late arrival.

"ABOUT TIME YOU STIRRED YOUR STUMPS, AMOS LAPP."

Amos cringed. "Morning, Hank." He looked at Fern. "Is the coffee still hot?" Oh no. The minute the words left his mouth, he knew they were a mistake.

"NEPHEW, YOU CAN'T EXPECT BREAKFAST WHEN YOU GET UP AT NOON."

Head down, Amos reached for an empty coffee cup and filled it with coffee, no longer caring if it was hot or stone cold.

"THE RACCOON IS PLAYING MIND GAMES WITH POOR OL' LUKE."

Amos settled into a chair. "So I hear." Land-o-mercy, did he ever hear. The whole town could hear Hank Lapp's bellowing voice. He peered at Luke over his coffee cup. "No luck with the trap?"

"Oh, there was luck all right. Plenty of luck for the raccoon. He scored with a bacon breakfast." Luke leaned forward. "Amos, can't I put a lock on Bob's latch for one night? To get just one good night's sleep?"

Amos took a sip of coffee. "It goes against my better

judgment. Especially when we've been getting so many lightning storms." He looked out the window to see a bright blue cloudless sky.

"FEAR NOT. I'VE GOT A TRICK OR TWO UP MY SLEEVES, BOYS."

Amos and Luke exchanged a look that said much.

That afternoon, the sky darkened with rain clouds, and it almost relieved Amos to see them. He felt a little sorry for Luke, but he simply would not, could not allow him to put a lock on Bob's stall. He loved that horse like a member of the family. No way was he going to put that fine horse in harm's way. No way.

As Amos stood outside the house to watch the clouds gather, he realized Fern had slipped up beside him. How did she manage to do that so quietly? He thought he was alone, and suddenly, there she was.

A metaphor, he realized. That's just how it was when they met. He was alone, needing a partner, and one day, she arrived. He hadn't expected Fern to fit into his household the way she did, to nurture well his three daughters, nor did he ever expect to grow to love her like he did. But she did, and he did, and she was a treasured gift to him. Someday, he would tell her so.

"Amos, what would you think if we let Luke sleep in the house? Maybe a night or so."

"Nope."

"All day today, I've been wondering if we aren't being a little too tough on him. He's been working hard for you. And he's trying to get through his fence-mending list. He's doing well, Amos. Other than that first slip-up, he's been making strides. It's pretty remarkable, to see him not excusing himself like he used to. Look how concerned he's been with Alice Smucker's welfare."

"Yup."

"But you still won't let him sleep in the house."

"Nope."

"Because of Izzy?"

"Because he's doing well out there. He's got a problem, caused by living creatures, and he needs to find a solution. He doesn't need anyone to rescue him. He's had too much of that. You know how soft Rose has always been on Luke. She can't bring herself to draw a line in the sand with him. She felt sorry for him, losing his father at such a young age, and ended up hobbling him with kindness. I'm actually glad she and Galen are in Kentucky. If she were here, imagine what she'd be doing right now."

Fern sighed. "She'd be camped outside of Bob's stall all night long, just to make sure her boy got a good night's sleep."

Amos laughed. "Rose King is a fine woman, but it's God's gift to Luke that she's away right now. I'm not sure he'd be making these changes if she were here."

Fern crossed her arms against her thin chest.

"Still disagree with me?"

"No. No, I don't. I see your point." She tucked her arm around his elbow. "However did you get so wise, Amos Lapp?"

He covered her small hand with his big one and gently squeezed. "By living with a difficult woman."

She yanked her hand away in mock horror and he reached

out to hug her and they stood there, watching the gray clouds above them. *Say something, Amos. Don't miss these opportunities that God has given you to say what needs to be said. Time is running out.* He swallowed. Speaking from the heart had never been easy for him. *Say it, Amos.* He could feel God's Spirit practically giving him a kick on his backside. *Say it.* Again, he swallowed past a lump in his throat. "Fern, you know, don't you?"

"What?"

He cleared his throat. "You know all you mean to me, don't you?"

"I do."

"Good."

They stood in that spot for a long, long time, his arms around her, his chin tucked on top of her head, woven together like woof and warp in a comfortable hug, until the rain began. First one big drop, then another, and soon they broke apart and hurried into the house.

⁓

Two nights later, Luke set a foolproof, much-too-expensive live trap near Bob's stall. He had bought it at the Hay & Grain, reassured by the owner that it was guaranteed not to kill the wild animal. "Use bacon," the owner said. "Raccoons love raw bacon."

And didn't Luke know *that*? This time, he stuffed the bacon to the far edge of the trap, making it more difficult to get to. The sky was clear, the forecast predicted no rain, so after a lengthy discussion over supper, Amos relented. Luke could fasten Bob's stall latch with a lock and key, as long as he slept with the key on a cord around his neck. Luke thought it best not to overthink that Amos was willing to risk his potential strangulation.

All that mattered was that Luke was finally going to get a good night's sleep, after a solid week of nighttime Bob visits. His weary eyes sagged shut, colossally relieved. He had finally outsmarted that cunning raccoon. He yawned once, twice, and rolled over, pleased with himself, as he slipped into sleep.

Sometime in the middle of the night, Bob stood over his cot, breathing heavily.

"NOOOOoooo!" Luke winced. "What in thunder is going on in this barn?"

Izzy waited impatiently on the porch for Luke to come out of the barn. When he did, she cupped her mouth to shout down to him. "Did it work?"

He lifted his head at the sound of her voice. "No! He picked the lock. Then he helped himself to the bacon without tripping the trap."

"What?"

As Luke reached the bottom of the porch steps, he lifted his palms in the air. "I surrender. The raccoon has a higher IQ than I do."

Izzy raised a finger in the air. "Do *not* think like that. We're not giving up that easily. That raccoon is going to be evicted from Windmill Farm."

Luke gazed at her, sleepy, disheveled, in a pair of old pants and a badly wrinkled shirt. "But how?"

She lost some of that guarded edginess she always had in his presence, and felt herself soften. "That I don't know. But I'm going to figure it out."

Slowly, Luke's tired face eased into a smile. He was smiling sweetly and not grinning like he was laughing, and she couldn't help it, she felt her lips lift in a smile in response.

Now, why did she do that? She didn't want to give him any encouragement.

FOURTEEN

L uke replayed that moment at the porch over and over in his head. Izzy Miller had actually smiled at him. It hadn't lasted long, but it was a real, honest-to-goodness smile. She'd laughed plenty of times, mostly at him, but never once had she smiled. He thought of that smile, of how it spread slowly across her face. It felt like a gust of sun-warmed air on a cold winter day, coming at you when you least expected it. It was that astonishing to him, that memorable.

He pulled his attention back to the book about phobias he was reading and his smile faded. The plight of Alice Smucker continued to plague Luke. As he came to the end of the chapter, he read of a method that might help acclimate Alice Smucker to snakes. He paced around the little tack room, working out the details in his mind. However, this method would involve Big Teddy Zook. As soon as he finished his chores for the day, he scootered over to Teddy's.

"What do you think?" Luke thought this idea of his was pretty amazing.

Teddy seemed less impressed. "So let me get this straight.

You want me to bring over a cage full of nonvenomous snakes to Alice Smucker's house."

"Yes, but not for a while. We have a couple of stages to go through before we get to that."

"We? Like, I'm in on this?"

Luke bit the corner of his lip. "I was hoping you'd help. Being the snake expert that you are."

Teddy liked that. "So what are these stages?"

"This psychologist, the one who's had such success with overcoming phobias, says to start with a series of experiences of graduated difficulty, starting with having the phobic—that's what he calls his patients—become very knowledge-able about whatever they fear. He says the more the phobic knows, the better." He paused to make sure Teddy was following along. He seemed a little guarded, but interested. "So the first stage is simple. I thought you could tell Alice what you know about snakes."

"What makes you think she'll listen?"

"Because she took that children's book I left on her door-step. You could tell her the things you taught me—like how to tell if they're poisonous or not. Their habits and habitats. What they like to eat." The experience of feeding the fro-zen mice to the snakes danced through his mind. "Hold on. Scratch the food thing."

Teddy's bushy eyebrows puckered together. He was turn-ing skeptical, so Luke picked up his pace.

"If that works, if she'll listen—and I think she will—then we move on to the stuffed snake. After that comes holding a toy snake. Those rubber types, the kind that can wiggle at the end of a stick. Then comes a snake skin that she can look at. Maybe even touch." He clapped his hands together. "And *then* comes your snakes in a cage."

"See, I don't get that part."

"So she can look at them, first from a distance. Then she can get closer and closer."

"Snakes are pretty boring in a cage. They don't snap or snarl or bite or hiss. They sleep most of the time."

Luke pointed at him. "Teddy Zook, you're a genius. That's exactly the kind of thing Alice needs to know."

"So, let me get this straight. The end result is that you want me to bring snakes in a cage to her house."

"Maybe just one. Now that I think on it, too many might scare her."

"And you want me to leave the snake in the cage at her house."

"Outside her house. So she knows exactly where it is."

"This is a lady who hates snakes. What if she tries to kill it?"

"No, no. I'm sure she won't try to kill it. And it's just for a short while, Teddy. I'm trying to help her overcome her phobia. The book I've been reading says that if a person feels safe around the object of fear, it'll help take down those fears a notch or two. Like, if she can actually look at the snake, in the cage, on her terms, she'll become comfortable with it." Unlike when he had the garter snake in the bag, only to have Alice open it and get freaked out. That was not good.

Big Teddy wasn't buying Luke's logic to overcome snake phobia, that was apparent. "Teddy, come with me. Tell Alice why you love snakes so much." He was banking on the fact that Teddy was a tenderhearted man and at least willing to give it a try. He loved snakes *that* much.

But Teddy was not so easily swayed. "You find me a Massauga rattlesnake in that marsh, and then I'll help you with Alice's phobia." He took a few steps out and stared at the swampy creek, hands on his hips. "I know she's out there."

Luke glanced behind Teddy at the murky creek that lined his acreage. Oh, boy. "Teddy, that could take a while. What about this? I promise to help you look for this snake, for as long as it takes. But in the meantime, we get started on overcoming Alice's phobia." He stuck out his hand for a shake. Teddy eyed him carefully. "Alice Smucker . . . she needs our help."

On that note, kindhearted Teddy returned Luke's handshake.

Luke and Teddy stood on the front step of Alice Smucker's house and knocked. Knocked and knocked.

"She's not home," Teddy said.

"Oh, she's home all right. She's always home." Luke saw the curtain move. He knocked again. "Alice, we just want to talk to you."

A voice behind the door finally called out, "Do you have any snakes?"

"No. None. I promise. We just want to talk. I brought Teddy Zook along with me."

The door cracked open to reveal an eye.

"Alice, I've been wondering something. Why is it you don't like snakes?"

The door shut.

Luke knocked again. "Alice, I don't have any snakes with me. I promise."

Teddy frowned at him, then knocked on the door. "Alice, it's Teddy Zook. I have a better question. What is it about snakes that frightens you?"

Luke jabbed his elbow at Teddy. "Good question, man." He leaned closer to the door. "Alice, what do you think? Why do snakes bother you so much? Other than that time when I tossed that snake in your buggy. I can see how that took you over the edge."

Teddy's eyebrows shot up. "You did *what?*"

Luke lifted a palm. "Long story. Harmless snake."

"You don't treat snakes like that. Or women, either."

The door opened again, a little bit wider. Alice eyed Teddy. He noticed. "Alice, I'm sorry if you've had a bad experience with snakes." He glanced at Luke with a scowl. "Most of them are completely harmless. Not only harmless, but beneficial to farmers."

The door opened wide enough to show Alice's entire face. "If snakes are so harmless, then why did Satan use it to tempt Eve in the Garden of Eden?"

"Well, that's an interesting thought, Alice."

"And then it was cursed. Had to slither on its belly. It's right there in Genesis."

"That's true."

It was? Luke hadn't read that part of the Bible before. Now that he thought about it, he hadn't read much of any Scripture. That was going to change, though. He scratched his head. First he needed a Bible.

"Alice, I don't think the serpent was the problem. It had

been created by God and called good. That's right there in the first chapter of Genesis."

The door opened wider still. Teddy was handling her so well that Luke knew enough to keep his mouth shut.

Alice poked her head through the door. "What about the time when the Lord sent venomous snakes among the Israelites? They bit the people and many died. Numbers 21."

"Well, that was similar to the situation in the Garden of Eden. The problem wasn't the snakes—they were just a vessel for God to use, or for the devil to use in the Garden. The problem was that the people had been complaining against God and Moses. Remember that God told Moses that the people were to take that which had hurt them and lift it up to him. He turned even a snakebite into a blessing and victory. It's a metaphor, Alice. The 'snake' in our life can be redeemed and turned to power."

Alice was listening, and Luke was amazed. She'd lost that haunted look on her face and was focused entirely on Big Teddy Zook. On what he was telling her.

"Alice, if a snake has hurt you, we'd like you to give us a chance to redeem it. If you're willing, we'd like to help you get over your fear of snakes."

She narrowed her eyes. "How?"

"By showing you how good they are, what purpose they have in God's creation. I can teach you all about that, so you can understand them better. They're quite beautiful, Alice. I think a sensitive person like you could appreciate the wonder."

Alice's hand went up to the tendrils of curls on her neck. She was blushing. Alice Smucker was actually blushing at a compliment paid to her by Big Teddy Zook. Well, well. Wonders never ceased.

On the way home, Luke glanced at Teddy. "I didn't realize you were such a Bible student."

Big Teddy shrugged. "I do listen to the sermons."

"I listen." Most of the time. Not always. But Luke did usually listen to David's sermons. His thoughts drifted off when it was the other ministers' turns. *He* drifted off. "In fact, I'm going to look up those verses you talked about with Alice."

"Good."

"Genesis and Numbers, right?"

"Right. Exodus too."

"Uh . . . Old Testament or New?"

Teddy squeezed his eyes shut, cringing. "Old Testament."

"Got it. I'll read it today."

"Genesis, Exodus, and Numbers?"

"Yes. Today I will read them. You've got my word on it."

"The whole books? Every chapter?"

"Of course, the whole books." He glanced at Teddy. "Why? Are they long?"

$\mathcal{F}$IFTEEN

July slipped into August. Just before the bishop wrapped up the church service one Sunday, he announced that baptism classes would begin soon. Any who wanted to be baptized this fall, David said, should join the classes. Jenny was sitting next to Izzy and jabbed her with her elbow. "You should do it."

Izzy hadn't given much thought to baptism. None. "What would that mean?"

"That's how you become Amish, Izzy. For good."

"Just like that? I'm Amish?"

"Well, that plus a couple of weeks spent listening to the ministers explain the 18 Articles of the Dordrecht Confessions."

"What are those?"

"Um, well, doctrine, I guess you could say. Mainly, you hear what it means to be Amish."

"You've done it?"

"Of course. Can't get married without being baptized." Jenny squeezed Izzy's hand. "Think about it."

So she did. Izzy thought of little else. Later that week,

David stopped by to speak to Amos about deacon business, so Izzy kept an eye on his buggy while she was in the farm stand, hoping to catch him before he left Windmill Farm. When she saw the buggy come down the driveway, she waved him to a stop. "David, I'd like to ask you something."

David climbed out of the buggy and tied the horse's reins to the fence in a loose knot. He walked around the farm stand, giving it a once-over. "This is impressive. So Luke designed it?"

"He did. And Teddy Zook helped build it."

David smiled. "Quite a team. Wouldn't have expected that." He looked it over once more, then turned to Izzy. "So, what's on your mind?"

"I've been thinking . . ." She fiddled with the edges of her apron. "I'd like to join the baptism classes."

He nodded once but made no comment.

She waited for him to say something, anything, but after a long moment, she lifted her face. "Would that be all right?"

"You want to bend at the knee?"

Bend at the knee? Oh, he meant to kneel. Last fall, she'd seen a baptism. And she'd seen Luke kneel to make his confession, back when he first returned to Stoney Ridge in May. "Yes. Yes, I do."

"Tell me why, Izzy."

"Why?" *Because Jenny said that's how a person becomes permanently Amish. I want that more than I have wanted anything in my life.* But Izzy had a sense that wasn't the answer David wanted.

"Yes. I'd like to know why."

Why? She wasn't sure how to answer him. "It feels right. Like it's the right thing to do. The next step." She was actually quite proud of her answer. It sounded like the correct thing to say.

"Izzy, when a person bends at the knee, it's more than posture. It's bowing to God. It's making him the Lord of your life." He leaned his back against the counter of the farm stand, crossing his arms, thinking over something. "I don't want to discourage you from attending baptism classes. But when the time comes to bend at the knee, it must be a sincere, authentic confession of faith. A total dedication. Each person has to get that right with Christ *before* baptism. I've seen too many people get baptized for the wrong reasons and end up leaving the Amish. It creates enormous pain for so many. If you're not ready to make that kind of commitment, when the time comes, don't do it. Not until you're ready, heart and soul and mind." He smiled at her and climbed into the buggy.

She watched him drive off, then returned to the farm stand and packed up for the day. She carried a few bags of unsold fruit up to the house where Fern would turn the excess into cobblers or crumbles or pies or something she called grunts, which sounded dreadful.

Fern was pulling clothes off the clothesline as she crossed the yard to the house. "Much extra today?"

"Not much. Only two bags of plums."

"Good. I want to make a cobbler to take to Teddy Zook. To thank him for his help on that farm stand." She tucked a towel under her chin to fold it in thirds, then folded it in half and dropped it in the laundry basket. "You don't look very happy. Did it have something to do with David?"

Izzy kicked a pebble with her bare toe. "I'm not so sure David wants me to get baptized."

Fern stopped folding laundry. "What makes you think that?"

"He asked me why." It wasn't just the question. It was the impossible-to-discern look on his face when he asked her to explain why she wanted to get baptized. When she'd told Fern her plans, she seemed almost overcome with joy. Her eyes had grown shiny and she had to swallow a few times before she said anything. She'd thought David would've been pleased. "It was almost as if he wanted me to rethink it."

"Oh honey, that's not it at all. There's plenty of bishops who would be pushing you up to that bench as fast as they could. David, he has that same talk with every single person who starts the baptism class, young or old. Every one. He always says God doesn't want a halfhearted, lukewarm church. It's all or nothing." Fern took down the last towel and folded it. "Honey, if you're not ready, nothing has to change. You're welcome to stay right here, until the Lord tells you otherwise. You were invited to Windmill Farm without any strings attached." She bent down to pick up the laundry basket. "No strings." She took the two bags of plums out of Izzy's hands and plunked them on top of her laundry basket before heading to the kitchen.

Izzy sat down on the porch, watching the clouds move across the sky, mulling over what David had said. About going Amish, that she had no doubts. Thoughts about God, they weren't as clear, nor as simple. More like a ball of Fern's yarn after a barn cat found it. Tangled and knotted.

After supper, Amos asked Luke to sit with him on the porch for a moment. "Every time I turn around," Amos said, "you're back at Alice Smucker's with a new idea to cure her. David and I, we're concerned you might be using her problems to avoid the rest of the list."

Luke thought that was a little harsh. Part of the problem was that the list kept getting longer and he was the reason why. He made new mistakes, like scaring Alice Smucker, and felt a burden to fix old mistakes, like finding a Massauga rattlesnake in Teddy Zook's swamp.

But he did listen to Amos. He knew David and Amos were watching his progress on that list and it was pretty slow.

The next day, after finishing his chores, he drove the buggy over to Carrie and Abel's house. A passel of boys were on the front lawn, running through a sprinkler. They froze when they saw him and stopped to watch him pull the buggy to the side of the driveway. Then, when they realized who had come calling, they scattered. Disappeared. All but one boy who slowly walked toward Luke.

"Nothing better on a hot summer day." Luke pointed his thumb toward the abandoned sprinkler. "Are your parents at home?"

The boy stared at him. "Depends. Are you friend or foe?"

Huh. Luke recognized this boy. He was the boy who had the audacity to ask if there was a pistol in Luke's boot. At *church*. Luke admired that kind of pluck in a boy. He held his hands in the air. "I come as a friend."

"Then follow me."

Luke walked behind this boy—only ten or eleven years old, he gathered, yet he walked with bold confidence. No, he didn't walk. He strode, this one. The boy stopped at the house and pointed to a pair of mismatched rocking chairs.

"You wait here. I'll go get Dad."

He shot off in another direction and Luke sat down in the rocking chair. He could feel pairs of eyes watching him from hiding spots all over the yard. Why were children so frightened of him?

He rocked the chair back and forth as he waited, thinking back to how his reputation had grown to such disrepair. To such disproportion. It reminded him of something his mother had said after his father's business went under. De lenger as en Schneeballe rollt, de dicker as er waert. *The farther a snowball rolls, the larger it becomes.*

People acted as if he had tormented them. That wasn't how he'd seen himself back then. Mischief maker, yes. A bit of a bully. He never really meant to hurt anyone, not intentionally. Not until Patrick Kelly and that bird of his. And then Galen's horse had to be put down after he'd stolen it for a joyride, tried to jump a fence, and it broke a leg in a tumble. Luke had crossed the line of mischief making at that point; he knew that much for himself. It was the reason he'd agreed to go to rehab. He had scared himself.

That was it, he realized in a flash of insight. People didn't know how far he could or would go. The Amish were a gentle people, and they didn't fight back. They probably felt very victimized, and by one of their own. Shame settled over him, a feeling that was becoming all too familiar. He took off his hat and ruffled his hair, and as he put his hat back on, he noticed Abel striding toward him, that boy striding along beside him, though he needed two steps for every one of his father's. "Hello, Luke. My son Rudy said you wanted to see me."

Luke rose. "If you have a minute to spare, Abel, I wanted to talk to you about something."

Abel bent down to whisper to Rudy, and the boy scurried into the house. "Let's sit here, in the shade." He sat down next to Luke in the rocking chair. "Hot day."

"It sure is." Luke cleared his throat. "Abel, years ago, I put sugar in the gas tank of your lawn mower."

"I remember. Ruined the engine."

"I wanted to apologize to you. It was an immature thing to do, and I'm sorry for it. I'd like to buy you a new lawn mower."

Abel watched him as he spoke. Those hidden children were watching him. Luke felt an inch tall, like he was sitting underneath a magnifying glass. The door opened and out came Carrie and Rudy, holding glasses of cold lemonade. Carrie handed a glass to Luke and then turned to face the yard, calling out, "Boys! Come out from your hiding spots and start feeding the animals their supper."

It was astonishing. From trees and bushes all over the yard, boys emerged. They trudged slowly down to the barn, disappointed.

Luke looked at Carrie. "All boys?"

"We have three girls, but they're over at the neighbor's." She laughed. "They aren't all ours. Some of the boys belong to the Blanks. They have the farm that backs up to ours." She tapped Rudy on the brim of his hat. "You too, young man. Off to tend to the chickens."

Rudy's confident gait was gone. Shoulders hunched, feet dragging, hands in pockets, he obeyed his mother and joined the others.

Carrie turned to head back inside. "Stay, honey," Abel said. "Luke came to tell us something."

Luke jumped up and let Carrie sit in the rocking chair beside her husband. "I just wanted to apologize for putting sugar in your lawn mower's gas tank."

"So you were the one who did it," Carrie said. "I was never quite sure."

Abel had not doubted the culprit, Luke could see that. He still hadn't said much. "I'd like to buy you a new lawn mower, if you'll let me." He licked his lips. "And I wanted to ask if what I'd done—the sugar in the tank—if it might have had any adverse effect on you."

Abel and Carrie exchanged a look. Carrie spoke up first. "The only effect was to make us get rid of that terrible old dangerous lawn mower. We ended up buying two hand-push lawn mowers, and since then I felt better about having the boys mow the lawn." She gave Abel a nudge on his knee. "And finally this old man could get a nap on a summer afternoon."

Abel leaned forward in the rocker, looking earnestly at Luke. "We thank you for coming. We forgive you. And we encourage you to keep going on the path you're on."

As Luke drove away from Abel and Carrie's farm, he felt some relief. But he also thought, *It shouldn't be that easy. It just shouldn't be so easy.* Something didn't feel right, deep down.

Twenty minutes later, he turned the buggy into another driveway. Years ago, he'd cut the rope on a swing hanging off an old tree at the home of Mattie and Solomon Riehl. Just like he'd done with Carrie and Abel, he offered them an honest confession and heartfelt apology.

When he asked how his mischief had affected them, they insisted that it ended up being a blessing in disguise. "Our children were so disappointed to lose their tree swing," Sol said, "that I made another. When I threw the rope up and over the branch, I tugged down hard on it, to make sure it was safe. Would you believe that branch snapped off? Turns out the whole tree was rotting from the inside out. I'd never noticed. So in a way, Luke, you did us a favor. One of the little ones could have been hurt."

Luke knew they were being gracious. He hadn't tried to do any favors. That tree swing had always made him mad. Many times he'd passed the Riehl house and noticed Sol patiently pushing one child or another on that very swing. The sight of a father and a son together churned up that gutted feeling inside Luke, and it was only relieved when he took his anger out on something or someone. Why couldn't he have had a father who would've taken time to push his son on a swing? It wasn't just because his father had died. Even when his father was alive, he never gave any of his sons that kind of personal attention. Something was always more important.

Mattie and Solomon Riehl only had one son, though they wanted more. They ended up raising foster children. Sol wasn't even pushing his own children on that swing. He was pushing other people's children.

Luke felt a deep shame come over him, worse than any remorse he'd felt after talking to Alice or Teddy or Carrie and Abel. He turned the horse toward the Bent N' Dent and pulled Bob to a stop when he saw David's horse standing in the shade. Before he opened the door, he braced himself for a loud greeting by Hank Lapp, who spent most of his free time at the store. Most of Hank's time was free.

The store was empty. Relieved, Luke went to the back room and knocked on the doorjamb. David was at his desk and looked up when he heard the knock. "Come in. Sit down. It's been a quiet day today. I welcome the company."

David smiled in that way of his, the way he did everything in life, a look of acceptance and understanding, of offering margin. It made Luke feel good, deep down, that look on David's face. He hadn't realized how accustomed he'd become to people bracing themselves when they saw him coming. He used to like having that kind of effect on others, but no longer. It bothered him. He felt like he was different than he used to be, but those cautious, haunted looks remained.

Not with David, though. He recognized the changes Luke had been working on. He affirmed them. He sat across from David and stretched out his legs. "I just came from Mattie and Sol's. Working down the list." He lifted his hand to make a checked-off sign in the air as if it was no big deal. It was a very big deal. David knew.

David leaned back in his chair. "How'd it go?"

"Good. Fine. They were very understanding. Very forgiving. Even said that I'd done them a favor." He explained about the tree swing and the rotting tree.

"Yet somehow you don't look very . . . forgiven."

Luke sighed. "Their kindness . . . it almost made it worse. As I was driving away, I realized that I used to target people or families that had something I wanted. So I took it from them."

"What was it they had that you wanted?"

"There's not one answer to that. The tree swing, that had something to do with my own father. Wishing things were different. When I used to see Sol pushing children on the swing, it upset me. Made me mad at my own father for not being that kind of dad. Same with Abel and the lawn mower." He glanced at David. "I put sugar in the gas tank of Abel's lawn mower. Ruined it."

"Go on."

"I used to see him pushing that lawn mower around the yard, holding the hand of some small boy. It made me furious. Mad at my own father for not being the kind of dad who spent time with his children. And my father was dead. Silent and absent. I had no one to take my anger out on." He rubbed his face with his hands, then slapped his knees. "David, what a jerk I've been. To such good people. What a fool! You shouldn't have let me come back here."

David was watching him carefully, in the same way that Abel had looked at him, as if he could peer right into his soul. "This is exactly why I wanted you to come back, Luke. You're finally getting outside of yourself, showing genuine concern for other people. That's a big step of growth."

Tears stung Luke's eyes. "It makes me feel . . . terrible."

David's chair squeaked as he leaned forward and propped his elbows on his desk. "What's happening is that your conscience has woken up. You've gone from having an underdeveloped conscience to one that is finally aware. Responsive to God's Spirit."

Luke covered his face with his hands. "But this . . . it's a horrible place to be."

"It is. It is. But there's a far worse place to be. It's the hard heart, the shameless man, who has a disregard for God, who glories in his shame. That's the worst place to be."

Luke choked up and had to swallow a few times to get out the words he needed to say. "How do I . . . live with myself? The more I see of what I've done, the more I understand how I've hurt others, the worse I feel." This experience of mending fences . . . it was the hardest part of recovery he'd had to face. It was the hardest thing Luke had ever done.

"Accepting the forgiveness of God is meant for ourselves too. Maybe that's when confession takes on new meaning, because there's a full understanding of the depth of sin.

"This is a good pain you're feeling. The pain of conviction takes you to the feet of God to seek forgiveness. It's an awareness of how flawed and sinful we are, compared to a holy and good God. You're not alone in this awareness. There's plenty of things I've needed to receive forgiveness for, to truly believe I am forgiven after I've confessed my sin. The feeling might take time to come, but it does come. Look at Psalm 51. 'Purge me with hyssop, and I shall be clean. Wash me, and I shall be whiter than snow.' That was written by King David, a man after God's own heart. Look at how utterly remorseful he felt. Don't you think he was feeling the same way you're feeling now?" He handed a box of tissues to Luke.

Luke snatched a tissue out of the box and dabbed his eyes.

David waited a moment. "I've found there's a number of things in life that boil down to a simple concept."

He exhaled a deep, painful breath. "What?"

"It's pretty simple, actually. An easy phrase to remember. 'You know better now.' Isn't that what life is all about? God wants us to keep growing in holiness. You know better now, Luke. Hold on to that."

Sixteen

When Luke returned home, he discovered that some creature had gotten into his tack room. The floor was littered with peanut shells. A jar of peanut butter, nearly empty, lay on his cot. All over his pillow were tiny little peanut-butter claw prints. "Blast! That blasted raccoon!" Just when Luke had a few nights of solid sleep, with Bob securely in his stall all night long, and he thought the raccoon had left the barn for good, back it came. And now . . . his very room was invaded by that conniving beast.

He stomped into the center of the barn. "That's it! I've had enough!" The two cows lifted their heads to peer at him curiously over their stanchions. Bob the buggy horse shuffled his hooves in the stall's straw.

Luke looked up toward the rafters and shook his fist. "Raccoon! Hear me. You're not getting away with this. I am going to trap you and release you so far from Windmill Farm that you'll need a taxi to get back." Something landed on his head and he swiped it away with his hand. A peanut? He lifted his head to scan the rafters. Blast! That raccoon!

It threw the peanut at him. He pointed a finger up at the rafters and turned in a circle. "This is personal, Raccoon. I'm coming after you."

⌒

It was past six thirty in the morning, but Fern and Amos were still upstairs. It seemed to be taking Amos longer and longer to get up and going in the morning, and it troubled Izzy. Neither Fern or Amos talked about this change, so Izzy tried not to think about it much. Instead, she focused her attention on outsmarting the raccoon that was messing with Luke's head. She'd found an article about raccoons in one of Amos's farming magazines and set it at Luke's breakfast setting.

When he came inside, grumbling about peanut butter, she pointed to it. "I dog-eared an article that says raccoons are easy to trap."

Luke looked bleary-eyed again. "They're wrong. They have a diabolical intelligence."

"It says that they're curious, they're always hungry, and they're not afraid of human scent."

"Don't I know it? That raccoon walked all over my pillow. I think it took a nap on it." He squinted. "Where did it find peanuts and peanut butter, anyway?"

"Not from me. But . . ."

"But what?"

"Hank Lapp was in the barn yesterday afternoon. He came to the kitchen, pleased with himself. Then again, he always does seem pleased."

Luke clunked his forehead on the table.

She was glad he couldn't see how big her smile was. "It

also says raccoons have excellent memories. If they get in and out of a trap, they'll remember how they did it. So you have to change your tactics."

Luke lifted his head and slapped his palms on the tabletop. "I'm ready to change my tactics. I want to kill it."

"No. You can't, Luke. We have to catch it live and release it somewhere else."

"So it can terrorize someone else?"

"I couldn't live with myself if I killed a wild animal." Kill something? Stop a life? Never. No way. She sat down across from him. "This article has a plan to trap a raccoon without killing it or causing it to suffer. Read it. I underlined that section."

Luke yawned, then picked up the article to read it aloud. "'Find a barrel or round trash can. The taller, the better. It also needs to have smooth sides so the perpetrator cannot get a grip once caught inside.'" He put down the article. "I like that term, 'perpetrator.' Sounds like a convicted criminal."

"Keep reading."

"'Place the barrel near the edge of any flat surface taller than the top of the barrel. Pour water into the barrel.'" He looked up, surprised. "Drown it! What a *great* idea."

"Wrong. Keep reading."

"'The barrel needs to be approximately one-third full, depending on the size of the raccoon. If your raccoon is smaller, use less water, as you don't want the critter to drown if you forget to check the trap in the morning.'" He set the magazine down again. "Yes, I do want to drown the critter. And what happened to calling it a perpetrator? Critter sounds too cute."

Izzy sighed and grabbed the magazine to finish the article. "'Place a board half on the table or solid surface, and halfway hanging over the barrel. Make sure the end of the board is exactly centered in the middle of the barrel. You want to try and balance the board so that it will tip into the can when the raccoon walks across it.'"

"I love this," Luke said.

"'Bait the trap. Place a tasty raccoon treat such as fish or peanut butter—'"

"We know it loves peanut butter."

"'—at the end of the board hanging over the barrel. The idea here is that the unsuspecting critter will 'walk the plank' trying to get the food. It will then unbalance the board and go crashing down into the water.'"

"And then it drowns. I'm in!"

Izzy ignored him. "'The water is a key component because, without it, the little sneak would jump and crawl right out of the barrel. When it splashes into the water, its fur becomes wet and heavy, and its claws lose traction. Those two things combined mean that it will stay stuck in the barrel until you check it.'"

Luke clapped his hands together. "I'll make the trap right after breakfast."

"I'll help," Izzy said, without thinking first. That was a mistake.

Luke looked delighted at that news. Too happy.

She frowned at him.

After breakfast, Luke went straight back to the barn to find an empty barrel and fill it with water.

"Only one-third full," Izzy said. "I'm not letting you drown this raccoon."

He swiveled around to see her. "Why are you suddenly interested in helping me get rid of this raccoon?"

"Just because."

"Hold on. You've changed your tune. Something's happened. What?"

"That wily raccoon got into my henhouse. Stole all the eggs. Every single one."

He was sorry to hear that, but not too sorry. At least someone finally understood how frustrating this raccoon had been.

"Something has to be done, Luke."

She gave him a look as if he'd been taking the whole thing as a joke. Him! The one who kept getting woken up by a horse.

"I forgot to add one more thing that was in the article. It said that if a mother raccoon is protecting her babies, she will fight with a ferocity."

Oh great. It hadn't occurred to Luke that it might be a she, and there might be more of them up in the barn rafters.

It worked. To Luke's amazement, the barrel trapped the raccoon. He had used two haystacks for the solid surface, with a board leading down halfway over the water filled barrel. At the end of the board, he rolled a raw piece of bacon around a blob of peanut butter. It was Izzy's idea. Bacon plus peanut butter. In the middle of the night, Luke heard a big *splash!* followed by thrashing and clawing and angry spitting sounds. He jumped out of bed, grabbed the flashlight, and ran to the barrel. Lo and behold, there it was. The perpetrator.

Luke tipped the barrel over so that the raccoon wiggled his way down into the foolproof, way-too-expensive wire trap he'd bought from the Hay & Grain. Using leather gloves, he latched the cage and locked it with a padlock. Then, carefully, he wove wire around the opening. The raccoon was furious with him, glaring at him, spitting and squeaking, shaking his wet fur so that it sprayed Luke. He didn't know that raccoons squeaked. He almost felt sorry for it. Almost. Satisfied, he went back to bed.

In the morning, Luke carried the cage with the angry raccoon out to the buggy.

Izzy yoo-hooed to him from the house. "Did it work? Did you catch him?"

"I got him! Tell Amos I'll be back. I'm taking this rodent ulcer as far from Windmill Farm as I can go."

By the time Luke had backed Bob up between the shafts and was fastening the buckles on Bob's harness, Izzy had come down to join him. She held out a piece of thickly cut toast, lathered with butter and jam. "Thought you might be hungry."

He lifted his head. "Well, thank you, Izzy."

"It was Fern's idea."

"Put it on the driver's seat. I'll eat it as I head to the hills."

She patted Bob's nose and walked to the buggy. "Luke."

Her voice sounded weird. Luke braced himself. "Yeah?"

"Where's the raccoon?"

"Back seat. In the trap."

Izzy cringed, the way you tighten up after lightning strikes and you're waiting for the thunder. "I see the trap. It's empty."

"No! No no no no no." Luke ran back to the buggy and

grabbed the edge of the buggy with both hands. The cage door was wide open. The trap was empty.

It was a glorious day, the sky as blue as a robin's egg, with a gentle, light breeze. On a summer morning like today, Amos liked to drink his first cup of coffee on the porch, soaking up the beauty of the day. The earth was full of the goodness of the Lord, he would think to himself. Today, unfortunately, he couldn't appreciate any of it. He sat at the kitchen table, bothered.

Fern handed him a cup of coffee. "What's eating you?"

"Have you seen what's going on between Luke and Izzy lately?"

"The raccoon eviction?"

"Fern, it's not funny. There's something brewing between them. I have three daughters. I know what it looks like when something is brewing."

"They do seem a little less combative with each other."

He thumped the table with his fist. "I was afraid of this happening. It's just what I worried about when we agreed to bring Luke here."

Fern sat down across from him. "Let me get this straight. You'd rather that they didn't even talk to each other. Not even be friends."

He frowned at her. "There's no such thing as a boy and girl, at their age, being friends."

"Are you worried about Luke? Or Izzy?"

"Both! They're broken, Fern. The two of them, they both had messy childhoods. How could two broken young people end up helping each other?"

"They can't."

"So you agree?" He felt a little better. He thought this would be a more difficult conversation than it was. "I'll ask Luke to find another place to live."

"I agree that two broken young people can't help each other. I don't agree that we make Luke move away from Windmill Farm. He's been a huge help to you, Amos. We've needed him this summer and we'll need him even more come fall. It's not fair to him to make him leave. He hasn't done anything wrong."

"What about Izzy? You're the one who always says she's been sent here to heal."

"I do believe that. And I believe the same thing for Luke."

Amos huffed. "Then what are we going to do?"

"We're going to trust God in this, Amos Lapp. We're going to continue to pray mightily for the two of them, and rest in God's sovereignty."

"Fern, I'm not doubting God. But their brokenness . . ."

She reached out and squeezed his hands. "God brought those two to us. They're part of our bundle of responsibility. We're seeing them both make great strides." She rose and went to the door, scooping up an empty laundry basket on the ground. "I'm going to bring in the laundry before the rain starts."

Amos looked out the window. The sun was shining. Only one small gray, wispy cloud hung in the bright blue sky. "Fern," he said, annoyed. "You think you can see the future. You can't. You can't forecast the weather. You can't foresee what might happen with Izzy and Luke."

"Now, did I say that I could? I never said such a thing. I said I trusted God with them." She left the kitchen, now equally annoyed.

Not an hour later, the sky turned a dark, bruised blue and the rain came down in thick gray curtains.

It had started sprinkling as Luke left Windmill Farm, but now rain was coming down hard. As he neared the Bent N' Dent, he hopped off the scooter and leaned it against the edge of the store. As he opened the door, he heard a loud, "LUKE SCHROCK. JUST THE MAN I WANTED TO SEE."

Oh, boy. "Morning, Hank."

"How goes the raccoon trapping?"

"Ineffective."

"You mean my peanut butter concoction didn't work?"

"No, it didn't work. What were you thinking, anyway?"

"Raccoons love peanut butter! It's a solid-gold fact."

"That, I know. But why would you try to bait him in the tack room?"

Hank sputtered and pointed at him. "THAT'S WHERE YOU SAID IT SPENDS ITS NIGHTS."

"No, Hank. That's where the horse goes. After the raccoon unlatches its stall. You got it all wrong." He caught himself frowning at Hank, exasperated at the man's indifference to his plight. He briefly wondered if this was the same reason people were always frowning at him so much. "I need to get some cinnamon for Fern. She's spending the day canning pears."

Hank licked his lips. "TELL HER I'LL BE STOPPING BY LATER TODAY for SAMPLES." He closed his eyes and stretched out his legs. "I'LL SIT HERE and PONDER MORE WAYS to TRAP A COON."

"You do that, Hank. Just let me know *before* you try

something. It took me hours to get that peanut butter off the floor. I don't know what you put in it, but it hardened like dried oatmeal paste."

Hank's eyes opened. One eye peered at Luke. The other eye drifted off to the side. It was a disconcerting experience. "THAT'S EXACTLY WHAT I PUT IN IT. That's the BEAUTY OF THE PLAN. Like WET CEMENT. The RACCOON WAS SUPPOSED TO GET STUCK IN IT."

Luke shook his head as he passed Hank. How did Edith stand him? But then, how did Hank stand Edith? She was as tough a woman as they come. Hank, for all his bluster, was as soft a man as they come.

Love. It was a mystery of dynamic proportion. What was it that made two people feel something special for each other? As he walked to the back of the store, his mind thought of the way Teddy Zook and Alice Smucker had been casting sideways glances at each other the last few days during their sessions of snake conditioning, cheeks blushing furiously. Both of them! Could something be stirring between them? Another mystery.

⁓

For the last two weeks, Teddy Zook and Luke had brought snakes, in cages, over to Alice Smucker's house. At first, she would only look at them through her window. Then, on the porch. And then, one rainy afternoon—probably because of the rain—she let Teddy bring a cage inside. Standing halfway across the room, she peered curiously at the snake, and listened as Teddy described it.

"It's kind of pretty, isn't it?" Alice said. "Its color, I mean. Not its beady eyes."

Teddy explained how a snake's eyes were designed, how you could tell if it was venomous or poisonous by how its pupils were shaped. Alice took a step closer to the cage. Just one. "So this one, then, it's not poisonous."

"Exactly right, Alice." Teddy smiled at her, and she smiled back at him, and Luke felt as if he was watching a miracle unfold.

A few days later, Alice Smucker held that same little bright green snake in the palm of her hands. Held. It. In. Her. *Hand.* What a day, what a day!

But it got better still. Luke overheard Teddy ask Alice what time she wanted him to come for Saturday supper. Blushing beet red, Alice told him to come at five o'clock, without a snake.

On the drive home, Luke was grinning from ear to ear. So much so that it annoyed Teddy. "Wipe that smug look off your face."

"Can't help it," Luke said, still grinning. "Here I was trying to cure Alice of her phobia, and along came an additional gift. Love. Two birds, one stone."

"If you think you've cured Alice, then why won't she leave her house?"

Luke's grin faded.

SEVENTEEN

Luke had told Big Teddy he would read through Genesis, Exodus, and Numbers, back when Teddy first quoted out of them, but then the raccoon distracted him from that intention. Today, Teddy reminded him of his promise, so he set aside time to read through the books after supper. He read them quickly at first, and then he went over them slowly, underlining certain parts. Despite loving to read, he'd never really considered the Bible to be captivating. It was, though. The more he read, the more it became a story. One long story. Over and over, he kept noticing a theme: God seeking, man responding. God calling man out of his situation and into a new one. A better one. God imploring man to believe and obey. It was a phrase David used often in his sermons. Believe and obey. He also noticed a theme of "all in." God wanted his people to be "all in." It was another subject matter David stayed camped on. "Heart, soul, and mind," he called it.

Luke yawned, stretched. He wanted to grab a quick shower before he turned in for the night. In the house's bathroom, standing half in, half out of the tub, he waited for the water to warm up. A shock went through him, as real as a bolt of lightning. One foot in, one foot out. It's what his life had been all about. Even at his lowest point, he'd never turned his back on God, not entirely. Now it seemed as if God was sending him a message through those Bible passages. "It's time, Luke. Time to decide. You can't have it both ways. I want you all in."

Luke stilled. If he chose God, if he gave himself to God all the way, it would mean the end of "one foot in, one foot out." He would never go back. This moment, right now, it would become his point of no return.

Return to what? What kind of a life was it? Living on the fence meant he didn't enjoy either side.

He took a deep breath and said aloud, "I'm in, Lord. All the way." Then he got into the tub and pulled the curtain and had the best shower of his life.

⁓

Late Friday afternoon, while milking the cows, Luke couldn't stop thinking about Alice Smucker. Her refusal to leave her house weighed heavily on his mind. Then he had a strange sense of a message pressing down on him: *Go. Go now. Tell Alice what you've just learned.*

The hair on the back of Luke's neck stood up. The voice wasn't audible, not at all, but it sure seemed loud and clear. He leaned back on the milking stool and gazed around the barn. "Hold on a minute. Is this what it means to be 'all in'?" he said out loud. "You're not serious. You can't be serious." Sage turned her head toward him, batting her thick eyelashes.

Again came the message: *Go and tell Alice what you've learned.*

"But I can't! She'll think I'm crazy. It'll set everything back. All her progress."

Bob poked his big head over the stall door to see who Luke was talking to. Who, indeed.

Again came the message. *Go. Go now.*

Heart pounding, hands trembling, he finished milking Lemon Thyme, fed Bob, and scootered over to Alice's house.

She looked surprised to find him knocking on her door, but not suspicious like she usually did. And she even invited him inside without him having to ask. As she poured a glass of lemonade for him in her little kitchen, he noticed that the gray top of the kitchen table had those squiggly black lines all over it. Kind of like a jigsaw puzzle. Going-nowhere kind of lines. This tabletop . . . it sort of symbolized Alice's life.

He thought of how much progress she'd made these last few weeks in facing her fears. Or maybe he was the one who'd made progress. He'd worked hard to show her that he was a changed man. Maybe both of them had changed.

She handed him a glass and sat across from him at the little table. "Something on your mind?"

"Yes. Yes, there is." He took a sip of lemonade, swallowed, then set the glass down. "Alice, I've been reading the Bible a lot lately. To be honest, spending so much time with Teddy has made me more interested in it."

Two streaks of pink went up her cheeks as soon as he mentioned Teddy's name. "He does seem to be quite knowledgeable about a great deal of subjects," she said, carefully avoiding his eyes.

Aha! He knew it. Something was brewing. Well, that wasn't why he was here. "I've been reading about Abraham, and Isaac and Jacob. Of Joseph in Egypt. And then a lot about Moses. Quite a lot."

"Well, that's good to hear."

"Moses is why I'm here."

"Moses?"

"Moses made a mess of his life—and it was a pretty sweet life he'd been handed. He killed an Egyptian soldier, was found out, and ran for his life. Even then, God hadn't abandoned him. Just the opposite. It seemed like God kept waiting for him to get his stuff together." He knew he had to come to his point soon; he could tell he was losing Alice's attention. "Each one of them, Abraham, Isaac, Jacob, Joseph, and Moses . . . especially Moses . . . they were all called by God to leave their comfortable life and go someplace."

Alice froze.

"Hold on, Alice. Stay with me. I'm almost done. I promise. I just want you to think this through—God called those Bible guys to get out of the house, each one, and he never let them down."

Her eyes were glued to the table, on those going-nowhere-jigsaw-puzzle kind of lines. Her lips set into a tight line. This wasn't going well.

"Those Bible guys, they were full of fear. Especially Moses. Look at how he tried to talk God into using someone else . . . right in front of that burning bush. I mean, *that* is a man hobbled by fear. Imagine telling God that you'll pass on what he's asking." He leaned forward. "Alice, you can have a story that ends like Moses's. You can trust God at his word and go out in the world. Even if it's uncomfortable and hard to do." He finished off the glass of lemonade. "That's what I

195

came to say today. That's all." He rose. "Oh, and thank you for the lemonade."

Outside, he reached down to pick up the scooter, troubled by the look on Alice's face when he'd left her at the table.

Her face was drained of color. She looked as if she'd seen a ghost.

On Sunday, church was to be held at Mattie and Sol Riehl's farm. Luke still felt awful about Alice. That look on her face, so shocked and troubled, it haunted him. He wondered what Teddy would have to say to him today. Chew him out, was his best guess. He was pretty sure he'd messed everything up and set Alice back. Again.

During breakfast, he could feel Izzy's curious glances in his direction, sensing something was off with him. Normally, her interest would make him sit up and take notice, but not this morning. He kept his eyes on his plate.

He was silent on the drive to the Riehls', replaying that talk in the kitchen with Alice over and over. Things had been moving along pretty well. Why did he put pressure on her? David and Amos had told him, numerous times, that he was not qualified to act as a counselor. What was he thinking?

But I thought I heard you, God. I thought it was you.

More likely, it was indigestion.

"Well, I'll be," Amos said, turning his head to look at the back seat. "Fern, honey, would you look at that."

"Oh my," Fern said. "I never thought I'd see this day again, but lo and behold, there it is."

Luke was concentrating on turning the horse into the Riehls' driveway. Boys were running up to meet them, to take the horse and buggy. It was when Bob came to a complete stop that he realized what Amos and Fern were staring at. Right in front of them was Teddy Zook's buggy. Teddy stood beside it, helping Alice Smucker climb out.

A gasp burst out of Luke, then his eyes filled with tears as he watched the two of them walk toward the house together. *Lord*, his heart prayed, *you didn't give up on Alice Smucker.*

All through church, his whole being felt a growing sense of awe, like a campfire that was gaining strength. He couldn't even look in Alice's direction without his eyes filling up again. He hardly spoke to the men on either side of him during the fellowship lunch. He didn't trust himself to carry on a conversation. He felt—oh, what was the word? euphoric!—so much so that he worried if he tried to speak, he might break out in a song of thanksgiving, and that would be weird.

Even on the drive back to Windmill Farm, Luke remained silent. Fern and Izzy chatted quietly in the back seat. Amos sat beside him, glancing at him now and then.

"So," he said, as they neared the road that led to Windmill Farm, "Teddy Zook gave you credit for getting Alice to church today."

Luke swallowed. He felt his eyes well up again. He didn't dare look at Amos.

"David and I, we've been trying to get her to come to church for well over a year now." He put a hand on Luke's shoulder. "I'm not sure what you said or did, but whatever it was, it was the right thing."

That big gentle hand on his shoulder, affirming him, wiped Luke out. The tears dripped down his face. He wiped them away with his coat sleeve, but they kept coming. He pulled Bob to a stop in front of the house so everyone could climb out. Amos went first, then Fern, then Izzy. Luke kept his hat brim down, head turned to the left, hoping Izzy didn't realize the state he was in.

He heard the buggy door slide shut behind Fern and Izzy. He flicked on the reins to get Bob turned toward the barn. He kept telling himself to hold it together, but as the buggy pulled over in the shade of the barn, before he knew it, he was doubled over the dashboard, sobbing so hard that his chest hurt. It took a few minutes before he could calm down and take in some deep breaths.

"Here, you big baby."

His head jerked up. Izzy stood beside his open window. She gave him a look that was for once not a smirk but one of real sympathy, and she handed him a little package of tissues.

$\mathcal{E}$IGHTEEN

Windmill Farm was hosting the August quilting bee, so Jenny came over on Wednesday afternoon to help get things ready. Fern and Jenny and Izzy made chicken salad with grapes and slivered almonds, bread sticks, and plenty of other good things. While they worked, they talked and talked. The kitchen had grown so warm that as soon as they finished their baking for the day, they sat on the porch and drank iced tea. Izzy and Jenny did, anyway. Fern never sat. She filled two glasses with iced tea and stood in front of them, the pitcher dripping with frost. "You girls sit here for a spell. I'm going to the basement to finish ironing tablecloths for Friday."

Izzy looked up in surprise. "Fern, it's so hot. You can't iron in this heat."

"Basement is cool."

"I'll help you later. Sit and visit with us."

"Can't. Too much to do."

Izzy started out of her chair to stop Fern until Jenny put a hand on her arm. "You won't be able to change her mind."

"But it's much too hot to iron."

"Maybe. I don't think that's what's on her mind. She's giving us time alone to talk."

Izzy sat back in the chair. Jenny knew Fern and Amos much better than she did. She wasn't completely clear on Jenny's story, mainly because she didn't ask any questions. It's not that she wasn't interested in others, she was, but she didn't want questions asked in return. She listened, though. From what she could figure out, Jenny and her brother Chris had inherited a nearby home from their grandfather, a man named Colonel Mitchell. Chris had worked for Amos as a field hand and later married his daughter M.K. They lived in Ohio now, where Chris raised horses. Jenny had slipped into Fern's life like a favorite niece, shadowing her every move. Where Chris and Jenny's parents happened to be—that Izzy did not know. No one discussed them. She understood *that*.

"So . . . what's it like having Luke Schrock live here?"

Izzy's eyes widened in surprise. "He doesn't. He lives in the barn."

Jenny frowned. "You know what I mean. What do you think of him?"

"Nothing." That wasn't exactly true. She had trouble keeping Luke out of her thoughts.

"Well, do you think he's handsome?"

"I think *he* thinks he's handsome." And he was. She had seen girls cast their eyes in his direction at church.

"Does he act like a gentleman?"

"No," Izzy said. *Sometimes*, she thought.

"Does he talk much?"

"Yes. Too much." It seemed that Luke just filled up a room with himself.

"Does he make you laugh?"

"Maybe." *Totally.* Sometimes he meant to and often he didn't. She tilted her head and narrowed her eyes. "Why are you asking so many questions about Luke Schrock?"

Jenny leaned over to whisper. "Because I think that Luke Schrock is smitten with you." She sat back in her chair with a grin. "So what do you think of that?"

"Nothing."

"One thing I know," Jenny said with certainty, "if a man can make a woman laugh, then he is worth paying attention to."

What? Izzy had never heard of such a thing. "Is that in the Bible?"

Jenny laughed. "No, but maybe it should be."

"Jesse makes you laugh." Izzy had often observed them together.

Jenny's eyes grew soft around the edges. "He always has. You and Luke . . . you remind me of Jesse and me, before we stopped pretending we disliked each other and started courting." She swept the yard with a glance, as if to make sure no one was listening even though no one was around but Fern, and she was down in the basement. Then she leaned in close to whisper, "Jesse wants to marry me."

"When?"

Jenny put a finger to her lips to hush her. "This fall. That's when the weddings happen. Jesse says he's going to talk to Amos soon."

"Why Amos?"

"He's the deacon. That's the way it's done. The deacon is the go-between. Amos'll talk to David about it, since he's Jesse's father. And then"—she shrugged—"I guess he'll have to talk to Fern about it. She's the closest thing I have to a mother." She smoothed out her apron over her skirt. "And then it'll be published, two weeks before the wedding happens."

"Published?"

"Announced in church. That's the way things are done." She glanced at Izzy. "You won't say anything, will you? It's supposed to be a secret until it's published."

"Of course not. I won't say a word to anyone." Izzy took a sip of her iced tea. So, here was another set of traditions she hadn't considered. Weddings. A nameless longing filled Izzy.

"I'd like you to be my bridesmaid."

Izzy was swallowing her iced tea and practically choked on the swallow. "Me?" *Me?*

"Yes, you. You're my best friend."

Izzy's eyes filled with tears. She'd never been anyone's best friend.

Jenny reached out and squeezed her hand. "I hope you'll say yes."

Izzy couldn't get the word past the lump in her throat. Instead, she gave a short nod.

Then Fern came back out, one hand holding a freshly ironed tablecloth, and the other hand holding a fresh pitcher of iced tea. "Kitchen's cooling down," she said. "We need to start on pies soon."

"Fern Lapp," Jenny said in a firm tone that sounded just like Fern's. "Sit down with us and rest for a moment." She poured her a glass of iced tea and made her sit down in a rocking chair.

"Maybe I will just sit a spell." And the talk turned away from weddings and laughter and on to whether adding vinegar to a piecrust made all the difference in flakiness. It turned away from Luke Schrock and did not go back to him. Izzy was glad. And yet, she thought of everything Jenny had said, about Luke being handsome, and that he was smitten with her. And how he made her laugh.

No. Jenny was wrong. So so wrong. Luke was unpredictable and bad-mannered and then there was his terrible reputation that followed him everywhere. No, no, no. Too risky, that one.

She squeezed her eyes closed, as if to force him out of her mind. And yet he persisted, as if he was right there on the porch with them.

As Luke walked up the porch steps to the house, the kitchen door was propped open and he heard Izzy laughing with someone. It surprised him, he hadn't heard her laugh much. Once or twice, she had laughed at him, but mostly, she frowned around him.

As he stepped into the kitchen, he saw Jenny and Izzy standing side by side, rolling out dough into piecrusts. They were giggling over something silly, and for a split second, they seemed oddly alike. And then the moment passed and he saw how very different from each other they really were—Izzy, tall and shapely, olive skinned and brunette, while Jenny was fair, almost elfishly small. Jenny, blue-eyed as a summer day, while Izzy's eyes were dark as coffee beans. Still, something in their profiles struck him as remarkably similar. Maybe it was the way they laughed. If he closed his eyes, they sounded one and the same.

Jenny spotted him first. "Hi, Luke. I'm teaching Izzy how to make piecrusts. Can you believe she's never made one? Not one time."

"Nor have I," Luke said, letting a broad smile escape. "But I've eaten plenty and will be happy to give you my humble opinion."

Jenny threw a lump of pie dough at his face, but he caught it midair. "There's nothing humble about you, Luke Schrock." She went back to rolling the dough. "By the way, Hank Lapp stopped by earlier to offer more raccoon trapping tips."

"Should I be worried? Did you let him in the barn?"

"No. He just stayed in the kitchen and sampled our baking."

"And provided rather a lot of unasked-for advice," Izzy added.

Luke took a bite of the raw pie dough and spit it out. "Jenny, did Izzy tell you she's signed up for baptism class?"

"Of course she did." Jenny grinned at him. "So I suppose you signed up right away."

"I believe I was first to sign up." That, actually, was the truth. He had put his name on the list on that very Sunday David had announced that classes would start soon. "Izzy signed up after me." He exhaled a dramatic sigh. "Like most women, I suppose she just can't get enough of me."

"See what I mean?" Jenny shook her head. "There's nothing humble about you, Luke Schrock."

Izzy ignored their banter and kept her attention focused on rolling out the pie dough until it was paper thin. Her face, he happened to notice, had turned a crimson red.

What was that about? The kitchen was warm, but not *that* hot.

An afternoon hush lay over Stoney Ridge, pushed in by a hot spell that hovered over the town in late August, triple digits and high humidity, so hot that Amos told Luke they needed to work early in the morning and late at night, but not during the middle of the day. Luke decided to head to the marsh and see if he could figure out where Teddy's elusive rattlesnake might be hiding. He scootered over, looked for Teddy in his carpentry shop but couldn't find him, so he went down to the marsh alone.

Marsh. That was a kindness. It was a stinking swamp. The smell was rank, with pond scum hanging on to the surface of the water. The air was noisy with the music of insects: dragonflies, whirligigs, water striders, and, of course, mosquitoes. He walked along the edges, his boots slipping in the muck. Then around one bend he found a flat area of grass and there was Rudy Miller—Abel and Carrie's son—lying on his back, his hat covering his face, hands behind his head as a pillow. Luke watched him for a while. He was barefoot, with a fishing pole held between his knees, snoring lightly. Quietly, Luke crept up to him. He yanked a few times on the fishing pole's string until Rudy jerked awake. He blinked a few times, then jumped to his feet and grabbed his pole.

"You!" His eyes went wide. "It's you."

"What are you doing?"

He shrugged. "Fishing."

"Looked like you were sleeping."

He yawned. "Both, I guess." He stretched.

"Does your mom know you're here?"

"She sent me to get something at a neighbor's. I'm just taking my time getting home."

Luke swallowed a smile as he sat down on the grassy spot where Rudy had been caught snoozing. "So, is fishing your favorite thing?" It was a nice spot the boy had found for himself. Quiet, peaceful, with a widened area for the water to pool. It was still a stinking swamp, but this part was better than the rest of it.

"Yup." The boy puffed up his chest. "I usually bring home dinner from this spot."

Luke doubted that. He hadn't seen any sign of fish in this murky water. But it was a nice, cool, shady place to be on a hundred-degree day, and he was amused by the boy's bravado.

Rudy sat down next to him. "You want to try to catch something? You can use my pole."

"Thanks, but I'm looking for something."

"What? Maybe I can help."

"A rattlesnake."

Rudy's eyebrows shot up. "Most folks stay clear of rattlers."

"Yeah, that's good advice." Luke stretched himself out, hands clasped behind his head, ankles crossed.

"Were you really as bad as they say?"

Luke opened one eye, then shut it. "Sometimes."

"Hank Lapp calls you the Jesse James of Stoney Ridge."

"Hmmm." Sounded like something Hank would say.

"Who's Jesse James?"

"He was an outlaw." It was so quiet, so still that Luke found himself drifting off. And then he woke with a gasp to the smell of smoke. Rudy sat beside him, trying to light a cigarette. "*What* are you doing?"

"Having a smoke. Want one?"

"No. How long have you been smoking?"

"Oh, years now."

Luke had to bite his lower lip not to burst out laughing.

Rudy had trouble lighting the match and dropped the cigarette twice. The boy kept nervously glancing over at him. Finally, it lit, and he took in a deep draft of smoke, first one, then another, and coughed so hard that he doubled over, scrambled to the edge of the scummy pond, and gagged. Luke's shoulders were shaking with quenched laughter, but he didn't want to risk injuring Rudy's tender pride. He knew all about tender pride.

Had he been like that as a boy? Probably.

The cigarette floated off into the pond scum. Rudy leaned back, his knees folded under him. He didn't dare look at Luke.

"Rudy, do you know much about this . . . marsh?"

The boy wiped his mouth with his shirt and turned to face Luke. "Every nook and cranny."

Luke must have looked skeptical, because Rudy crossed his heart. "I'm telling the truth. I've been coming here for as long as I can remember."

Luke sighed. "Okay, then tell me everything you know. Leave nothing out."

Rudy beamed. "How much time ya got?"

"As much time as you have knowledge." Luke didn't think it would take long. But it did. Turned out the boy actually knew his way up and down this swamp, and even made some sense as he talked. When Rudy finally exhausted himself of information, he paused and looked at Luke.

"So, then, Rudy, how'd you like to help me catch a rattle-snake?"

The boy looked like he'd just been given the moon.

207

Luke stared at David's long fence-mending list. He'd made it through four pages. Sixteen families. He'd written a long letter of apology to his stepfather, Galen King, asking him to forgive him for causing the death of his prize horse. If there was anything he could do to make amends, he offered to do it. So far, he hadn't heard back. That was not a surprise.

The last apology he'd made was surprisingly easy. He had ridden his scooter over to the Sisters' House, five old sisters—now four—who lived together in a house as old as they were. Long ago, he'd broken an upstairs window with a baseball. He apologized to the old sisters, quite sincerely, but they only stared at him with blank looks on their wrinkled faces.

"We don't remember," one of them said.

"And if we don't, then you shouldn't either," said another. They sent him home with a paper bag full of freshly made chocolate chip cookies. He would have to do something nice for them soon. Mow their lawn, maybe. Fix their rotting porch steps.

With the Sisters' House crossed off the list, there were only two names left. *Ruthie Stoltzfus and Patrick Kelly.*

It was time to face Ruthie and Patrick. He'd taken pains to avoid both of them for the last few months. It wasn't difficult to do because Ruthie had been avoiding him too. He knew her that well, or at least, he had known her that well.

Luke had always thought he and Ruthie would end up together, had counted on the bond they had in common to be unbreakable. Both had lost a parent. Both were middle children who'd been overshadowed by older siblings with big, consuming problems. For Ruthie, that meant Katrina and Jesse. For Luke, that meant Tobe and Bethany. Their younger siblings were adorable and uncomplicated. Luke and Ruthie loved their families, but they both grew up feeling invisible.

Hold on, Luke Schrock. Hold it. There I go down that well-rutted path of self-pity. Blaming parents has an expiration date, his counselor told him. Own your choices, own your problems.

He "recalibrated" his thoughts, almost like shuffling a deck of cards in his head. David called it taking every thought captive to God. When he took time to respond to that inner jab, to take captive those dragging thoughts, he literally felt lighter, like he'd dropped a stone out of a backpack.

Okay. He took in a deep breath. The time had come to face Ruthie and Patrick. He spent some time on his knees, then took the scooter and headed over to the Inn at Eagle Hill. It was his family's home, a bed-and-breakfast business his mother had started after moving here. She was a survivor, his mother. Rose Schrock King didn't have an easy path, but she was a faithful woman. As a widow with four children, she had to find a way to support her family, and she figured out a way to do it.

The Inn at Eagle Hill was a beautiful old farmhouse set against a hillside. As he scootered up the gravel driveway, he saw Ruthie and Patrick coming down from the hillside, holding hands. A swirl of envy rolled around in his stomach. They looked so happy. This was what he had wanted for himself. She was the one he had wanted. The Inn at Eagle Hill was his own family's home, and yet he wasn't welcomed here, not really. His mother had asked Ruthie to run the inn while she and Galen were in Kentucky. She hadn't asked Luke.

He didn't blame his mother. Fresh out of rehab, Luke wasn't ready for the burden of running the business. Galen probably had an opinion too. It wasn't that Luke didn't have a high regard for Galen. He did. But Galen had little tolerance for Luke, especially after he hurt his horse on that awful night—the night it all came crashing down. The bottoming-out night.

Ruthie spotted Luke first, and came to an abrupt stop. He lifted his hand in a light wave. Patrick looked down at him and gently tugged on Ruthie's hand. Luke could read their thoughts. She didn't want to have to talk to him, but Patrick would insist. He was that kind of a guy. A good guy. A very good guy.

He met them at the bottom of the hill. "Were you eagle watching?"

"We were," Patrick said.

Luke had used English for Patrick's sake, but was surprised by Patrick responding back in Penn Dutch. So, then, he had mastered the language in the last year. Pretty impressive. Izzy was still struggling with it, hesitant to speak it, though Luke could tell she understood most of it.

"There's two nests now," Patrick said. "Last year's babies have returned and made their own home."

"Two of them?" Luke said. "I remember when that first nest was built. Took the pair a couple of weeks to build it. It ended up as big as a bathtub. A tangle of sticks, but on the inside, lined like velvet. Supposed to weigh a ton, a full ton. Hard to believe." He pressed his lips together, suddenly aware he'd been talking too fast, too nervous. Pressure talking.

Ruthie's eyes were fixed on him in a hard glare. He looked right at her. "I came to talk to you both, if you have time."

"We don't," she said in a cold tone.

210

Patrick's elbow nudged her. "Yes we do." He pointed to the house. "Let's go sit on the porch and get out of the sun."

The three of them walked to the porch and sat down. Luke had to admire the well-cared-for condition of the house. Ruthie sat on the far side of Patrick, and Luke pulled the rocking chair out a little, so he could face her, too, and not just talk to her profile.

He cleared his throat. "I came to apologize to you for the ways I hurt you. I know I did some terrible things."

Ruthie snapped her head around. "Why? Why did you do such terrible things?"

Luke took in a deep breath. "To be honest, I was jealous of Patrick. I saw how close you two were getting. I felt as if my life was out of control."

"You killed his pet bird."

Nyna the Mynah. Patrick had patiently taught Scripture verses to that bird, and somehow that bird kept preaching them at Luke. He felt like it was throwing rocks at him. He had hated that bird.

He could hardly believe he was once *that* guy. But he had been, and he needed to confess this sin and ask for their forgiveness. "I am . . . so sorry. Truly, I am." He cleared his throat again. "No excuses. It was a dreadful thing to do. It was downright evil. Hurting you, Patrick, that was so wrong." He turned his gaze to Ruthie. "I hurt you too, Ruthie. I tried to drag you into my downward spiral. I saw that you were finding peace inside, and feeling settled about joining the church, and it made me panic. I felt kind of . . . abandoned."

He wished she would say something. It would be easier if she expressed her anger, her disgust for him. The silence, that was harder to take.

"All I can do is let you know that I am truly sorry, that I wish there was something I could do to change the past. But I can't. I can only make a better future. I'm asking you both to forgive me. I know the Amish have to say they forgive . . . but I don't want you to do that until you truly believe it." He rose. "I'll wait for it." He let out a breath. "Okay, that's what I came to say."

"Luke," Patrick said, "if it's my forgiveness that you need, then you have it."

There was a pause, an opportunity for Ruthie to chime in. She didn't.

"Ruthie," Patrick said, "we're all sinful in God's eyes, each one of us. You and I, we aren't any less sinful than Luke. If we think we are, then we're fooling ourselves."

Ruthie looked at him, jaw dropped. Then she snapped her mouth shut.

A long, quiet moment passed, broken when Patrick stood up. "Luke, thank you for coming. I know it wasn't easy. Consider yourself forgiven by me. I hope we can be friends." Standing there on the porch of the Inn at Eagle Hill, Luke felt blessed by Patrick's humility. By the mercy Patrick handed to him. Why had he waited so long to come? How had he misunderstood Patrick's character so entirely?

He glanced at Ruthie.

"It's going to take me some time," she said, arms tightly crossed.

"I understand, Ruthie. Take all the time you need." But Luke felt encouraged. He put his hat back on, nodded to them both, and turned to leave. He had to leave fast because he could feel tears clogging his throat. He made it to the scooter before they started coming. One by one, then a steady stream. All the way home, the tears kept coming. Hard tears, deep tears.

By the time Luke reached Windmill Farm, the tears felt less like they were coming from a deep pit inside him, and more like a refreshing summer rain. He leaned the scooter against the barn and stopped for a moment to watch the sun drop behind the orchard hill.

Confession brought such sweet relief. Why hadn't he known that? Probably because he had always carefully avoided it. Yet it was the most wonderful gift he could imagine, to feel cleaned up and right before God. The tears kept coming, pouring down his cheeks, but now they weren't the painful type. They were the good kind. Those wash-the-soul-clean kind of tears.

NINETEEN

Two more unable-to-forward-return-to-sender letters arrived in Windmill Farm's mailbox. As Izzy walked back up to the house with those returned letters in her hand, she felt thoroughly defeated. Her list of Grace Millers in Ohio was now exhausted, without a single lead left to chase down. Not one. She had no idea what to do next.

She went upstairs to her bedroom and flopped on the bed. She lay there, eyes staring at the ceiling, when she heard the faint jingle of a buggy arriving. Normally, she would hurry to the window to see who had come. Not now. She couldn't budge. She was too discouraged. She put her elbow over her eyes, wondering how much it would cost to pay a detective to look for her mother. But where would she find a detective, anyway? Certainly not in Stoney Ridge.

Maybe she couldn't find her mother because there was no longer a Grace Miller to find. But then, wouldn't Izzy be able to track down some kind of death record?

She was thinking through all that and more, when Jenny burst into her bedroom. "Look what I have for you," she announced gaily. She held up a brown bag.

"What?" Izzy said weakly.

"Buttermilk doughnuts. Glazed. I've been experimenting all week and think I finally developed the right recipe. To sell at your farm stand." She shook the bag. "They're still warm."

Izzy sat up. Doughnuts were, in fact, the most comforting food she could imagine. And Jenny was an exceptional baker.

As she looked into Jenny's face, something occurred to her. Here she was, feeling sad and sorrowful about a woman who had walked away from her, when she had a friend who walked right into Izzy's life. And kept walking into it. Jenny had an uncanny ability to find a way to break through Izzy's impenetrable shell.

She studied Jenny's face thoughtfully, her small, patient face, made with more precision, more fineness than ordinary faces. She'd never told Jenny about her search for her mother. She'd never told anyone. Maybe someday, she'd tell Jenny about her mother. Maybe not, though. It suddenly seemed less important. Maybe it was time to give up the hunt. At least . . . for right now.

"How did you know?" Izzy said. "I've had a craving lately for buttermilk doughnuts."

"Glazed," Jenny said.

Izzy smiled. A true, deep-down smile. "Even better."

For the last few evenings, after supper, Luke had put on Amos's fishing boots (which were two sizes too large for him—Amos wasn't as tall as Luke, but he sure had big feet), wore heavy leather gloves, and waded through Teddy Zook's stinking swamp. In one hand was a long stick to push around the reeds. In the other hand was a sack full of empty plastic juice bottles, and in a backpack were fresh eggs from Izzy's henhouse. Rudy had joined him a few times until his mother caught wind and put an end to it. Since then, Luke was on his own. He missed him, though. It was nice to be admired by someone, even if that someone was only ten years old.

He'd learned how to make a humane trap from a book in the library. He cut a flap out of the bottle, just big enough for the snake to get in but not out. The first time he waded alone through the swamp to position the traps, he felt so jumpy that he thought he heard rattles everywhere. The next evening, he grew more accustomed to the sounds floating around the swamp. Most of them were startled birds, and he knew he was the reason they were startled. If he scared off a bird, what made him think he could find and capture a clever Massauga rattlesnake? If there even was one to be caught.

By the third time, his anxiety about being in a swamp at dusk was nearly gone and he could relax a little as he waded through the murky water. He checked each trap and released two turtles, but no snakes. By now he had a sense of the swamp, its unique sounds and smells and boundaries. He'd learned enough from Teddy to identify most of the snakes he'd come across, and found plenty of them, but no Massauga rattler.

On the fourth evening, he put on Amos's galoshes and gloves but couldn't find the scooter to ride over to Teddy's. He had to trudge up to the house to ask Izzy where she'd left it. It was a beastly hot night, and Fern and Amos sat in rockers on the front porch, fanning themselves with paper fans.

"Any idea where Izzy put the scooter?"

Fern pointed to the marten houses up on the hill near the

orchards. "She went to check on the birdhouses." The marten houses stood guard on the hillside, large vertical wooden "bird condos"—as Amos called them—that sat on top of metal poles. The martens were Windmill Farm's insect patrol, and Fern and Amos made sure the birds were treated well for their labor.

"Thanks," he said, dreading another hike up a steep hill in the hot rubber galoshes. By the time he reached the top of the hill, he saw Izzy pick up the scooter and start down the hill's narrow path. She didn't realize Luke was on his way up the hill until it was too late. His wading boots were so cumbersome, above his knees, that he couldn't move quickly. At the last second, she jumped off the scooter and released it, causing it to crash right into him, knocking him flat on his backside. He looked up, caught his breath.

Izzy stood over him, peering down with a worried look. It reminded him of the way Bob the buggy horse stood over his cot, breathing down on him with his hay-breath.

"Luke, I didn't see you. Are you hurt bad?"

He blinked a few times, seeing stars. "Who's Luke?"

Her dark eyebrows shot up in concern.

"I'm kidding." He pushed himself up on his elbows. "I'm fine. No harm done."

"What were you doing?"

"I came to borrow the scooter."

"Why?"

He sat up and brushed off his shirt. "Going swamping."

"That's where you've been going each night?"

Well, well. So, she had noticed his absence. "Yup."

"Why?"

"I need to find something for Teddy Zook."

"What?"

"A snake."

She put her hands on her hips and narrowed her eyes. "Is that why my hens have been laying less eggs this week? Are you using my eggs to bait the snake into a trap?"

"Maybe."

Izzy frowned. "And you haven't caught a snake yet."

"No. I haven't found it yet, but I have found plenty of birds."

"Birds?" Her interest was piqued. "Well, if you're seeing birds, then there's probably no snake where you're setting the traps. Birds are too smart to feed or nest near snakes."

Argh. How had he not thought of that?

Izzy let out a long-suffering sigh. "I guess I'll just have to go with you."

To the creepy, noisy swamp? To trap a snake? Luke was shocked, absolutely stunned, but kept his face as neutral as he could. "Well, Izzy Miller, I knew you had a bite to you, but I didn't know you were a fan of snakes." He put his hat back on and started grinning again. "Or maybe there's something going on between us." He wiggled his eyebrows.

"There's nothing going on here." Her hackles rose. "Go by yourself, then."

"Hold on, hold on. I'm not trying to get you mad." Slowly, he stood up. "I'd like your company, Izzy, but it's just not safe in that swamp. I'd never forgive myself if you got hurt. I'm looking for a rattler."

"What? Why?"

"It's something I need to do for Teddy." He bent down and picked up the scooter. "Mind if I take it?"

"Be my guest." He climbed on the scooter, stiffly, because

his knees couldn't bend in the fishermen's waders. He hoped he didn't look quite as ridiculous as he felt. As he started down the hill, he heard a shout burst out of Izzy, "Be careful, Luke!"

He lifted a gloved hand in a wave. Maybe there *was* something going on here.

The baptism classes were held after church, with David and Amos taking turns to lead them. David encouraged questions, even debate. It shocked Luke. He had expected a passive experience of listening to long doctrinal statements, and that was one reason he'd avoided signing up. Like so much in life, he'd been wrong. Not even close. The classes were filled with vigorous discussion.

Take the last class. Luke always had plenty of questions about Amish traditions that had no biblical basis, even innocuous ones. He asked why the Lancaster Amish observe Easter Monday. "There's no mention of Easter Monday in the Bible. Other Amish don't observe it. So why do we?"

David countered with an excellent point. "Always look to the heart of a tradition. Easter Monday might not be in the Bible, but pay attention to its intent. It's meant to celebrate the first week of Christ's resurrection. And as for why Lancaster Amish do and others don't, well, that's because each church makes its own decisions. Lancaster is one of the oldest settlements. Many of those traditions arrived from the Old Country with our ancestors."

Put that way, it was hard to dispute the value of such a tradition.

Others spoke up too. They weren't as controversial as

Luke, but they were curious and invested in the process of baptism. But Izzy, she never said a word. Something about her silence was unsettling to Luke, although he couldn't put his finger on the reason and say, *That's it. That's the problem, right there.*

Fern needed some pickling spices at the Bent N' Dent one afternoon—she wanted to make pickles out of the garden's abundance of zucchini—and Luke volunteered to scooter over there. He hoped the store might be empty and give him a chance to talk to David. They hadn't talked in a while, not one-on-one like they used to, and he missed those talks.

Alas, alas. There sat Hank Lapp in the shade of the store's porch.

"WELL, WELL, WELL. It's the NEW AND IMPROVED LUKE SCHROCK. I hear YOU'RE GETTING DUNKED."

"If by that you mean I'm taking baptism class, then, yes."

"THE RACCOON! WHAT'S HAPPENED? HAS HE MOVED ON YET?"

"Not exactly. Soon, I hope." In truth, Luke had just about given up. The only good thing was that the horse seemed to be coming in just once a night now to wake him up. Under the circumstances, that felt like a considerable improvement. Once a night to be greeted with Bob's whiskers felt oddly manageable, which was a strange thing to realize. The raccoon—he had beaten Luke. Beaten him. It was appalling. And yet, he had too many other things on his mind to care much.

But he didn't want to go into any of what was on his mind with Hank Lapp. No sir. "David in?"

"HE IS. HEAD ON BACK THERE." Spoken like he was David's personal assistant.

Luke knocked on David's door and opened it when he heard him call out to come in.

"Sit down. What's on your mind?"

"There's something I wanted to talk to you about, but I feel a little funny. It might not be my place. And who am I to suggest such a thing? I mean, look at the way I used to handle church." He was rambling, and completely confusing David.

"Luke, I'm not following you. Start again. At the beginning."

Luke leaned forward in his chair. "Have you noticed how quiet Izzy is during baptism classes?"

"Sure, I've noticed. She's a quiet person."

"I just wonder if . . . maybe she's joining the Amish because she thinks it's the right thing to do. And not because . . ."

"Not because of . . . what?"

"Well, you've always told us to not join the church unless our whole heart is willing."

"That's true. I stand behind that." David steepled his hands. "So you think Izzy's whole heart isn't in joining the church?"

"I hope it is. I want it to be. It just seems as if, well, as if she would be sharing more if her heart was a part of the decision. I know her well enough to know that when she has an opinion about something, she'll let you know."

David nodded, thinking carefully. "I think I know how to find out the answer to that question."

"Good." Excellent. Luke stood up.

"You need to talk to her. To ask her."

Luke sat down. "Me?" His voice rose an octave.

"If the Lord has put this concern on your heart, Luke, you need to see it through."

"Me?" It rose still another octave.

"Assuming your concern for her is genuine. Is it?" With the lift of an eyebrow, David said much.

"Yes, it is. I mean, she's a beautiful girl, but that's not what's been worrying me."

"I think it's significant that you feel worried about Izzy, Luke. And I believe God wants you to act on it."

"But"—he slapped his chest—"me?"

"Yes. I'll be praying for you, Luke, so that you'll approach Izzy with a humble and contrite heart. And I'm pleased that you're growing aware of your sensitive heart."

"Sensitive?" He'd never in his life heard himself described as having a sensitive heart. Not once.

"Yes, of course you have a sensitive heart." David looked genuinely surprised that Luke didn't consider himself in such a way. "Why else do you think you've had so many lingering issues from your father's death?"

"I've never thought that it might be because I'm sensitive. I just assumed it was easier to be angry with my father than to grieve for him."

"That probably was the root cause of your anger. It became a way to cope for you. But no longer."

"No. Not any longer." At long last, he was coming to peace with his father, forgiving him his flaws, which were many, and recalling his virtues, which were few. But there *were* some virtues. His father had had a nice way with people, which made him a good salesman.

"Luke, at any given moment, your life is going to be determined by your view of you, or God's view of you. I've never doubted that there's a God-given destiny for you. Perhaps this is the start of it. The one thing I'd caution you is not to preach at Izzy."

"Preach at her?"

"Yes. The way you did with Alice Smucker. She said she felt like she'd had the bishop come calling one evening, quoting all kinds of Scripture at her. I believe she said it felt like you were whacking her on the head with the Bible."

"She said that? Huh. I thought I handled it very delicately." Luke sighed. "But she did come to church."

"She did. And it might have been just the right way to work with Alice. I think you wore her down. Izzy's different, though. She's not going to respond well if you approach this topic with her like a bull in a china shop."

Luke left David feeling a little dazed. This meeting hadn't gone at all the way he'd expected.

TWENTY

A flock of geese flew overhead, honking loudly enough to startle Amos. He'd noticed more and more birds heading south. Another summer was wrapping up. His last one, perhaps? He hoped not, but only God knew that answer.

Time was passing so quickly. Too quickly, but he brushed that thought off and tried not to dwell on it. There was time enough to do the things he needed to do.

Jenny and Jesse's wedding was just a few weeks away. Fern must have had an inkling about its coming last spring. She always seemed to have a sense about these things.

The church ladies met yesterday to plan the wedding dinner. Every female in Stoney Ridge would bring a dish or two to share. That's one of the things Amos loved about these people. All hands on deck, all the time.

Not long after Jenny's wedding, Izzy and Luke's baptism would follow. So many important, life-changing moments in the lives of these young people. He never tired of it, nor did Fern. It spoke to their hearts in a profoundly meaningful way.

Fern loved every minute of these big events, especially the preparing part. She'd always reminded Amos of a hummingbird, flitting from one flower to another, moving so fast its wings were invisible. He didn't think Fern had sat down to read the *Budget* or work on a jigsaw puzzle in months. And she was running poor Luke ragged with a never-ending to-do list.

Poor Luke. Ha! Now wasn't *that* evidence of a change in his attitude toward the boy. He'd never share that thought with Fern, of course. He could imagine the look she'd give him, that smug "I told you so."

Maybe he should tell her, though. She'd always had a soft spot for Luke, even when he was at his worst. Amos never had anything for Luke but disdain and distrust.

He never could've imagined the strides Luke had been making toward becoming the man he was meant to be. Even Hank called him "the 2.0 version" as if he understood computers, which he didn't. Luke wasn't making excuses for himself the way he used to. That self-pity tone in his voice was gone. He went above and beyond the call of duty for his fence-mending list—others had commented on it. Look at Alice Smucker! She'd been at church twice now, and Fern said she was seen at the Bent N' Dent, buying a bottle of Clorox bleach.

But there was one thing Luke did, and kept doing, that really spoke to Amos's heart—he had started to care for Windmill Farm like it was his own. He did much more around the farm than his daily chores, and even more than Fern's to-do list. She'd come up with the idea of letting Luke turn the buggy shop into a fix-it shop, and Amos was actually considering it. Amazing. And he saw for himself how Luke treated those trees in the orchard, just like Amos did—as if they were made of glass.

Amos had three sons-in-law, fine men, but not one of them loved his trees like he did. Even his daughters didn't understand the importance of those trees—their history and legacy, the ongoing burden of caring for them through every season, and their blessed fruitfulness. To his surprise and delight, to his shock—of all people, of *all* people!—Luke Schrock did.

It was a beautiful September day, not nearly as hot as it could have been, nor as cold as it would soon be. Some of that comfort could be credited to the sheltering roof on the new farm stand. Izzy appreciated that sloping corrugated metal roof more than any other feature, and some day she might even tell Luke so. She didn't want him to get a big head, though. It was plenty big enough.

How could fall be here so soon? Time seemed like a fast-moving river ever since she'd come to Stoney Ridge. The moment she'd set foot at Windmill Farm, she wanted the days to slow down. Instead, they sped up. Jenny's wedding was right around the corner—early October.

Prior to coming here, Izzy had always wanted life to hurry up, to gallop past the awful years to get to the good times, when she would be free to do what she wanted to do. No social workers deciding where she'd live and with whom. No depressing group homes. No more living hand-to-mouth on the street.

It might seem strange, but Izzy considered this new farm stand to be her first true home. Luke and Teddy had outdone themselves and designed details with her in mind. Even the countertop was the perfect height for her 5 foot 9 inches. She didn't have to bend over like she did at the old farm stand. Or even worse, at the card table. There were extra shelves placed along the back wall, providing space for jewel-colored jars of jams and jellies.

Those would be coming in soon from the church ladies, now that the harvest was in full swing. Jenny's baked goods were a big hit, and she'd started selling some handcrafted goods made by church ladies—potholders, tea cozies. She'd asked David first, because the goods had been displayed on a dusty corner shelf inside the Bent N' Dent. She didn't want to steal his business.

"Steal it? You'd be doing me a favor," David had said. "I want the Bent N' Dent to stay focused on food. It was never meant to be a handicrafts store. I just didn't have the heart to say no to those ladies." He seemed overjoyed. "Now I can send the ladies right over to you."

Not a minute later, David had packed everything on that dusty corner shelf into a cardboard box to move to Izzy's farm stand. If anything sold, he explained, Izzy would get a 5 percent commission.

Everything did sell, and quickly. It was all about presentation. Who would want to buy a dusty tea cozy? No one! But dust it off, and display it next to a delicate china teacup. Snap! Sold.

Izzy had been mulling over the notion of asking Amos if he might consider converting the buggy shop into a store. The only problem was that the shop was jammed full of stored seldom-used equipment. Amos's attic, Fern called it. Farmers, she said, couldn't throw anything away. They never knew when they might need something, so they kept everything.

If the tour buses continued to come through the fall and spring, Izzy could imagine a path from the driveway that led right to the store. And there was still another idea that was simmering in the back of her mind, something that sparked when Fern told her that saying of her father's: Es nemmt en schlecht schof as sei eegni Woll net draage kann. *It's a poor sheep that can't carry its own wool.*

It still troubled her to think of her woollies being sent off to market. Amos raised Polypay sheep, known for their meat and wool. *And* wool. She wanted to try to talk Amos out of raising sheep for their meat and let Izzy sell their wool. In the store she envisioned in the buggy shop.

Stoney Ridge didn't have a yarn shop. Even Edith Lapp complained that she had to take the bus all the way to Lancaster to buy yarn. There was a market here, just waiting to be tapped. A vision of the interior of the store was taking shape in Izzy's mind—skeins of colorful wool, like a rainbow, hanging off wooden wall pegs.

Thinking about the yarn shop made her happy. But the thought of talking about it made her anxious. Amos and Fern had never indicated how long she could remain at Windmill Farm. She pulled her weight, she knew that, but it was one thing to have a long-term houseguest. It was another thing for that long-term guest to ask to convert a buggy shop into a permanent place of business. As she thought about how to say what she wanted to say to them, she heard someone call her name.

"Izzy, can I talk to you about something?"

She spun around and saw Luke Schrock standing there,

holding a basket of fresh-picked apples in his arms, an awkward look on his face. "What's wrong? Did I do something?"

"No." He tilted his head slightly. "Why do you do that?"

"Do what?"

"Why do you always think something's wrong?"

She shrugged. Usually, it was.

He set the basket on the counter and she started looking through it for the best apples. Whatever it was that was on his mind, she had a sense that she didn't want to hear it. She decided to take charge of the conversation. "Do you know how to shear sheep? And how to card wool? And dye it?"

He seemed confused. "I've sheared some. Scalped the poor things might be a better description of it. But I've never carded wool or dyed it. Why do you ask?"

She examined a bruised apple and put it in the Fern-to-make-applesauce pile. Nothing went to waste on this farm. "Just wondering. But if you happen to be at the library sometime, could you bring home some books about raising sheep for wool?"

"Whoa. Really? Is that what you're thinking to do?" he said, not surprised, indeed almost smiling. "What does Amos say about it?"

"He doesn't know yet. So please don't say anything." She started on a pyramid display of apples. This took some concentration. "The bus should be coming along in a few minutes, so I have to keep setting up."

"But there's something I'd like to talk to you about."

"Talk while I work. As long as you talk fast."

"It's about the baptism class."

"What about it?"

"You don't say much in it."

"I'm listening, that's why."

"Is that the only reason?"

She stopped to glare at him. "What does *that* mean?"

"I just wondered . . ." He cleared his throat. "I've spent a lot of time listening to preachers and never really taking it to heart."

Izzy could feel a swirl of anger start in her belly. "I need another basket of apples before the next bus comes."

Typical of Luke, he kept plowing on, oblivious to how uncomfortable she was with this topic.

"I'm speaking from my own experience. I know there's a difference between listening to God and, well, having God's Word go deep. It had to start changing me from the inside out, changing everyday situations. It's like . . . the difference between—" he scanned the farm stand until his eyes landed on a glass jar of fresh-cut flowers—"those flowers in water, looking good for a few days before they start wilting because they lack nourishment. Compare it to a flower planted in the ground, with roots going deep in the soil. Growing and blooming and lasting."

She stared at him.

"The flowers in the jar, they might look pretty, but there's so much more to being a flower than just sitting in a jar. A plant, that's what the flower wants to be. What it's meant to be." Looking concerned, he added, "Am I making any sense?"

She glanced behind him when she heard a loud rumbling. "The bus is coming and I still have work to do. And you do too. I need another basket of those apples. Fast."

"But you know what I'm trying to say, don't you?"

"Luke," she said in an expressionless tone. "Those apples. I need them in time for the tour buses."

The problem was, she knew exactly what he was getting at. It was the last question in the world she'd expected to come from *him*.

⌒

Thunder rumbled across the ridge to the north. The morning's blue sky was gone, replaced with heavy, leaden-gray clouds. Izzy closed up the farm stand and made a dash to the house before the rain thickened to a downpour. During thunder and lightning storms, Amos insisted she close up shop, and Izzy didn't argue. The metal roof worried Amos, but it was the lack of customers in pouring rain that sent Izzy up to the house.

As Izzy ran up onto the porch, the rain started coming down hard and fast. Down the hill, she saw Luke bolt to the barn. Amos stood at the open barn door, waiting for Luke, watching the storm unfold. Inside the kitchen, Fern sat by the window, absorbed in mending a rip in Amos's white shirt. The yeasty fragrance of freshly baked bread filled the kitchen. In that moment, everything was so lovely, so perfect, it almost hurt. Izzy couldn't help wondering how different life would've been with Fern Lapp as her mom.

"Yum," she said, inhaling.

"Dry rags are on the counter," Fern said, not even looking up.

Fern was actually sitting down, Izzy thought. The house was quiet, Amos and Luke were in the barn, and the bad weather would keep everyone right where they were. Now was the time. "I've been thinking about something for next summer," she said, wiping her wet face off with a rag. "What would you say if I turned the buggy shop into a shop? I've been thinking about . . . selling yarn."

Fern stared over the top of her glasses. "Yarn? In the buggy shop?"

"Knitting is becoming a popular thing to do. Among the English, I mean." Her hands dropped to her side. "There's a growing demand for hand-spun wool. Edith Lapp was talking about it during the last quilting. Hand-spun wool sheared right off the sheep."

Fern's sparse eyebrows shot to the top of her prayer cap. "You mean . . . our sheep?"

"Yes. I don't know if you and Amos realized this when you started the flock, but Polypay wool is ideal for yarn. Luke says he's sheared before. Once, he said. And I'm going to read up on spinning and dying wool. I think it might work. And then, maybe Amos wouldn't send Lucy and Ethel out to slaughter this year."

One of Fern's eyebrows went down and one stayed up—a bad sign. "So is that what this is about? Sending sheep to slaughter?"

"No. Well, yes and no. The farm stand has done so well this year, even with the crash. And you know how David agreed to let me sell handicraft consignments from the Bent N' Dent—well, it's all been sold." She snapped her fingers. "It got me thinking that I could sell even more. But if I did, I'd need more space. Even more than the new stand allows."

Fern set down the shirt. "The buggy shop."

"Yes. It's an ideal location. Since Jesse moved out, it's just sitting there, storing equipment. I really don't think it would cost much to convert it into a shop. I'm pretty confident it'll pay for itself within one summer. And I'll pay for the spinning wheel and carders."

"Oh Izzy." Her name came out of Fern on a sighing breath.

"Really, it wouldn't cost that much! Edith Lapp said she could teach me how to spin. She says it's not difficult. It just takes a while to gain skills, but it's not supposed to be hard."

"I don't know," Fern said. "I just don't know."

But she did. Izzy could see it in her eyes. An uncomfortable feeling started in the pit of Izzy's stomach. "Jenny's wedding is just around the corner. I shouldn't have asked during such a busy time. Never mind. We can talk about it some other time."

Fern set down the shirt. "Izzy, it's not that . . ."

She thought Fern would be pleased about this idea. Before, she'd always championed Izzy's ideas for the farm stand, encouraged her to rise above her self-imposed limitations. Why wasn't she enthusiastic about this? Had Izzy asked for too much?

A memory flashed across her mind. A time when she'd asked a foster mother if she could take swim lessons in the summer, and the foster mother had hedged and stalled in the same way Fern was doing now. It turned out the foster family was going on a summer vacation and had no intention to take Izzy with them.

Her hands twisted the wet rag nervously. She shouldn't have gotten her hopes up. A dashed hope was worse than no hope at all. If she thought about Fern's reluctance—or was it rejection?—much longer, she'd tie herself into a knot. She spun around to set the rag on the kitchen counter. "It's all right. I shouldn't have asked." She started up the stairs.

"Izzy, wait up. It's a good idea. A very good idea. It's just that . . ."

Izzy stilled, one foot on the step. She braced herself. *It's just that . . . we aren't planning to have you still be here next summer. You've stayed here long enough. It's time to go.*

Fern moved closer to her. "It's just that Amos told Luke that he could start a fix-it store in the buggy shop. They've talked about converting the shop this winter, after the harvest is done. They've been working on some sketches."

Izzy lifted her chin a notch, still facing the stairwell. "Luke Schrock." Of course.

"It was my idea. Luke's been working so hard around the farm, helping Amos with far more than he's asked of him. He's got a natural bent to fix things. It's been such a good thing, to see Luke show that kind of care and diligence. We want to help keep him on that path."

The words were gentle, hopeful, affirming, but they still hurt.

So this fix-it shop had been Fern's idea. Did Luke ever have to work for anything in life? Everything seemed to get delivered right to his doorstep. That wasn't fair, she thought to herself. Fern didn't know about Izzy's idea for a yarn shop. *Besides, be realistic. Luke is Amish. Born Amish. He's one of them. You are not.*

Something welled up inside of her and was threatening to burst out. She hurried up the rest of the stairs, feeling tears burn the back of her eyes. She didn't want to show weakness. Never, ever show weakness.

"Izzy!"

At the sharpness of Fern's tone, Izzy flinched slightly, as if suffering from a physical blow. At the top of the stairs, she turned to face Fern, who stood at the bottom of the narrow stairs with her shoulders pulled back. "It's all right, Fern. I understand." Her voice had dropped to a whisper.

"Understand *this*. There is no scarcity of love in this house," Fern said. "Love is not finite. Most everything else in life is finite . . . but not love."

The full sense of what Fern said struck her like a thunderclap out of a clear sky. Everything in life, everyone Izzy knew, she'd viewed through the lens of scarcity. Everything! If Amos and Fern had grown to love Luke, it meant that their love for Izzy had to diminish. "How?" Izzy said, her voice cracking with emotion. "How is that even possible?"

"How is that possible? Oh honey. Haven't you learned this by now?" Fern gave her a look that said "you're missing something," but what she said aloud was, "'We love because he first loved us.' You got to believe this. God *is* love."

That kind of thinking . . . that love was not finite, that God was love . . . it was a massive shift in the way she thought and felt about . . . everything.

Izzy had come to Stoney Ridge to change, but she hadn't really changed at all.

TWENTY-ONE

Luke had never paid much attention to weddings before. This one, Jenny and Jesse's, felt different. First of all, he was the one who had to whip Windmill Farm into pristine condition to get ready for the wedding. Fern was a stern taskmaster. For the last month, she met him at breakfast with the day's chores, added to all his other chores. Thank heavens that raccoon had left the barn. If he had to cope with Bob's wake-up calls in the night, and Fern's ruthless tasking all day, he'd be a shell of his former self. He was hardly sleeping as it was.

He felt pleased with himself for finishing off Fern's list with a task she hadn't even put on the list. The red windmill. Three days ago, early in the morning, he'd shimmied up the windmill and measured the remaining blades. Two blades showed signs of rotting wood near the bolts. He scootered over to Teddy Zook's and ordered three new red blades made for the windmill. Pronto. Teddy said he'd have them ready on Monday, Luke begged him to make it Friday, and Teddy, being Teddy, hemmed and hawed and finally agreed. After supper on Friday, Luke scootered back to fetch them. He installed them on Saturday morning, just as dawn broke the morning sky. Just in time for the wedding. He wasn't going to tell Fern. He was going to wait and see if she noticed. He felt pleasure spiral through him.

But back to this wedding. There were two more reasons he found himself paying close attention. Unlike other weddings he'd attended, Luke knew Jesse pretty well. He'd seen him grow up from one of Fern's Wayward Boys to a pretty good guy. A very good guy, actually. Luke hadn't really known Jenny until these last few months, and only knew her as Izzy's closest friend. Her only friend, now that he thought about it. How many times had he walked into the Windmill Farm kitchen to find those two with their capped heads together, cooking and baking, laughing and whispering?

That was the third reason he was paying special attention to this wedding. He wondered how Izzy was feeling, deep down, about Jenny getting married. There was no way those two girls would have the kind of time together like they once had. No way. He knew how it worked. Soon one baby would come along, then another and another. Jenny would be thoroughly preoccupied with her family—as she should be—and there'd be little time left for Izzy.

Throughout the wedding meal, Luke watched Izzy. He was seated far across the room from her, with a perfect vantage point to observe her next to Jenny at the front table. He noted again how attractive she was, especially lovely in that pink dress she wore, his favorite. She seemed happy, smiling, leaning close now and then to Jenny to catch a whisper. But then Jenny turned away from her to talk to Jesse. For a moment, Luke saw something in Izzy's eyes—pain? loneliness?—but it vanished before he could put a name to it. He'd seen it before in those incredible eyes, and whatever it was, he felt an almost unbearable urge to fix it, to make it better, to be the one who filled the emptiness he saw in there.

He forced himself to look away, tried to shake those thoughts right out of his head. Why did he have such mixed-up feelings for Izzy? The problem, he heard a little voice answer, was that she had no feelings for him. Not good ones, anyway. Most of the time, she either ignored him or snapped at him. Like a fool, he kept coming back for more. Was he falling for Izzy? That would be crazy. That would be like trying to make friends with a lioness.

"So, it's fixed."

A voice cut into his thoughts. He looked up to see Fern standing over him. By now he should be accustomed to her ways, sneaking up on a man the way she did, but she still startled him. He cleared his throat. "Fixed?"

"The windmill. The squeak is gone. I looked a little closer and discovered three new blades had replaced the old ones." She patted him on the shoulder. "You did good, Luke."

So she *had* noticed. It felt good, doing good.

Here, in October, was the weather Amos had been wishing for in September. Blue skies, crisp air, slanting golden sunlight. He walked through the orchards on a mission to examine the late-bearing apple trees. A few more bushels, and that would be the end of this year's growing season. The trees would be empty, preparing for winter's rest. The leaves that remained on the trees were turning a riot of color. Those that had fallen carpeted the orchard floor red and gold. Luke had been raking leaves each day to keep insects from multiplying, but the nights were cold enough now that insects had no chance. The leaves could just decompose on the ground. He needed to remember to tell Luke that information. Other things too. This afternoon, he planned to show him how to press cider.

"I just got a call from Dok."

Amos jerked like a fish on the line. "Fern! Why can't you give a man notice that you're coming, instead of slipping up behind him like a coyote?"

Fern ignored him. "Dok said you told her to take your name off the transplant list."

Amos frowned. He had planned to tell Fern that news himself, after the wedding fuss had come and gone. But it had come and gone and he still hadn't told her. "I've given this a lot of thought, Fern. I've prayed long and hard. My time is coming to an end, and I'm at peace with that."

"You don't think I might have something to say about that?"

Oh, she'd have plenty to say. That's why he hadn't told her. "Fern, I've had a good long life. I'm sixty-seven years old."

"Sixty-eight."

"See? Even more of a reason to take my name off that list. I'm done. I've had a happy life, and it's time to go."

"That's the most selfish thing I've ever heard in my life." She was red-hot mad, jamming a finger at his chest in her fury. "Dok says you are a viable candidate for a transplant. God is giving you a chance to live a longer life, and you're just throwing it all away. Well, Amos Lapp, you may be ready to meet your Maker, but has it occurred to you that we might need you here a little longer?"

To his surprise, she burst into tears. He pulled her close

to his chest, wrapping his arms tightly around her, and let her sob.

This he hadn't factored in. Fern's tears.

The air in the kitchen was hot and sticky and humid, though the weather outside was cool. All afternoon, Izzy had been canning jar after jar of Fern's applesauce. These apples were the last of the season, the very last, but more than they'd anticipated. Amos and Fern had gone to the Bent N' Dent to buy more canning supplies, and more cinnamon, and some secret ingredient Fern added to her applesauce. Cloves, maybe?

Izzy pushed a stray lock of hair off her forehead with the back of her hand and turned when she heard the door open, thinking Fern had returned. But there stood Luke in the kitchen doorway with a question on his face of whether he should come in. Izzy felt her heart quicken. Ridiculous! She willed her heart to slow down. It didn't work.

"Are you busy right now?"

Was she busy? She was standing over the stove with a pot of water bubbling away, jars of applesauce in a water bath, waiting patiently until she heard the lids pop and knew the lids had sealed. Was she busy? Of course she was busy! But he did look nervous. Jumpy. Insecure, which was a rare look on Luke Schrock. He held his hat brim in his hands, squeezing it, circling it round and round. "Not really."

His eyes were now locked on Izzy. "Jenny's married now. I figure she won't be coming around so much."

She wanted to say, "Well, that's a keen insight of the obvious," but swallowed down the snippy retort. She promised herself that she wouldn't be impatient or mean to him, like she usually was. "That's the way it should be. She's somebody's wife now."

"You're going to be needing a friend, Izzy." Luke took a deep breath. "So what's it going to take to be friends with you?"

What kind of a question was that on an afternoon of canning applesauce? Good grief. Luke Schrock was always doing that to her. Tossing questions at her that he had no business asking. Questions that felt like arrows aimed at her Achilles heel. She shook her head so hard that her capstrings bounced. "I don't need any friends of the male kind, least of all a smart-alecky one like you."

"Izzy, I'm not like that." In his eyes was a plea, like he wanted things to be nice between them. But also like he didn't know what to make of her.

Something caught in her throat and she felt like she was choking. "I've got a lot on my mind, Luke Schrock. Lots of plans. I don't want anyone messing that up."

His face grew even more serious. "I'm not trying to mess anything up. I'm just looking to be your friend. Why not give me a chance?"

Izzy felt burning tears flood her eyes and turned her head from his hard gaze. She felt foolishly self-conscious. "Because I know what you'd do."

"What?"

"Once you get what you want, you don't want it anymore. I don't need that kind of friend. Nobody does." A part of her wanted him to get mad at her, really steamed, just to prove to her he was that kind of a guy. But no, he wouldn't do it.

"I don't deny I've been that kind of guy in the past. But no longer, I hope." Luke Schrock would not leave well enough alone. He sighed. "I'm asking you again, Izzy Miller. Isn't there something I can do to prove myself to you? Something that tells you I could be a good, faithful friend to you?"

One by one, the lids on the jars of applesauce made a *pop pop pop* sound. Izzy got the clamps to lift each jar out of the water bath and set them on the counter to cool. By the time she had taken the last jar out of the pot, she turned to the door to say something, but Luke was gone.

Later that afternoon, Izzy went down to the barn while Luke was milking Sage. She handed him a piece of paper. "I thought of something you can do for me."

He opened it. Izzy had written a name on it. *Grace Miller.* "Find her."

"Who is she?"

"My mother."

"Your mother?" He stared at the paper. "When did you last see her?"

"Years and years ago. I was only four or five."

"Can you tell me anything more about her? Where she's been living?"

"No."

"Your father?"

"Never mind him."

Luke rubbed his chin. "It's not much to go on."

"It's all I've got. Find out where she is . . . and maybe then we can be friends."

He looked up. "You can count on it."

Yeah. Right.

Luke would never admit it to Izzy, but giving him permission to find her mother could not have been more fortuitous. Grace Miller was the last name on his fence-mending list. He'd hemmed and hawed about how to track her down over the summer, unsure of where to begin. Mostly, he was unsure of whether he should involve himself in something that might bring more trouble to Izzy than goodness. But then . . . she handed him permission! A green light from God.

As soon as he had some spare time, Luke went to the library to see if he could get the nice librarian to help him find out some information. She wasn't working that day, which was very unfortunate. Betty sat at the desk, scowling at him as he approached, so he veered off into the book stacks. He watched two boys at a computer. They looked to be only ten or eleven years old, but they sure knew what they were doing. They were playing some kind of video game. Each time they laughed too loudly, Betty looked up and glared at them.

When the game was over, Luke walked over to stand beside them. "Can one of you help me locate someone?"

The boys looked up at him, then did a double take. They exchanged a look. One boy said, "You mean . . . on this computer?"

"Can you try and find someone's address?"

"Easy." He kicked the leg of the chair next to him, indicating Luke should sit down. "What's his name?"

"A woman."

The boy snickered. "Of course." He grinned at his friend. "See? They all have a secret life."

"No, no. It's nothing like that. She's an older woman."

Then they both howled with laughter.

Luke rolled his eyes. "She's my friend's mother."

That took their amusement to another level. More boys came out of nowhere to crowd around the computer. This wasn't going well.

"Her name is Grace Miller. I don't know much about her."

"She's in Pennsylvania?"

"I don't know. She has a daughter who's been in foster care."

The boys whipped out their phones and started tapping away at them. He wondered what barrel he had just pushed over the waterfall. There was no getting it back.

One boy's head popped up. "Grace Miller?" He held out his phone for Luke to look at. It was a picture of a woman, staring straight ahead, with a blank look in her eyes. Luke examined the picture more closely. He could see hints of Izzy in her face—the forehead, the eyebrows.

"I think that might be her. Does your telephone say where she is?"

"Telephone? He called it a telephone. Dude, it's a smartphone. Where you been this last century?" That got them all laughing again, so loudly that Betty the librarian rose to her feet.

Luke looked at the smart-mouthed boy with the smartphone. "Hurry up. The librarian's on her way. What does it say?"

The boy scanned the story, running his finger down the phone's face. "Grace Miller was arrested on DUI charges."

Arrested. "She's in jail? Where?"

The boy read further. "She's here, man. Down the road. Right over there in the Lancaster pokey."

Without any warning Betty was upon them, arms akimbo, and the boys scattered like buckshot into the aisles of books. Luke was the only one left. He tried to hold her mean, hawk-like stare, but he buckled. "I was looking for something. They were helping me."

She shook a finger at him. "You shouldn't be fiddling with computers. You'll be getting into big trouble with your bishop. Technology is a tool of the devil, your people think." In a doomed voice she whispered, "You'll be shunned."

He cocked his head. He thought about trying to clarify her misconceptions, but then decided it wouldn't matter. She believed what she wanted to believe. "Thank you for your concern for my welfare."

She'd done her duty—scolded the errant teens, warned Luke of his spiritual jeopardy. Satisfied, she dropped her arms and returned to her guard post.

Luke sat down at the computer. He'd never actually used one before, but he had watched others use them. The boy who had been at the computer had typed in Grace Miller's name and up came a number of bullet posts about her. The smartphone boy was quicker, so all eyes had turned to him. Luke pressed the first bullet point and highlighted it. Up came an entire newspaper article about Grace Miller's DUI. It had happened last week. Just last week! Luke looked around for paper and a pen to write things down. He heard a hissing sound and looked up to see the smartphone boy.

"Dude, don't you know anything? You can print that out." He looked over to see where Betty sat, saw that she was talking to someone, so he zipped out of the bookshelf and pressed a few buttons. "The printer is over by Ol' Bag

Betty," he whispered. "You'll have to go get it from her. It'll cost you a dime."

A dime, plus a grim warning of his fate. "Thanks." Luke smiled. "Thanks for helping."

The boy vanished.

TWENTY-TWO

Luke went straight to David at the Bent N' Dent with the information he'd learned about Grace Miller. He hoped he might find the store empty, but there was Hank Lapp, sitting inside, drinking root beer. "LUKE SCHROCK. SIT YOURSELF DOWN and PLAY CHECKERS WITH ME."

"Thanks, Hank, but I need to see David."

"HE'S NOT HERE. I'm MINDING THE STORE for him."

"Where'd he go? Will he be back soon?"

"THAT'S THE PROBLEM WITH YOUNG FOLKS. Always in a hurry. EVERYTHING is an EMERGENCY."

"Hank, I really need to see David."

"HE'LL BE BACK IN TWO SHAKES of a LAMB'S TAIL. Now SIT DOWN."

Two shakes of a lamb's tail ended up being two long games of checkers. Luke was so distracted that Hank easily won, which delighted him. Finally, David walked in the door and Luke bolted up from the rocking chair. "David, can we talk?"

"Sure. Let's go back to my office. Hank, do you mind watching the counter?" There were no customers.

"OF COURSE NOT! I'm EAGER to help." With that, Hank stretched out his legs, crossed his ankles, and closed his eyes.

In the office, David sat down and motioned to Luke to sit down, but he couldn't sit. He could only pace. "David, I happen to know that there's something Izzy's been trying to do as long as I've known her, without any luck. I thought I might see if I could help. And I could. I found out what she was looking for. Something important."

"Sit down and tell me what's so important."

"I'm not sure you would approve."

"Try me."

"Izzy's been trying to locate her mother."

"Her mother? Why hasn't she asked me about her? Or Fern and Amos?"

Luke stopped pacing. "Wait. Do you know where her mother is?"

"No, I don't. I don't even know her mother's name." David tilted his head. "Why does Izzy want to find her mother?"

"I'm not sure. You know Izzy. She doesn't volunteer much. I've seen her write letter after letter, and most got returned. That's when I asked who she was writing to, and she chewed me out for butting into her business."

David smiled. "So why are you trying to butt into her business now?"

"She asked! Don't look at me like that. She really did. I asked her what I needed to do to prove I could be a worthy friend to her, and she told me that if I could find her mother, then she'd consider it. Izzy thinks I'm . . . let's see . . . she says I am self-centered, and self-pitying, and annoying, and . . . anyway, you get my gist. I thought if I helped her find her mother, she might realize that I might be all those things, but I can also be a good guy."

"You are a good guy, Luke."

Luke grinned and seesawed his hand. "Getting there. A work in progress, mostly, thanks to you, and Amos and Fern. For not giving up on me."

"All thanks belongs to God. It really does, Luke. It all starts and ends with God. He's the one who doesn't give up."

"So speaking of not giving up," Luke said, "I think I found Izzy's mother."

"You're sure?"

"I'm pretty sure. Not 100 percent sure. But I did see her picture and noticed a resemblance."

David held up one hand. "Back up. How did you happen to find this woman?"

"On the library computer. I typed her name into the search line and up popped this newspaper article about her. Probably because it was so recent."

"What do you mean, recent?"

"Grace Miller was arrested for a DUI just last week. And get this part . . . she's in Lancaster."

David's jaw dropped. "Tell me what you've learned."

Luke pulled out the paper he'd printed out and handed it across the desk to David. "The picture printed out pretty blurry." Really fuzzy.

He sat back in the chair as David read, picked up a pencil, and underlined a few sentences. "It says here she's being held at the Lancaster County Prison. Waiting court action."

Luke peered at what David had underlined and tried to read it upside down. "Are you going to contact someone?"

"I might make a phone call or two. See if her arraignment

is on the court docket." He stilled his pencil and looked up at Luke. "Have you told Izzy any of this?"

"No, nothing. I came straight to you."

"Do me a favor and hold off for now. I want to find out more about her mother." More to himself he added, "She's come so far from when she first arrived."

Luke would've liked to ask David more about that particular topic, about what Izzy was like when she first arrived, but he knew what the answer would be. David was careful about guarding others' privacy. He appreciated it for his own sake; he needed to respect it for others. He glanced at David. "I won't say a word to Izzy. But will you let me know what more you find out about this Grace Miller?"

"I'll tell you what I can, Luke. I just want us both to keep in mind that Izzy is our first priority. If it isn't in her best interests to meet her mother right now, if her mother isn't in good shape, then this subject is closed. Got it?"

Luke lifted his hands in surrender. "Got it." And he did. Not saying anything about Grace Miller for now, and maybe indefinitely, was the noble thing to do. But being noble meant he had nothing to show Izzy to prove his friend-worthiness.

After church on Sunday, David crossed the yard to speak to Luke. "I spoke to someone at the courthouse. They set up an appointment for me with the judge."

"The judge?" Luke felt a familiar trickle of discomfort. He had a healthy respect for the law, having brushed against it a few times. "Why?"

"To find out more about Grace Miller." He crossed his

arms against his chest. "Would you be free to go with me? Monday at ten in the morning."

Luke was so pleased to be asked that he didn't know how to respond, until something Fern always said popped into his mind. "Well, you never say no to a bishop."

David laughed. "I'll have to remind my children of that. Meet me at the bus stop at nine."

Luke hardly slept that night. These encounters with the law brought up all kinds of uncomfortable memories. Sitting in the judge's chambers was a sobering moment. It was very official, the walls lined with shelves full of thick legal books. He and David waited in two leather chairs, and Luke wondered how David could look so at ease in an environment where they were so ill fitted. They looked like what they were—old-fashioned farmers, sitting in a law office. But in came the judge, a woman who greeted David warmly.

"I haven't seen you in a while, David. How have you been?"

"Very well, Rebecca. This is Luke Schrock. He's the one I was telling you about."

Guilt seized Luke. What had he done that a judge needed to know about him? Nothing came to mind. Nothing recent, anyway.

"So you're the one who tracked down Grace Miller. When David told me there might be a family connection—a daughter, right?—I realized that might be why she came to Lancaster." She sat down in her chair behind the desk, shifted her glasses from the top of her head to the bridge of her nose, and opened a file. "Last week, Grace Miller was picked up on a DUI charge in downtown Lancaster. She wasn't actually driving. She'd pulled over to the side of the road, though the car's engine was on." The judge made a rocking motion with her hand. "It could be argued in court as a technicality, but she's at a critical point in the system. Because she has a prior criminal record, the DA could try to get her sent to prison for a very long time. It's all about Pennsylvania sentencing guidelines." The judge closed the file and took off her glasses. "I spoke to her probation officer. She said Grace Miller has been making real progress in getting her life together. She's kept a job, reported in regularly for drug testing, and has been clean for the past two years. That's pretty significant. And then *this*." The judge let out a weary sigh, like she'd heard this story before. "Something happened to her, is my guess. Some kind of stressful situation that took her right back to her old habits."

Ah, that scenario was one Luke was well familiar with.

"David, when we spoke on the phone last week, you said you might have something to offer Grace Miller. I really don't want to send her to prison. I'm not ignoring the DUI, but her car was on the side of the road without an incident. She hadn't hit anything or caused any damage. If there had been, we wouldn't be having this conversation."

David leaned forward. "If you're right, that she's actually trying to turn her life around, but then was hit by some stress and couldn't cope—well, to me, that says she hasn't learned *how* to cope. Rebecca, I'd like to suggest Grace be placed in the Mountain Vista Rehabilitation Clinic. I think she could get something out of the clinic that could help her for the rest of her life."

The judge shook her head. "It's a nice thought, but there's no funds to pay for it."

"Our church. We'll pay."

The judge snapped her head up. "Why?"

"Because, if she is indeed the Grace Miller we're seeking, she has a daughter who is joining our church. This woman has been brought into our lives through her daughter, and I believe God wants us to pay attention to her. To give her another chance."

"You'd do that for a stranger?"

"For a church member's mother. Yes, we would. Gladly."

"Even though it may not turn out the way you hope."

"Even so. At the very least, we will have peace before God that we've done all we can for this woman. And for her daughter too. In a way, she's joining the extended family of the church."

The judge paused for a long moment, chin tucked. Then she lifted her head. "David, I'm going to do something I wouldn't do for most people. I'm going to let you go to the prison and ask Grace if she's willing to consider rehab. I want her to see you face-to-face. If she agrees to go to rehab, I'll work with the DA and PD to find a satisfactory plea bargain. I have to warn you—if she's like most addicts, she'll check herself out of rehab and skip town. If so, there'll be a warrant out for her arrest and that'll be the end of it. But if a miracle occurs, and she sticks with it, then I take my hat off to you."

"Not to me, Rebecca, but to God. He's in the business of making miracles."

She smiled. "In this case, I sincerely hope you're right."

As Luke and David walked out of the courthouse, he glanced at the bishop. "How do you know the judge?"

"She's my third cousin on my mother's side."

Luke jabbed a finger in the air. "I knew it! She reminded me a little bit of Dok."

David grinned. "Good eye. They're no-nonsense women."

"Exactly." He liked no-nonsense women. Fern, Ruthie, Izzy too. He liked their sharp wit. You knew right where you stood with them. He didn't do as well with soft-hearted types, like his own mother or even Birdy. They made it too easy for him to take advantage of their kindness. The thought shamed him, but it also made him realize he was starting to have a greater self-awareness. And wasn't that something the counselor encouraged him to develop? He would have to remember to tell him in the next phone call—*I had my first glimmer of self-awareness!*

How pathetic was that?

Still, it was a start.

TWENTY-THREE

It took just twenty-four hours for David to receive the call from the judge's office that he was cleared to see Grace Miller, and once again, he asked Luke to come with him. Luke was overjoyed to be included, a feeling that lasted until he was inside the Lancaster County Prison. Even though it was in downtown Lancaster, its exterior looked like a charming European castle. As he passed through all kinds of ominous security checks, his excitement quickly faded. There was no doubt it was a prison.

They were led to a sterile waiting area—called the greeting room but it looked more like a concrete bunker with armed guards at every corner—while another guard went to fetch Grace Miller. Luke felt his stomach swirl. Around him were visitors, women mostly, who had come to visit inmates for non-contact visitation, which meant a wall with glass divided inmate from visitor, and they spoke through a phone. The whole experience made the hair on Luke's neck stand up. David, though, seemed pretty at ease.

"Have you done this before?" Luke asked.

"Yes, in fact, I have. The prison encourages clergy to come. Bishops, ministers, and deacons, we have to get used to all kinds of things. Even if it's uncomfortable."

Luke didn't want to get used to it. When Grace Miller was led through the door and to a chair at the glass wall, he quickly stepped back to let David be the one to speak to her. She was a petite woman, very thin, all angles and bones. Too thin. She looked careworn. Luke tried not to stare at her, but he couldn't help himself. As he studied her, he started to see a few signs of Izzy in that face—the shape of the eyes, the full mouth.

Grace Miller kept shifting her gaze from David to Luke, as if she couldn't grasp why these two Plain men were here, visiting her in jail. She picked up the phone.

Luke looked to David to start the conversation and watched the color drain entirely out of his face, like someone pulled a stopper from a sink. David handed the phone to Luke and quickly rose, bolting for the door.

"Whoa, David." A red flare went off in Luke's head. He held the phone receiver against his chest. "Hold on! Where are you going? What am I supposed to do?"

Without turning around, David stopped at the door and said, "I need a minute, Luke. Talk to her about . . . I don't know. About anything. I just . . . I need to go check on something."

Luke sat in the chair David had vacated, baffled. He had no business stepping into the bishop role! He needed David here. "Uh, I'm Luke Schrock. He's, that guy who bolted, he's the bishop. David Stoltzfus. We, uh, we're Amish." Okay, that sounded stupid.

"Yeah, that I can see. Why do you keep staring at me?"

Luke blinked several times and swallowed. "I guess, um, you remind me of someone."

"So what do you want?"

Luke shot up an arrow prayer of *Help! Really, God. I need help like I've never needed it. Right now.*

Acting braver than he felt, he said, "I understand you have a drinking problem. Or drugs? Maybe both?" Okay, that was another stupid thing to say.

Grace's eyes narrowed in a suspicious way. "I'm clean and sober."

"What I mean to say is, if you ever get out of jail, how are you planning to stay clean?"

Wrong tack again. Angry now, Grace got up to leave just as David came back in the room. The color had returned to his face, and he seemed strangely calm, purposeful. Luke wondered how David could do that, gain control over himself. Self-control had never been a strength for Luke. Just the opposite. Highly impulsive tendencies, the counselor had once described of him.

Luke jumped out of the chair to hand David the phone. Grace hesitated and sat back down. David held the phone between them so Luke could hear the conversation and, in a calm, measured voice, explained why they were here. "Grace, we came to see if we can provide help to you so that you're able to continue in your path of sobriety."

That! Now *that* was what Luke should have said.

She shook her head, her cheeks bright. "I'm clean now."

Luke swallowed a smile. Of course she was clean now; she was in jail. It's what would happen when she was released—that's where addiction had to be faced down.

She had her eyes on Luke, as if she could tell what he was

thinking. "Like I told the kid, I'm clean and sober. Almost two years now. I just had . . . a slip-up. One."

David nodded. "Have you been taking part in any program while you've been at the county prison?"

She shrugged. "There's not much here."

Well, not much was better than nothing.

"I understand you were picked up by the police in Lancaster," David said. "May I ask what brought you here?"

Grace's bravado disappeared and was replaced with a shocking vulnerability. "I came to . . . make amends."

David's eyebrows lifted. "That's a fine place to start. I'd be interested in knowing more."

"Is that why you're here? You want some kind of confession out of me? Look, I'm not the same person I was back then. I've changed. I served my time. I just had one mistake. Just one. That counts for something, doesn't it?"

Luke felt as if he was watching two trains pass each other. David's train was going one direction, Grace's was going another. David must have had a similar thought. "Grace, could we back up a moment? Let's start at the beginning. What brought you out here? To whom were you making amends?"

"My daughter. In Stoney Ridge. She's one of you. She sent me a letter, asking me to come. She asked me to come." She patted her chest. "She *asked* me."

Oh my. Wow. So one of Izzy's letters had made it to Grace, after all. Luke was impressed. She shifted in the chair and light from a huge mirror on the far wall limned Grace's profile. *Man oh man*, Luke thought. *From a certain angle, she sure looks like Izzy. Rather*, he corrected himself, *Izzy sure looks like her.*

"So," David said, "you came to make amends."

She lifted her chin when she spoke in a way that reminded Luke again of Izzy. "That's what I told you."

"But something stopped you."

She sighed. "I was almost there." She lifted her hand and pinched her thumb and index finger nearly together. "I was *this* close. But then I lost my nerve. I stopped to call my sponsor, but she didn't pick up. And as I hung up the phone, I saw a bar across the street . . . and I thought that maybe if I had a drink, just one, I could better handle facing my kid. It was a big deal, you know. I hadn't seen her in years. And the last time I saw her, I didn't do right by her."

Luke knew the rest of the story. If she was looking for courage from a bottle, it would take a very big bottle. One drink led to two, to three, to four. And then, somehow, the police showed up. It was a familiar story, one Luke had heard at the rehab clinic plenty of times.

David was watching Grace carefully as she spoke, so intently that Luke wondered what was running through his mind. "What made you want to make amends?"

"The Twelve Step program. I've been going regularly to AA these last two years. It says you gotta make amends to people you've hurt."

And didn't Luke know all about *that*.

"I'd done my best to avoid it, but my sponsor told me I couldn't keep dodging my past. When I got that letter from my daughter, it seemed like the universe was trying to tell me something."

"Grace, if you might be willing, there's a clinic that has wonderful results. It's in the country, not far from here."

"I can attest to the clinic's success," Luke said. "I'm a recovered alcoholic."

She shot a look at Luke and blinked a few times, confused. "You?"

"Yes. Me."

She considered him for a long moment, then turned to David. "My probation officer said I was facing jail time."

"The judge might be willing to offer you a deal," David said. "Rehab, effective rehab, versus jail time. Your probation officer can explain more."

"Hold on." Her interest was piqued. "So you're saying that I have a choice. Jail or rehab."

"Correct."

"Look, obviously, I don't want to spend more time in jail. But I really don't need another stint in rehab. I've been clean for two years. Two years! That's gotta count for something. I've never stayed clean that long."

"I think you do need rehab, Grace," David said. "The reason you relapsed was because you faced an important part of healing without any scaffolding to support you."

"Not true! AA has helped me. Trust me, I've tried it all."

"Alcoholics Anonymous is a wonderful structure, if you embrace all twelve steps."

"I have. I've tried. I told you. One slip-up, that's all."

"What about step 11?"

"What about it?"

David repeated step 11 from memory. "'Sought through prayer and meditation to improve our conscious contact with God, as we understood him, praying only for knowledge of his will for us and the power to carry that out.'"

Grace looked away, frowning.

"You said the universe was sending you a message. Is that your understanding of God? A nameless universe? Because I think of the universe as a very hostile place. A broken world. But there is a loving God who made the universe, who is always at work to redeem those he created."

Grace folded her arms against her chest. "So that's why you're here. You're out to convert me. Just like you did with my girl."

David shook his head. "Not at all. I want you to be prepared to live the rest of your life without drugs or alcohol. I want you to have the life God intended you to live. But it can't come apart from God's help. I think this clinic would be able to help you find the life you're looking for."

Grace rolled her eyes. "Look. I don't have money for rehab."

"Our church might be willing to help you. We have funds available. The clinic is run by Plain people. They have such good results *because* faith is part of the program. There is no true healing without God involved."

"So let me get this straight. You're offering to send me to rehab. To even pay for it." Her eyes narrowed. "Why? Why . . . why would you be willing to do this?"

"Grace, your daughter would like to have a relationship with you, but we can't let you be a part of her life if you're not clean and sober."

Grace's face blanched. "She still wants to see me? Even though I missed her wedding?"

"Wedding?" David and Luke exchanged a look.

"Yeah. That's why I came back to Stoney Ridge. For her wedding."

A wedding? Luke could almost see the gears turning in David's mind, just like they were in his own head. She wasn't talking about Izzy and her letter. She was talking about—

"Grace," David said, "what's the name of your daughter?"

TWENTY-FOUR

David asked again. "Grace, what's the name of your daughter?"

"Jenny. She went by the last name of Yoder. I don't remember what her married name is."

Quietly, Luke said, "Stoltzfus."

Grace blinked. "Wait." She pointed at David. "Isn't that what you said your name was?"

David hesitated. "Yes. It's a common name."

Not all that common in Lancaster, Luke thought. He wondered if David might reveal more—that Jenny Yoder had married his son, Jesse, and that he was Jenny's father-in-law. But David kept a poker face and leaned back in his chair.

"Grace, we came here today on behalf of Isabella Miller."

"What?" Grace went blank, stunned. Several long seconds passed before she added, "She's . . . here?"

Something clicked in Luke's mind and it started to spin. Hold on, hold on. Then that would mean . . . Izzy and Jenny—they were sisters? He wanted to laugh, or cry, or both. But when he looked at David, he was shocked to see such stillness emanate out of him, utterly at peace. How did he do it? Somehow he was able to absorb any shock without obvious effect. Luke, he could barely contain a roller coaster of emotion.

Grace looked like Luke felt. Shaken and stirred. Even with the distance of the glass divider, Luke could see the hand that held the phone was trembling.

"When did you last see Isabella?" David asked.

"It's been a while." Her eyes grew shiny. "She was little when they took her away from me."

Took her away. Ah, how Luke recognized that tone! He could see it objectively now. Izzy was put in foster care because Grace was arrested for her drug habit. No wonder Izzy had no patience for him at first. She recognized that note of self-pity too.

Grace wiped her eyes with the back of her forearm, then took in a deep breath and let it out. "So *that's* why you're here." She looked at David. "Isabella, she's staying with you?"

He nodded. "She wants to be baptized into the church this year. She's been going through classes."

"I would think you'd want to keep me far away from her, then. She's right where you people want her, isn't she?"

David ignored that. "Isabella had a rough go of her childhood. She was sent from one foster family to another, and then to group homes. When she ran away, she ended up living on the streets in Lancaster. By the time she connected with our deacon, she'd developed a pretty serious dependence on alcohol. And she was only seventeen."

Luke was all ears. In the last thirty seconds, he'd learned more about Izzy than he had in four months of knowing her.

"She ended up going to rehab, Grace. This same clinic.

And when the time came to be released, we offered her a place in our church. No strings attached. Just a place to come and find her way forward. There's never been any pressure on her to go Amish—that's been her own choice."

Suddenly Grace's eyes went wide. "Then, do she and Jenny know each other? They must."

"They do. In fact, they're good friends. But they aren't aware that they're siblings."

"They had different fathers. All three of my kids did."

"Good grief," Luke whispered. "There's a third?"

"Chris Yoder," David whispered back, hand over the receiver. "Married to one of Amos's daughters."

Grace was watching them but couldn't hear. Nervously, she tucked a lock of hair behind her ear. "The other two, they're older than Isabella. She never knew them. They were taken away from me before I had her. When I got pregnant with Isabella . . . I tried a do-over. This time, I was going to do it right. It worked for a while. But then . . . it all fell apart." She shrugged, as if it was part and parcel of her life. "Isabella was too little to know she had siblings. I wanted to make a fresh start. Pretend I was a different person than I was."

"But it isn't possible, is it, Grace? We bring ourselves along. Thankfully, God can redeem even our worst failures."

Grace rubbed one of her temples with her fingers, as if her head hurt. "Maybe it's best if I just leave her be. Let her live her life. Sounds like she's making choices that will put her on a fixed path."

"In a way, she is doing just that. But I believe there's a part of her that's unable to heal without addressing some things in her past. And I suspect it's the same story for you. There are things in your past that need to be faced, not avoided."

Grace didn't respond to that. She had leaned forward on her elbows, with her chin cupped in one palm, eyes on David. She tilted her head and narrowed her eyes at him, almost squinting. "I know you from somewhere. I'm sure of it."

David ignored her stall tactic. "Grace, let's stay focused on Isabella right now. She needs her mother. Whole and healthy."

Grace lowered her eyes and traced the edge of the counter with a finger. "How do you know she's not better off without me?"

"She's not," David said firmly. "Every child needs a parent." His voice showed a hint of exasperation, the first Luke had noticed. "Look, we want you to have a place in your daughter's life. We want to help you stay clean and sober, and we don't think that's going to happen without gaining tools. The right kind of tools."

Grace dropped her head, and Luke realized she was crying. "Every time I try," she murmured, then swallowed hard, "every single time, I just mess it up." She banged one fist on the counter. "You don't realize the things I've done."

Finally, *finally*, the façade dropped and she was real. For the first time, Luke felt a glimmer of hope for this woman. David must've sensed the same thing, because he waited patiently until she lifted her head. "We're offering you a chance to make a new life for yourself, Grace. I'm not promising an easy path ahead, but it's a program that's helped a lot of people, if they're willing to be helped. If you want a life that includes your daughter, this is a way to get it."

"Are you sure," Grace said, "that she wants me in her life?"

"Oh yes," Luke said. That much he knew.

"She does," David said. "Very much so. She's the one who

sent us to find you. But I have to let you know that if you don't agree to the clinic, I won't let you see her. We Amish, we can be pretty protective of our own."

"So if I say yes to this clinic, then I get to see my girls? And if I don't agree, then I don't."

"If you agree to participating in the clinic's program, then you are saying yes to your daughters, to being the mother they've always wanted you to be."

The guard motioned that their time was almost up.

"Grace, I want you to think this option over. We'll be back to meet you on your arraignment day to find out what you've chosen to do."

"If I don't agree to this program, then I don't see my daughters. That's what you're saying, isn't it? You think I can't stay clean on my own."

"If you choose not to go to the clinic, then I hope and pray you will stay clean. I truly do. But we won't be letting you near your daughters, not until you've proven yourself. And yes, I think it will be much more difficult to stay sober if you don't have some kind of support."

"This place . . . they'll try to turn me into a Plain person, won't they? I'd have to wear those kooky clothes?"

Luke looked down at his shirt and pants. Kooky? Huh. He thought he looked pretty cool.

"No, not at all. There's all kinds of people there, English and Plain, but faith is an instrumental part of the process. It's a clinic that considers God to be the true Healer in this broken world. In people's broken lives."

"Seems like a lot of pressure to not say no."

There it was again, that tone of self-pity. It amazed Luke—to think this woman wouldn't grab a chance to reconnect with her children, whatever it might take. Was he once so selfish? Probably.

Grace glanced up at Luke. Her eyes, they seemed almost . . . beseeching. "This place . . . it really helped you?"

"Yes. Along with a caring community. I couldn't have licked it on my own. No way. Each time I tried to do it alone, I ended up worse than before. Hurting more people than I ever imagined. Addiction is powerful."

"It owns you," Grace said quietly.

"Yes, exactly that," Luke said without hesitation. "It wants more and more of you, until it's taken everything from you. But its hold can be broken. For good. It can, Grace. There's a whole new life ahead for you." He gave her a slight smile. "Maybe that's why your name is Grace. A life of grace waits for you."

Grace ducked her chin. "I'll think about it." She stood up. "I guess I should say thanks. You didn't have to come here."

"Don't thank us. Thank your daughter. She's the one who's been trying to find you. Think about Isabella, Grace. About Jenny. Get well for your daughters' sake."

Grace didn't respond. Carefully and thoughtfully, she set the phone back in the receiver and walked away. David watched her, and Luke watched David, wondering what he was thinking, because his lips were moving but he wasn't saying anything. Then he realized David was praying for her.

David put the receiver back and rose to his feet.

Luke stood and followed David to the exit. "Well, that was . . . a surprising encounter."

Over his shoulder, David said, "On many levels."

"What are you going to tell Jenny? And Izzy?"

"I need time to mull this over."

Luke expected David to need mulling time the way Amos needed mulling time—slow and deliberate. To his shock, David had it figured out by the time the bus reached Stoney Ridge.

"Okay, here's the plan. I want to wait to tell Jenny and Izzy the news about each other, and about their mother's whereabouts, until after Grace makes the decision to enter Mountain Vista. Or not. That way, we'll know how to prepare the girls and not mislead them with unfair expectations. If Grace chooses not to go to the clinic, at least they have each other. And if she does choose to go the clinic route, then they can get reacquainted with Grace together. But I don't want them disappointed. They've had enough of that."

"David, was Izzy abused?"

He sent him a sharp glance. "Has she not told you about her life before Windmill Farm?"

Luke shrugged. "You know Izzy. She's not one for questions. Never uses more words than is necessary."

"She doesn't want to go backward, only forward."

"I guess I just feel . . . sort of protective of her. I don't need to know details. I just wondered if she'd been hurt."

"What do you think, Luke? A young girl like her, living on the streets."

It was all starting to make sense to Luke—Izzy's defensiveness, her fierce independence, her suspicion about men in general. He wanted to singlehandedly punish the nameless men who had hurt her. To punish them, hurt them, even kill them. It was a horrifying thought for a man about to become Amish, that desire for revenge. He wondered what David would say if he knew Luke's thoughts. No, hold on. He knew David well enough by now to know. *Let a just God dispense*

269

justice. Instead of taking vengeance on them, pray for them, Luke. They are in danger of losing their souls for eternity.

"David . . . you know, an addict never fails to disappoint."

"Maybe, but I sensed a crack in Grace Miller's façade, just enough for the light of God to shine through. Maybe she'll surprise us."

Luke had to hand it to David—the man did not give up on people. Luke? He had plenty of doubts about Grace. Yes, there might have been a crack or two in the façade, but Luke knew how hard and deep that shell was. He could tell.

But then, what if David had given up on me? Where would I be? It had taken three times for Luke to get through rehab. Three times! He had to bottom out, to get to that point of no return. Imagine if he'd had a life of alcohol or drug abuse—years and years of patterned responses to stress of any kind.

"Pray for Grace this week, Luke. Pray for Izzy and Jenny too. This is an important week in their lives. It could be a fulcrum point."

"I just hope I haven't opened up a Pandora's box."

A look of sadness covered David. "Oh, you have. In more ways than you could possibly imagine. But closed boxes never did anyone any good." He folded his arms against his chest and closed his eyes, as if he was suddenly and thoroughly exhausted.

Another thought danced through Luke's head, a happier one. He'd found Grace Miller for Izzy. He was officially done with the fence-mending list. Done! Every name checked off. Hardest, most gut-wrenching thing he'd ever done in his life.

Best thing he'd ever done in his life.

Two days later, David and Luke went to the courthouse for Grace's arraignment. David didn't even have to invite Luke. He just assumed he would be going.

The two men sat at the back of the courtroom on a long, hard bench. They waited patiently through three hearings until the bailiff announced the next case number on the docket. Grace Miller was led in and sat at the defense table next to her court-appointed lawyer. Luke watched her carefully. Dressed in civilian clothing, she looked better than she did in her prison jumpsuit, softer, a little less brittle. Her hair was pulled back in a tight ponytail. The only sign that she was nervous was the way she kept tugging on the sleeve of her blouse.

The judge picked up the file, read through the first page, and looked up at Grace. "Ms. Miller, you've been arrested for driving under the influence. Your public defender has requested a plea bargain. He's asked that your DUI charge be reduced to a drunk and disorderly charge. You have a prior record of arrests and convictions, and I have the authority of the court to deny this plea bargain. But I'm taking into account that your probation officer has confirmed you've been clean and sober and gainfully employed for the past two years. The plea bargain would drop the charge from a felony to a third-degree misdemeanor. That means it would not be a criminal charge on your record, but it should be taken seriously. The maximum sentence for a drunk and disorderly conviction is ninety days. Ms. Miller, if you agree to this plea bargain, you'll relinquish your right to a trial by jury and go directly to sentencing. Is that what you understand you've agreed to?"

Luke saw Grace lean over to whisper something to her

public defender, then she straightened up and said a clear and loud yes.

"Ms. Miller," the judge continued, "you have another choice here today. If you are willing to check yourself in to the Mountain Vista Rehabilitation Clinic and successfully complete the program, then your sentence will be suspended. If you do not complete it, a warrant will go out for your arrest. Personally, I'd like to keep you out of jail and on a path to sobriety. But it's your decision to make."

Grace rose to her feet. "I accept the offer to go to rehab." She started to sit down, but her public defender whispered something to her and she straightened. "And I thank you, Your Honor."

The judge rapped her gavel. "Then your sentence is hereby suspended. Grace Mitchell Miller, I don't want to see you in this court again. You've got a chance here. Don't blow it."

Outside the courthouse, David and Luke waited in the cold for Grace Miller to get released. It took so long that Luke started to wonder if something had gone wrong.

David didn't seem at all anxious. The man amazed Luke. Whenever he was around him, he felt his heart and soul settle. Sometimes he wondered if that's what Heaven would feel like. Your whole self settled into a permanent and lasting peace.

Luke pondered where the money was coming from for Grace Miller's rehab costs, because he doubted the church would provide for an outsider. They were generous people, but not *that* generous. Then he realized the money was probably coming from David and Birdy's own pocket. It wouldn't surprise him.

Finally, the door opened and there was Grace Miller. She walked up to David. "So . . . you meant what you said."

"Absolutely."

"I'll try it. I'll give this place of yours a try. That's all I'm promising to do."

David smiled. "Then, let's head over there."

Amos and Fern sat across the table from David and Luke. David had stopped by Windmill Farm early this morning to ask if they could talk privately today. That wasn't out of the ordinary, for David often stopped by to discuss deacon business. But then he asked for Fern to be included, and Luke too. Amos's spine stiffened. And could Amos find a way to have Izzy be away from the farm when they talked? With that, the hair on Amos's neck stood up. He racked his brain, wondering what trouble Luke might have gotten himself into. The boy had been doing so well, he'd thought. So well.

After the midday meal, Amos had sent Izzy over to the Bent N' Dent on a fool's errand. "Fern needs salt?" she asked him, a skeptical look on her face. "Salt?"

"And sugar. Both." He had handed her a ten-dollar bill, feeling a little guilty, but David was due to arrive in ten minutes and he was anxious to get to the bottom of this. Whatever *this* was.

David was sipping a cup of coffee, calm as a man could be. Amos's stomach was twisted into a tight knot. What had happened? He glared at Luke. What had the boy done?

David set down his coffee cup. "Can you tell me what you know of Izzy's parents?"

Amos looked to Fern to answer. He knew nothing.

"Not much," Fern said. "She skirts the issue if I bring up anything about her background. Sometimes I think she wants to pretend her life started here, one year ago."

David put a hand on Luke's shoulder. "A couple of weeks ago, Izzy asked Luke to find her mother. And lo and behold, against remarkable odds, he did just that."

"So this meeting isn't about something Luke's done wrong?" Amos avoided Fern's frown. He could read her thoughts. She was sending him a silent scold for being so quick to assign blame to Luke.

David gave Amos a surprised look. "No. Not at all." Hands clasped, he set them on the table. "Are you familiar with the name Grace Mitchell?"

Amos sucked in a big gasp; he felt like he'd had the wind kicked out of him.

Fern glanced first at him, then at David. "That's a name we'll never forget."

David's eyes remained fixed on Amos. "Would you mind telling me what you know of Grace Mitchell?"

But Amos couldn't seem to gather the words. He closed his eyes, swallowed, and tried again. Nothing. After a long, awkward moment, Fern filled in. "She grew up in the house that backs up to Windmill Farm. She lived with her father, a man named Colonel Mitchell. She had two children, a boy and a girl. She got involved with drugs—I'm not sure about that part, but then—"

Amos held up a hand to stop her. This part of the story, he had to make sure was crystal clear. "My first wife, Maggie, she took pity on Grace Mitchell. Not so much on her, but on those two little ones. Maggie would go over to the house and try to help, but that woman, she was not an easy person to help. Maggie used to say that she thought the colonel named his daughter Grace because she was going to need so much of it in life."

Slowly, he eased out of his chair and went to the window. "One spring afternoon, Maggie had gone over to visit Grace. The little girl baby, she had colic like our Menno did. She wanted to take goat's milk over to Grace, to see if it might help with the colic. I expected her back within an hour or so, but she didn't come home."

His voice choked up and he had trouble getting the words out. "I knew something was wrong. As soon as Julia, my eldest, came home from school, I left the little ones with her, and I went over to the colonel's." The vision rolled out in his mind, vivid and clear, as if it were yesterday. "Maggie had fallen down the porch steps and hit her head on a rock. Her skull was fractured. The paramedic said she had died instantly, that she never knew what had happened."

Luke's eyes went wide. "Grace pushed her?"

"Colonel Mitchell confessed to pushing Maggie and she fell backward. The coroner ruled the death as accidental homicide. He went to prison and died there, from cancer."

David, Fern, and even Luke waited patiently, letting Amos continue at his own pace. He'd rarely spoken of that day since it had happened. "Colonel Mitchell, I believe, was protecting his daughter Grace. But I remained silent."

Gently, David said, "Why didn't you say anything?"

"Because I think I'd have done the same for one of my children." He paced around the room for a moment. "I suppose I wanted someone to be held responsible for my Maggie's death. I'm not saying Grace tried to kill Maggie. It might have been an accident, but she never owned up to it."

"Has she ever returned to Stoney Ridge?" David said. "So far as you know?"

Amos spun around. "Once. The colonel had left the house to his grandchildren. Somehow, she managed to swindle her two children out of their inheritance. As far as I know, she's never come back."

David sat back in his chair. "Amos, she's here now."

TWENTY-FIVE

Amos had to get out of the kitchen. His chest felt tight, as if he couldn't get enough air, and he thought he might pass out. He leaned his hands on the porch railing and took in big draughts of fresh air.

How could this be? Grace Mitchell, surfaced again.

He thought he'd dealt with the anger he'd felt for her when he found out that Chris and Jenny Yoder were her children. He thought he'd dealt with it again when he learned that his youngest daughter, M.K., was sweet on Chris. For a long while, he blamed Chris. He worked that through, or so he'd thought, after he and Chris had made amends.

But from the violent reaction he had to news that she was in Stoney Ridge, he realized he'd never truly forgiven Grace Mitchell for her role in his darling Maggie's death, not deep in his heart. And so the Lord had brought it to him again, while he still had time to face this hard thing.

Grace Mitchell. The mother of sweet Izzy? How could this be?

The door swung open with a squeak and out came David, holding a fresh cup of coffee for him. "You okay?"

"Yes. No." Amos took the coffee with one hand and rubbed his face with the other. "David, why am I responsible for Grace Mitchell's children? All three."

"Has it been so very difficult to love those children? Jenny, Chris, Izzy?"

"No, no, of course not. They've been a great blessing to us." He looked at the steaming black coffee. "But you have to admit that it seems strangely coincidental that they keep ending up at Windmill Farm. I want nothing to do with this woman, yet she keeps turning up like a bad penny."

David's mouth lifted in a smile that didn't reach his eyes. "I've had the same thought." He pointed to the rocking chairs. "Let's sit down."

Amos watched David select his words with some care. He leaned forward in the rocking chair, his fingers steepled together in a way that made Amos know something important was coming.

"Amos, years ago, while I was living in Ohio, a single mother and her daughter lived next door to us. Something wasn't right. The little girl, only four or five years old, she was left alone quite a bit and kept wandering over to our house to play with my children. My wife, Anna, scooped her in among our own brood. Anna tried to help this woman, but she wasn't easy to help. She had a drug problem, we thought. She didn't mind having her daughter cared for by Anna, but that's all the neighborly help she wanted.

"We had an open buggy that Anna liked to use on summer days. The buggy had a short in the turn lights. I'd been meaning to fix it, but something kept coming up. You know how that can go. Long to-do lists."

Amos knew. His whole farm was a long to-do list.

"Then came a day when I got a call from the hospital. There'd been an accident—Anna and Katrina, my eldest daughter, they were driving in the buggy and were hit by a car. Anna . . . she was killed instantly. Katrina was badly hurt." David choked up and couldn't speak for a long moment. He squeezed his eyes shut. Then he puffed out a long breath. "It turned out the driver of the car was our neighbor, and drugs were found in her car. She was arrested, and her daughter was put into foster care. This neighbor ended up getting convicted of a DUI vehicle-related manslaughter, a felony. She was sentenced to . . . I don't remember . . . maybe seven to ten years in jail. Long, but not as long as it could've been because of that short in the turn lights. She claimed she never saw the lights." He let out a puff of air again, as if this was taking everything in him to say the words. "I never knew what happened to the little girl. Until now. Amos, our neighbor's name was Grace Miller. Grace Mitchell Miller."

Amos experienced a tingling on his scalp and a sudden flush of heat that began at his breastbone and spread quickly upward to his neck and face, turning them red.

"The little girl," David continued, "her name was Bella. Short for Isabella. Amos, she's our Izzy."

Amos's heart gave one huge thump and started to beat wildly. He felt little beads of perspiration on his forehead. This wasn't good. Dok had said to avoid getting excited.

He tried to breathe in and out, tried to calm himself, but this was too much to absorb. His body was reacting faster than his mind could fathom the news. "Did you know? All this time, you knew who Izzy's mother was?"

"No. Not until Luke and I went to that jail last week and saw Grace's face. I never connected Izzy to the little girl Bella.

More than twelve years have passed since I'd seen her. She was a child. Now she's a grown woman. But the more I thought about it, the more I wondered if Izzy might remember me, and Katrina and Ruthie and Jesse, and the others."

"She must have. At the Lancaster Public Market, she asked me if I knew a family named Stoltzfus. I never could figure out why she was asking." Amos's heart was still pounding, as hard and fast as if he'd run a race. He wondered if he should get some pills to slow it down. He set the coffee mug on the porch before he spilled it. "Why did you have to turn this stone over? Why couldn't it just be left alone?"

"I didn't intend to. Luke's the one who found Grace."

"About that. How did he find her? Why couldn't he have just left things alone?"

"Izzy asked for his help. At the very least, the fact that Luke wanted to help her is a sign that our prayers for him are being answered." David rubbed his hands together, as if he was getting cold. Amos had no sense of whether it was hot or cold. He wanted David to stop talking. He wanted to forget this conversation.

"Look, Amos, there's more to this story than you and me, grief and loss. Grace Mitchell is in Mountain Vista, right now, trying to get her life together. She's been clean for two years, until right before Jenny's wedding."

Two years. Two little years. That didn't seem like much of a reason to welcome her into their lives.

"We have an opportunity to truly trust in the sovereignty of God. Grace Mitchell Miller matters. She is not lost in God's eyes. This could be a time of great healing for her."

Amos pounded his knees with his fists. "And what if she fails again, David? What about Izzy? That girl has been through enough. Do you know how long it took her to look me in the eyes? Six months! I can't imagine the kind of men who've been in her world. She's finally learning to trust . . . and you want to bring this kind of a *mother*"—he practically spit the word—"into her world?"

"Don't forget that Izzy's the one who started this. She's been looking for her mother this entire year, sending letters to every Grace Miller in the phone book. And another thing—even if Grace does fail, Izzy has a safety net. She's got you and Fern, she's got me and Birdy. And then . . . she's got a sister named Jenny. And a brother named Chris. We never would've put that all together, without this . . . strangely prophetic timing. I guess we have Luke to thank for that."

"When do you plan on telling Izzy all this? Seems only fair that she knows she has a sister."

"I don't know." David crossed his arms over his chest. "I want to wait and get guidance from God before the girls are involved. I don't want them to be needlessly hurt or disappointed."

"Don't forget that Izzy is getting baptized this Sunday. She should be told before then. It's only right."

"Believe me, I haven't forgotten. And I agree with you. She should be told. I just want to pray a little more about it." David squinted his eyes. "Are you going to be okay? You still look pale."

"I'm still trying to get my head around all this. For me. For you. It's a lot to take in." His heart was still reacting to the news, but it was slowing down a little.

"That it is. When I saw Grace behind the divider glass at the prison and realized I recognized her, I . . . well, to be honest, I nearly passed out cold. All those feelings that are swirling inside you right now—a desire for revenge, for making her pay, for wanting her to understand how deeply she hurt my family, how she robbed my children of their mother, my grandchildren of their grandmother. All those terrible and overwhelming feelings that you're dealing with now . . . I felt them too. I had to leave the greeting room and get some fresh air, just like you did."

"How in the world did you ever go back in to talk to her? To face her?"

"As I stood out in the hallway, praying desperately, it struck me that the chance of this meeting couldn't be an accident. It had to be a divine appointment. And if so, then God was going to have to give me the courage to get through it. And if this was a divine appointment, if God was at work, then he was doing something remarkable. Maybe even miraculous. I didn't want to interfere with that miracle." He paused, then took in a deep breath. "So here we are, my friend. On the brink of watching God's redeeming work."

Oh, David, Amos thought, his heart finally settling back to a normal pace. *How do you do it? How are you able to lead us toward right living despite your own pain?*

When the Lord brought David Stoltzfus to Stoney Ridge, *that* was a miracle in the making. There were times when Amos wondered if the Israelites had the same sense of respect and awe for King David as he, and many others, felt for their bishop. Yes, David Stoltzfus was a man with flaws, yet he was also a leader with a spirit deeply sensitive to God's leading.

If that man could seek this woman's best, having suffered the very same personal casualty from her that Amos had, then he would follow his bishop's lead. Amos knew he was not standing alone, but shoulder to shoulder with David.

The weather had turned cold and stayed cold. After breakfast Friday morning, Izzy was upstairs changing sheets on her bed, breathing in the scent of sun-dried cotton, when she heard the familiar sounds of a horse and buggy come up the driveway. She went to the window to see David Stoltzfus jump out of the buggy as Amos walked outside to meet him.

It was a sight Izzy'd seen many times over the last year, bishop and deacon, conferring together over church matters. They walked toward the house and stopped to talk at the bottom of the porch steps. Izzy stuffed a pillow into a clean casing and went downstairs to see if they wanted something to drink, and they did. The kitchen was strangely quiet as she poured two mugs full of Fern's fresh-brewed coffee.

"She puts chicory in with the grounds," Izzy said as she handed David a mug.

"Fern Lapp is the best cook in town," David said, then his eyes widened in alarm. "Please don't tell Birdy I said that."

"Es schmackt immer's bescht an annere Leit ihrm Disch." *It always tastes best at other folks' table.* "That's a Fern Lapp quote."

"Your accent sounded good." David smiled, but not with his eyes. They looked exhausted.

Izzy wondered what was weighing David down as she put the coffeepot back on the burner. She turned around to find the two men facing her with strange looks on their faces. Fern stood nearby. Where had she come from? Fern's eyes looked shiny, and she wondered whether she should offer to bring her a tissue.

It took an instant for Izzy's brain to register what was happening. Fern? Crying? "Something's happened, hasn't it?" The first thought that came to mind was that Luke had been hurt. And then she was annoyed with herself for even worrying one second over Luke Schrock. But she was! "Tell me what's wrong. Have I done something?"

"Izzy, sit down with us," David said. "We want to share some news with you."

As she settled into a chair, the worrisome thoughts came too fast, one after the other. Memories bounced through her head like popcorn in a skillet: social workers showing up at foster families' houses to tell Izzy it was time to pack up. Oh yeah, she thought. She knew this drill. "You want me to leave," she said in a crisp business tone, trying to sound in control of her feelings. She could feel her face grow warm, her heart pound, as she fought back the automatic panic that rose within her. Where would she go? What would she do? She had no idea. In a defiant move, she crossed her arms and tucked her chin to her chest. "So then, I'll leave."

"Leave us?" Fern's voice rose an octave. "Oh, Izzy, we don't ever want you to leave. This is your home."

Amos reached over to pat her shoulder with his big farmer's hand. The gesture was clumsy but tender, and it touched her deeply. Then he added a few words in his gruff voice that rocked Izzy's world. "You've become a daughter to us."

A daughter? Amos Lapp just said he thought of her like a daughter, and Fern was nodding furiously in agreement, like her head was on a coiled spring. *Someone* considered her to be like a daughter. First time. Tears pricked Izzy's eyes. She lowered her gaze as she asked, "Then . . . what's going on? What's happened?"

Amos cleared his throat. "Do you remember when I used to buy you a burger at the Lancaster Public Market?"

Slowly, she nodded. Where was this going?

"One time, you asked me if I knew a family named Stoltzfus. Do you remember?"

She lowered her glance, and gave a quick nod. *Oh no.*

"Back in Ohio," David said, "there was a little girl named Bella who lived across the street from us. Her mother would leave her alone for long periods of time, sometimes even overnight, and this little girl would wander over to play with my children. I remember that she was a sweet little girl, with big, sad brown eyes. She didn't talk much, and she never asked us for anything. My wife, Anna, she had a special fondness for this little girl. Anna had a phrase she used, and this little girl, only five or six years old, used to mimic her. Whenever Anna was surprised or overwhelmed or happy, she would say, 'Oh my soul.'"

Izzy's palms started sweating. She felt almost feverish, shaky and sticky and cold and hot, all at once. She kept forgetting to breathe. Her mind felt filled with barn swallows, swooping through her rafters with the most ridiculous contingency plan: *If I act fast, I can escape out the kitchen door and run to the road. Maybe hitch a ride to Lancaster? And then . . . and then . . . go where? And why? Why am I running? Who am I running from? These are the people I was running to, not away from.*

David's voice broke through her craziness. "Izzy, are you that girl? Are you Bella?"

Her hands twisted the edges of her apron as she struggled

to respond. "I never forgot your family." Her throat seemed to close up. She started, "Three years ago . . ." Her voice cracked and she had to start over again. "Three years ago, I went to your old farmhouse, and the lady who lived there gave me your new address. I hoped you could help me find my mother."

"Is that why you came to Lancaster? You were trying to find us?"

Izzy nodded again. She didn't dare look up. A fallen tear made a dot on the front of her dress. One dot, then another.

"Izzy," Fern said softly, "tell us why you've been so determined to find your mother. What is it you want from her?"

Everything. Nothing. "I have a question to ask her." Tears were falling fast now, splashing down her face.

"What question?"

"Why did she give up her parenting rights so I became a ward of the state?" Even to her own ears, Izzy could hear the faint note of hysteria in her voice. "I need to know. Not knowing has plagued me my whole life."

"Izzy, honey," Fern said, her face full of worry, and that made Izzy want to cry even more. "Can't you see how the Lord's been watching over you? He directed you right to Bob the buggy horse, just when Amos happened to be dropping Sadie at the market."

Oh no. Not that. Anything but that. Up came the misery, the loneliness, the anger. Up, up, and over. Out of her burst something aloud she had never dared to say before, something she barely allowed herself to think. "If God was watching over me, then where was he when my mother gave me up? Why did I have to spend a childhood in foster care?" She was practically screaming, even to her own ears, and she didn't care! "Where was he when I was living on the streets? Did he just show up that one day when Amos drove the buggy into town?"

"I don't know the answer to that," David said, as calm as a man could be. "You're not alone in experiencing hardship. All through the Bible are stories of good people who have been dealt difficult circumstances. Look at Joseph, sold off by his own brothers into slavery. He must have felt the abandonment that you feel. I can promise you what the Bible teaches, that God brings good out of everything for those who love him. Everything can be redeemed, and used for good. Izzy, I want to tell you something that I've told Luke, over and over again. At any given moment, your life is going to be determined by your view of you or God's view of you."

"Don't you see? That's my point exactly!" How could she make them understand? She had grown up adrift in the world, standing outside the current and watching it go by. Never belonging to it, nor to anyone. "The reason God hasn't noticed me is because I'm not worth it. I *know* that."

Amos, tough old Amos with his careworn face, even he was crying now. Big tears were running over his cheekbones and into his beard. "Oh no. No no no, darling girl. Just the opposite." His voice quavered as he spoke. "Do you remember what I told you once? You're a pearl of great price to God."

Fern handed Izzy an entire box of tissues, for she was sobbing now, big huge wracks of sobs. She was too deeply into crying to stop or feel embarrassed by the display of raw emotion, so she just kept on crying for a while. Now and then, Fern awkwardly patted her hand; David and Amos looked at her with eyebrows knitted in concern. It took a long time, but at last the tears slowed and her breathing eased from great gulps to a more normal sound.

Then, in the calm that resulted, at times so quiet a fly could be heard buzzing against the windowsill, David slowly rolled out the story of her mother, of Luke finding out where she was, of the conversation he'd had with the judge, and of meeting her in jail. "Grace Miller agreed to go to a rehab clinic to avoid going to prison. She made a plea bargain to reduce a DUI charge down to drunken disorderliness. She's still on probation, of course, and if she leaves the rehab, she'll be arrested. The judge was clear on that. But if she stays, then there is hope. If she stays."

Izzy just listened to the sound of his voice, like it wasn't happening to her. Like this wasn't her mother whom he was talking about. Why would David bother himself to help Grace Miller?

After David had relayed the entire story, he cocked his head to one side. "You're awfully quiet, Izzy. Do you have any questions? I'll answer what I can."

Oh, she had plenty of questions, an endless amount. Which one to ask first? What she wanted to ask was, *What is she like? Do we resemble each other? And . . . did she even ask about me?* Instead, as coolly as she could, she said, "So then, are you paying for her rehab?"

"No one acts alone in our church," David said. "We all work together. Our church will provide for Grace Miller. We have a fund for these kinds of special circumstances."

Special circumstances? Grace Miller was a stranger to them. She was a stranger to her own daughter.

Why? Why would those church people care enough to turn over their pennies to help a stranger? These Amish, they baffled Izzy. They ran counterclockwise to the rest of the world. "Why was my mother here? Why did she come to Lancaster in the first place?"

David and Amos exchanged one of their bishop-deacon looks. "She came for a wedding, she said. She'd been invited. She was trying to get to it when a police officer found her pulled over on the side of the road."

A wedding. Her mother was going to a wedding. Izzy twisted the edge of her apron with her fingers as she rolled those words over and over in her head. She felt scalded to the core. Grace Miller was in Lancaster County not because of Izzy, not because of the countless letters she'd sent. Obviously, her mother had no intention of coming to find her. She never had. All those years of hoping, wishing, wanting, even praying . . . and the one scenario Izzy hadn't allowed herself to think was the one that was true: her mother didn't care about her.

When she wiped her eyes again, David said, "Sometimes, the strangest things come out of great pain. You block the pain and you block everything. Izzy, something wonderful has been discovered in all this. It turns out you have two half siblings. A sister and a brother."

She blinked. Siblings? "Where?"

"Your brother, his name is Chris. He lives in Ohio. Married with children. But your sister, she's closer. Closer than you think." Outside, there was the clip-clop of a horse and buggy coming up the drive. David got up and looked out the window. "In fact, she's here now."

Izzy went to the door and opened it. She saw Luke driving the buggy and realized someone else was with him. Before he could even bring the horse to a complete stop, the buggy door slid open and out jumped a blur of a female. Her arms were lifted in the air as she bolted toward the house, shouting, "Izzy! Izzy! Izzy!"

Jenny?

"You! Me! We're sisters!" She ran straight at Izzy, almost flattening her in her joy.

Late that night, Izzy climbed into bed, but she couldn't sleep. In the course of one short day, she had multiple life-altering changes. She had a half sister, and a half brother. Family of her own. It astounded her. She still couldn't wrap her head around all that was revealed in the kitchen this morning.

Jenny had dragged Izzy down to the phone shanty to tell Chris the news. She tried to convince Chris to come to Stoney Ridge for Izzy's baptism this weekend, but he couldn't get away that quickly, he said. Thanksgiving, though. He promised he'd bring his family to Windmill Farm for the holiday. And that was just weeks away.

Something else happened today. A few words were said that struck to the marrow. Amos and Fern said they considered Izzy as a daughter. First time. *And* they wanted her to stay at Windmill Farm. She'd never been called a daughter before, not even by that one foster family who'd kept her as long as they could, until the father lost his job and they had to move away. Even them. They referred to her as a foster child, not a foster daughter.

Yes, today was the best day in Izzy's life.

And the worst day too.

When Izzy found out that Jenny's wedding was the reason

her mother had come to Lancaster, that she'd kept tabs on Jenny all these years but not on Izzy's whereabouts, she felt joy slip away. Jenny wanted to explain more about their mother, but Izzy stopped her. She felt as if she'd had all she could handle today. Her mind would explode if she heard anything more.

Jenny had asked David if they could visit Grace while she was in rehab. He said that he'd hoped there'd be a time for that in the future, but not now. Izzy felt relieved by David's answer. She no longer wanted to see her mother. Not now. Not ever.

Listening to the patter of rain on the roof, she finally drifted off to sleep, but it was not with a peaceful heart. She felt anxious about the past, anxious about the future, and then anxious about being anxious.

TWENTY-SIX

Izzy hadn't had a chance to privately thank Luke for finding her mother until Saturday afternoon. She found him down in the barn. He'd just finished a major cleanout of Bob's stall and was replacing old straw with new. He saw her come in and gave her a nod, but kept pushing fresh straw around the stall with a pitchfork.

"I appreciate what you did," she said, standing at the open stall door. "Finding my mother. Going to the prison. And to court too. I'm sure it wasn't easy."

Luke set the pitchfork against the stall door. "Couldn't have been easy to grow up in the foster care system."

"Well, that was then. This is now."

"I'd like to hear more about then. I'd like to know more about you."

She shrugged. "Now that you've met my mother, you might know more than I do."

"Are you going to go visit her? Your mother, I mean?"

"No," she said, a little too quickly. "No. David said to hold off for a while." She brushed some bits of straw off her arm. "I mean, I will, eventually. Jenny too. Just not now."

Luke tilted his head. "She can't fix you."

Izzy jerked her head up. "What's that supposed to mean?"

"Your mother. She can't fix you."

She stiffened. What did he know about it? About anything? She turned to leave but he reached out to stop her.

"Hold on. Listen to me for a minute. That empty feeling inside that drove you to find your mother—she's not going to give you what you want. What you need." He let go of her, although she hadn't tried to pull away.

"I know that." His gaze searched her face until she turned away.

"That need you have, it's not wrong, Izzy. It can be filled up."

"And I suppose *you*," she said, sarcasm dripping, "you think you can provide everything a girl needs."

His eyes went round with surprise. "Me? No. No, not me, Izzy. I was talking about God. He's the only one who can fix you."

She looked down at her sneakers so he couldn't see her face. She could feel the heat rising in her cheeks. "So now you're a preacher?"

"No, no. Don't get me wrong. I'm not trying to preach at you. I'm trying to tell you what it's been like for me, what I've had to figure out. Our childhoods can't be compared, that's for sure, but I know what it's like to want more from a parent. I kept looking in all the wrong places. It took . . . a lot, I guess, until I understood that only God can fix me. You know, fill up what's been missing." Leaning against Bob's stall, he watched her thoughtfully. "Tomorrow's the day. Baptism. You're going to make a promise to the church that'll set the course for the rest of your life. It's a big, big deal."

"I know."

"I'm not sure you do." She stiffened so visibly that he lifted a palm. "Wait. Before you get your knickers in a twist, just hear me out." He folded his arms against his chest. "I know you love the Plain life. It's full of habits and traditions . . . and even predictability. After meeting your mother, I can see why you'd be drawn to it. But you're missing the best part if you miss out on the faith part." He thumped his chest with his fist. "It's the heart of this Plain life."

She glared at him. "I've never said I don't believe in God."

"But it's one thing to believe in God. It's another thing to give ourselves to God." He pushed himself off the stall wall and took a few steps toward her, an earnest look in his eyes, almost pleading. "At the end of every baptism class, every single one, David's put this question to us—'Are you ready to love God with your whole heart and soul?'"

Izzy pulled her gaze away from him. Those blue, blue eyes of his. They were fixed on her like lasers.

"You really shouldn't be getting baptized tomorrow if you can't say yes to David's question." He waited a long moment, but when she didn't respond, he didn't press her. He turned and strode away, leaving her alone in the quiet of the barn. That was wise.

"Are you ready to love God with your whole heart and soul?"

Izzy kept replaying that question over and over again as she helped Fern with supper and then as she ironed her dress for tomorrow's baptism. A few weeks ago, Luke had asked her a similar question, and it had bothered her, on and off, but like a lot of other things that weren't quite right, she'd pushed it to the back of her mind and tried to forget about it. The fact was, she'd never wanted to face this question head-on. So tonight, as she tossed and turned in bed, she considered it.

Luke was not wrong. She loved the Plain life. She was at home in it, impressed by the simplicity, the priorities, the community, the reverence, the emphasis on humility. She wanted to say yes to Luke's question and mean it. But even she knew she'd left God out of becoming Amish.

There were plenty of times in her life when she wondered if there was a God. The problem was, if that were true, why was she so angry with him?

She thought back to the emotional outburst she'd had in the kitchen yesterday morning. It was *embarrassing*. But it was utterly honest. Why did she have to grow up the way she did? Rejected and abandoned and forgotten. She couldn't understand why God had dealt her such a harsh hand.

Then a thought hit Izzy like a thunderbolt. *Understanding.* She had always sought—no, demanded—understanding from God, made it a condition between them. Maybe that was why she felt so blocked from God. For as long as she could remember, she'd been shaking her fists at God, demanding that he explain himself to her. Blaming him for her troubles and never once thanking him for the good things. And there *had* been good.

Finding Sheila in that graveyard when she was so lost and frightened and alone. Coming across Bob the buggy horse when she did, and how it led to meeting Amos. David. Fern. Living at Windmill Farm. Then Luke, awful, wonderful Luke

. . . he had found her elusive mother. And now she had a sister in Jenny.

Instead of feeling resentful and sulky like she usually did when she thought about God, she felt ashamed. She'd been arrogant. The very quality she'd branded on Luke. The very one. Overwhelmed by feelings of remorse and relief, all mingled together, she burst into tears. Deep inside her came a need to pray, to say something honest to God, from her heart. First time.

Not like this, though. Slipping out of her bed and onto her knees, she wondered how to pray. The Amish mostly did their praying in silence, with chins tucked to chests. Was there a right way to start? A guaranteed way to get God's attention? She didn't know. "Father in Heaven, God of all Glory and Wonders, Creator of the Universe . . ."

She paused. Too much?

"Lord God, Sir." Not enough?

She took a deep breath and tried a third time. "Lord, I need you in my life more than I need understanding. I choose you, Lord. Amen."

Out the window, she saw the proud full moon hanging over the farm. She wasn't sure what time it was, but dawn couldn't be far off. Sleep was not going to come tonight. She grabbed her quilt off the bed and padded softly downstairs and out of the house to sit on the front porch.

In the dark and cold, wrapped up tightly in the quilt, she waited for the sun. Suddenly it emerged, bathing the hillside of Windmill Farm in a golden light, almost as though somebody had flipped a switch. A shaft of light, breaking through the darkness. She felt so thoroughly . . . what was the word? . . . thankful.

Luke wasn't sure why he kept waking before dawn, why he couldn't seem to remain in bed once he was awake, drowsing, dozing, the way he used to. He blamed the raccoon.

Winter was just around the corner. Knowing that, the raccoon had left the barn to find a warmer place. Luke was pretty sure he was gone, because two whole weeks had gone by and he hadn't been woken in the night by Bob's big nose. It irked him that the raccoon was smarter than him about moving on to someplace warm. At night, the barn was cold and so was Luke.

He yawned. Today was his baptism day, and he was ready and eager. The only mar on the day was that he had no family coming to witness the ceremony. He'd written his mother to tell her but didn't mail the letter until a few days ago. His fault, he knew. The letter might not even have arrived. He should've called. In a way, maybe it was good that this would be a private moment for him. A public confession, but private in its own way.

He stretched and sat up, ready to get the day under way. He wondered if Izzy was awake, if she'd thought about what he asked her yesterday. She hadn't come down for supper because of a headache, or so she'd told Fern.

He wasn't sure if it was right or wrong to push her about faith the way he did—probably wrong, but he couldn't get it out of his mind. It was the same way he'd felt when he'd spoken to Alice Smucker. He had to do it.

He knew that Izzy might be furious with him for asking, and their friendship, if you could call it that, might end. He knew that, but he still had to ask. What Izzy thought of him didn't matter. But it did.

He put on his coat and left the barn to go outside to get the clean milk buckets. The sun was just cresting the horizon, bathing the farm in golden light. And there, on the porch, was Izzy, wrapped up in a quilt.

He strode toward the house and stopped at the bottom of the steps. He needed to see her face for only a second to know something important had happened.

"Hi," she said shakily.

"Oh, Izzy," he said. In a moment he was at her side, arms wrapped around her, holding her close. He felt her soften against him and held her as tight as he could without crushing her, for the longest while. The world had shrunken to just the two of them.

Then the rooster started crowing and they separated, each heading to their day's chores. Before she headed into the house, Izzy turned around and gave him a real honest-to-goodness smile, and he felt pleasure spiral through him.

___

In church that morning, after the sermons, the time came for baptism. Izzy's throat began to ache and tears stung her eyes. Tears ran down her face and onto her dress as David asked baptismal questions to the applicants, then as they all knelt. They spilled down her face when Amos, as deacon, poured water three times through David's cupped hands, held over Izzy's head, and said those momentous words: "Upon your faith which you have confessed before God and many witnesses, you are baptized in the name of the Father, the Son, and Holy Ghost."

And then she cried when she saw Luke—awful, wonderful Luke—close his eyes and tuck his chin so reverently to receive the baptism. More tears. When would they run out?

She felt like she'd been crying nonstop since Friday. As if the tears had been collecting deep inside without her knowing it, and couldn't be stopped up any longer. She never used to cry. Not ever.

Fern nudged her arm and handed her a tissue. She tipped her head a bit, to make sure Izzy noticed something. Someone. There, down a long row of benches on the women's side, sat a woman with tears streaming in ribbons down her cheeks. "That's Luke's mother," she whispered.

TWENTY-SEVEN

Autumn ended as quickly as it had begun. Rain started to fall and didn't stop, turning the ground to mud. Today was the first day without steady rain since Luke's baptism, and with winter looming, he knew time was running out for snake hunting.

He waded through the marsh's edge, through the cold muck, gently moving the tall grasses with a big stick, checking on his traps. It amazed him that he'd been looking for a sign of that Massauga rattler whenever he had some time to spare . . . since August. Big Teddy was convinced she was in this swamp, somewhere, and Luke had a gut feeling he was right. Call it crazy, but he felt at times that snake was watching him, waiting. Grinning. A little like the raccoon.

Yeah, that sounded weird, even to him.

As he meandered along, his thoughts drifted to the visit he'd had with his mother last Sunday. It still touched him; she'd traveled all the way from Kentucky to be there for his baptism, all on her own. She was only able to stay for a few days—enough time to check on the Inn at Eagle Hill, and enough time for some good long talks with Luke.

Right before the bus was due to arrive to take her back to Kentucky, she started to cry. "I always knew, Luke. I knew you'd get to this good place."

And then he started to cry, which was embarrassing. But good, though. He hadn't cried in front of his mother since he was a boy.

Luke got to the last trap he'd set and found it empty, like the others. He let out a big, sad sigh. Teddy had warned him that snakes, like bears, went into hibernation during the winter months. The grass was covered with hoar frost in the morning, and the forecast called for a chance of snow this weekend. This snake-hunting venture had to come to an end. He was bummed. This, he had wanted to do for Teddy.

He bent down to pick up the trap to take back home. As he lifted the trap, he heard a strange sound. Under the trap—*his* trap—was a smallish snake. Not as small as a garter, but not as big as some of the water snakes he'd been finding in the marsh.

He watched it, not even daring to take a breath. The snake watched him too. A triangular head, pupils like slits, a coiled body, and then he saw the tail's end. *Rattles.*

Oh boy. Oh boy, oh boy. This was it. This was *her*! This was Teddy's Massauga rattler. He was sure of it. He thought. He hoped.

What to do? How to capture it? He had to capture her for Teddy, but he sure didn't want to get bitten.

He thought back to everything Teddy had told him about this snake. They're extremely secretive—boy, wasn't that the truth—and rarely interact with humans. They're surprisingly docile, he had said. Okay, that was good. That they would prefer to avoid humans whenever possible. Luke felt the same way about rattlesnakes.

Okay, okay. Deep breath. He needed to make a plan before she slipped away. Food. What did they eat? Rodents, Teddy had said. Small prey.

Slowly, slowly, he backed up. A few feet away from the trap, he'd noticed a dead frog floating on the water. He grabbed the frog and pushed it inside the bottle, then carefully moved it toward the snake, with the open door of the bottle facing the snake. Then he waited, and waited, and waited.

Ten minutes passed, then thirty, then more than an hour. His feet had gone numb. He tried to remain as still as he could, eyes fixed on that snake, but he was shivering from the cold, sure he was going to freeze to death before this snake made a move. Maybe snakes didn't even like dead frogs.

She didn't budge. She watched him, though, and flashed her forked tongue once or twice. Just often enough that he knew she was alive.

He tried to figure out Plan B—grab her head, hold her jaw from biting? But he remembered Teddy had said that this rattler was particularly venomous. Plan B sounded like a death ticket.

He moved on to Plan C—grab her and wrap her up in his coat and hope she didn't slither out. That, too, sounded like a potential death ticket—and then her head moved a fraction of an inch toward the frog, as if she'd gotten a whiff of it. Could snakes smell? He didn't even know. She moved another fraction of an inch, then another. Slowly, painfully slow, she slithered into the bottle. Luke closed the flap behind her, his heart pounding like a drum. He had found her! He'd found her for Teddy! He hoped this was her, anyway.

Holding the flap shut, he wrapped a piece of twine around the bottle to keep her in there, and ran as fast as he could through the muck to reach Teddy's carpentry shop. He didn't want to stop or look at the snake. He just ran and prayed, and ran and prayed.

Teddy looked up in surprise as Luke burst through the door of the carpentry shop. Gasping for breath, he held out the bottle and put it on the workbench. "I got her. I found the Massauga rattler. I think I did, anyway."

"No way. There's no possible way you found her." Teddy walked over to the bottle and examined it.

Still panting, Luke said, "Think it could be her? Maybe?"

Teddy didn't respond, didn't even look up. His eyes were glued on the snake in the bottle. The snake peered right back at him with her beady eyes. "Well, I'll be." A wide smile wreathed his face. "It's her all right."

Izzy wasn't at all surprised to hear that Luke had found the Massauga rattlesnake for Teddy Zook. She knew he would find it, sooner or later, if it was in that marsh to be found. That was how Luke was. He didn't give up. She was pretty sure he could figure out how to build a rocket ship to Mars if he put his mind to it.

She'd been wrong about Luke. Maybe not at first, not the way he acted when he arrived at Windmill Farm last May. But he started to change and she had been slow to believe it. She kept her defenses up around him. Finally, she was letting go.

For so long, she'd worn her defense like a skin, protective and impenetrable. Now she felt herself slipping out of it, not in bits, but as a whole piece, like a molted skin, it sat dry and weightless beside her. She thought of Luke again, awful, wonderful Luke, and of his Massauga rattlesnake. Was this how a snake felt when it shed its skin?

Since the weekend of her baptism, Izzy felt as if she'd fallen asleep one person and woken up another. She couldn't remember who she used to be. It was bewildering. It was *wonderful*.

Amos walked through the orchards, looking over each tree, noticing its condition. His heart started racing out of control, something that was happening more and more often, and he sat down under a tree, leaning his back against it. *Not yet, Lord. Just a little more time, please.* There was so much he still had to do, so many things to take care of.

After a few minutes, the rapid beating of his heart settled down and so did his breathing. Slowly, leaning on the tree for support, he rose and straightened the kinks out of his back. He stepped away from the tree trunk to look it up and down. He tied red ribbons around the branches that would need pruning this winter. Bright enough to see, sturdy enough to last until mid-winter, when Luke would climb the ladder to prune.

It was something he'd thought of while helping Fern clean up the greenhouse, getting it ready for winter. Fern always left things in such a way—pots, tools, seeds, notes—so that anyone coming behind her would know just what to do. He thought he should do the same.

Luke found Amos standing at the top of the hill overlooking the orchard, watching the sunset. Huffing from the climb, he exhaled loudly and dramatically. "Whatcha doing?"

"Breathing in crisp, cold air. Basking in the last sunrays for the day. What a moment. What a fine, fine moment." A V-formation of Canada geese scudded across the sky, honking in a way that sounded like rusty nails getting pulled out of dry wood, and Amos lifted his head to watch them.

Luke admired that. Amos was never too busy to miss the gifts of nature. After the geese disappeared behind the ridge, he turned to Amos. "Fern said you were looking for me?"

"David stopped by. Deacon business." He glanced sternly at Luke. "Don't tell anyone else the news."

"What news?"

"Teddy Zook and Alice Smucker want to get married."

Luke already knew. Teddy had confided the news to him after he'd found the Massauga, kind of a reward to him. But Luke could see Amos's delight in having a secret to share and didn't want to steal that from him. "How about that!" A satisfied grin covered Luke's face. How about *that*.

Amos smiled back, pleased, but then his smile faded, and a chill went down Luke's spine. Something else was on his mind and Luke wasn't sure he wanted to know.

"That's not why I asked Fern to send you up the hill. See those red ribbons on that tree? Those are all the branches that need pruning. I'm going to mark each tree for pruning. Come January, when the weather stays cold for a spell, pruning begins. It's critical to do it at the right time, and in the right way."

"Got it. We'll start in January." Amos didn't have to tell him what to do, because he already knew. "You've talked about pruning from the moment the last apple was picked. I've been listening. You don't have to worry. It's only November. We'll get it done, come January."

"It's time to talk about the future." Without meeting Luke's eyes, Amos said, "I don't know how much longer I'm going to be around. My heart, it's failing. My time's coming soon, I know that."

Luke was well aware of Amos's continued decline. He'd been napping more and more in the day, looking grayer, huffing for breath at the slightest exertion, halting every few steps up the driveway.

Luke's vision blurred beneath a wash of unexpected tears and his chest was suddenly choked with feelings—feelings of love and respect and sorrow. He swallowed once, then twice. "Isn't there something that can be done? A new heart?"

"Fern wants me to keep my name on the transplant list, but I'm also sixty-seven years old. Wait. Scratch that. I'm already sixty-eight, she said. I've had my chance. I don't know that it's right to take a heart from someone else. Besides, this heart"—he patted his hand over his chest—"this is the one I want to keep. I don't know if you're aware of this, but the heart pumping away in my chest is a transplant."

"I didn't know."

"It was my son's heart. Menno was his name. I just can't . . . give it up. Not this heart. It's my last tie to him."

Luke ducked his head. Tears were rolling down his cheeks. "How long?" He wiped his face. "How long do you have?"

Amos lifted a shoulder in a shrug. "There are some things that are on God's side of the fence. Dok wants to try some new tests, and she's talked about some new medicines. I don't know. Maybe I will, maybe I won't. One thing I have trust in, I won't be dying a minute too soon and not a minute too late. And for now, I'm still here. So don't start planning my funeral just yet."

"I'm not." He knew Amos was trying to lighten the moment, but those words felt like a solid slap. He couldn't bear the thought of Windmill Farm without Amos. Couldn't bear it. "I don't know what to say."

"Well, I do. There's something I want you to do for me."

"Anything. You name it."

"Fern has a dream. I promised her that I would do it but that she had to give me time to warm up to it. We had to go slow, so that's just what we've done. What I didn't realize was that time was the one thing I couldn't give her. I think I'm going to need to pass this promise on." He put a hand on Luke's shoulder. "I've prayed long and hard about this, and the Lord has shown me that you're the one to do it."

"Amos, you are making me really nervous. What are you talking about?"

"You know how Fern is about children who need homes. What is it you boys call Windmill Farm?"

"You know about that nickname?"

"Of course."

"We call it Fern's Home for Wayward Boys."

Amos chuckled. "Has a nice ring to it. Fern never had any children of her own. There are a few women, like my Fern, who have an unusual capacity to love other people's children. Mattie Riehl, she's another one like Fern."

Luke clasped his hands behind his back and squeezed. Amos always took a long time to get to the point, and he could tell this was going to be a slow rollout. *Patience, Luke.* Something he'd never had in abundance. Maybe that's another gift Amos had given to him—like it or not, he was building a muscle for patience.

"She wants to empty out Lancaster County of foster children."

Luke was so surprised that he couldn't answer for the longest while. He had that frustrating dreamlike confusion of racking his brain for the answer and then forgetting what the question was. There was a question, wasn't there? "What exactly does that mean, to empty out?" Then it dawned on him. "Wait. You mean, get those foster children into Amish homes?"

"That's exactly right. Empty it out."

"All of them?"

"All of them. Lots of siblings. They need to stay together." He lifted a hand and waved it in the air as if he were swishing away a fly. "Empty it all out."

"How? How in the world could I do that?"

"That's what's always stumped me. I don't know. But you're a smart fellow. You can do this, Luke." Amos suddenly looked drained. Fatigued. Worn out. "I'm asking you to do this. For me. After I'm gone."

Again, tears pricked Luke's eyes. He swallowed. "Amos, I . . . don't know how I'm going to get along without you."

Amos smiled. "You'll muddle through. I have faith in you." He put a hand on the back of Luke's neck, the way a father grasped a son. "Will you see it through? Help me fulfill my promise to Fern?"

"I'll take care of it, Amos. I'll take care of everything. Windmill Farm, Fern."

Gently, Amos gave Luke's neck a squeeze. "What about Izzy?"

Luke looked at Amos in surprise. "What about her?"

"How do you feel about her?"

How did he feel about Izzy? Luke hesitated. His feelings about Izzy were complicated. "She's . . . a challenge."

Amos laughed and clapped his hands together. "That's what I thought. Luke, I have a hunch she's the one for you."

The one? *That* one? Luke felt gobsmacked, as jolted as if he'd just gotten a kick in the gut. He felt himself unraveling before Amos. He'd tried so hard to stamp out feelings for Izzy, convinced she felt nothing for him. They'd had a moment together now and then, but mostly, like now, she avoided him. "Amos, you do realize that 99 percent of the time, she can't stand me."

"I do." He grinned. "But there is that 1 percent." He crossed his arms against his chest. "And you are a boy who loves a challenge."

"What makes you so sure Izzy is the one for me?"

"I see how you look at her. Your eyes, they're all for her. Your heart's in your eyes." Amos's gaze swept over the farm. "Ask any man, Luke, and he can tell you the moment he realized when a certain woman would be the one he wanted to spend the rest of his life with. It's the moment you realize she makes you a better man."

Watching the sun drop below the orchard, Luke mulled that thought over. For the first time it dawned on Luke why Izzy always set him off-kilter. That girl made him earn her respect. And he *worked* for it. In that way, she made him a better man.

"You're not the same fellow David dropped off last May. I think Izzy has had a lot to do with that. And you've been good for her too. Even if she won't admit it." Amos coughed a few times. "Izzy's tried hard to keep her heart small and contained and carefully guarded, but God wouldn't leave her be. Thank heavens that he doesn't leave any of us be."

Something shifted into focus for Luke, a vision that had been fuzzy for a very long time. Most of his life, in fact. In his mind's eye, he saw himself striding up the driveway to Windmill Farm, as Izzy was coming out of the kitchen, with a child or two hanging on her apron strings. A little girl who looked like Izzy, a boy who looked like him. The kitchen door's hinges didn't squeak.

In that moment, Luke had a plan for the rest of his life. He wanted to marry Izzy. He wanted to fill a house with children with her. He wanted to see her every single day for the rest of his life. She was the one for him.

Now he just had to convince her that he was the one for her.

After closing the fence behind the sheep, Izzy studied the hillside for a glimpse of Amos. She and Fern and Luke, they were all watching him these days, making sure he didn't need help.

Shielding her eyes from the sun, she let her gaze sweep the farm. The beauty of this place, the deep and abiding peace that existed here, it often overwhelmed her.

Fern came out of the house holding an empty laundry basket. Izzy watched her check the towels hanging on the clothesline for dryness, shake her head and drop the basket, water a potted geranium with a bucket of rainwater, then hurry down the driveway to get the day's mail. She moved from chore to chore like a bumblebee. By contrast, Amos was a slow-moving bear.

When Izzy saw Amos come out of the barn and cross the yard, she whispered a prayer that was becoming her daily plea. *Oh God, please don't take him. Not yet. We need Amos, Lord. Please. A little more time. Amen.*

Izzy was just now learning how to pray and trust God. Praying, she found, wasn't so hard. She had started to have frequent conversations with God. At least, she did the talking. It was the trusting—that was the hard part. Fern called it the important part. That's where faith began.

Watching Amos, she thought of the surprising conversation after supper last night, after Luke had gone to the barn.

Fern and Amos had asked Izzy to join them in the living room for a moment. They sat around the woodstove, cozy in its warmth, and drank peppermint tea from the garden. "We've given your yarn shop some thought," Fern had said. "The buggy shop—that's just the best spot for Luke to start his fix-it shop. The carriage doors of the buggy shop open wide and the driveway leads right up to it. Cars and buggies can come and go easily."

That wasn't the surprising part of the conversation. Izzy had known all that and wasn't sure why Fern felt the need to tell her. She'd assumed the yarn shop idea had been nixed. But then came the surprising part.

"I mentioned your yarn shop idea to Amos." She reached out to pat his hand. "He did a little research on it."

"Starting with Edith Lapp," Amos said. "The town boss." His eyes were crinkling at the corners, like he was trying not to smile.

"Edith thinks there's real potential in a yarn shop," Fern said. "Hand-spun yarn is getting popular, just like you told me. The closest yarn shop is in Lancaster, and they only sell acrylic yarn."

Amos chimed in. "Edith says using acrylic yarn is like eating ice milk instead of ice cream. No comparison, she says."

"And then Amos found out the price of lamb isn't worth much right now. Too many on the market. He's willing to forgo sending the lambs out this year, if you really want to give this yarn shop idea a go."

"Assuming you plan to stay at Windmill Farm, that is," he said, trying to sound gruff.

She looked from Fern to Amos and back to Fern. Were they serious? She blew out a startled breath. "Yes! Oh my soul, yes."

Amos lifted a hand. "Slow down a minute, Izzy. I've been reading up on raising sheep for wool too. Older sheep—their wool starts wearing down, thinning out."

"Like us," Fern said, eyes twinkling.

"Old sheep," Amos said, "they'll still need to be culled. Sold off as mutton."

"Scratch that," Fern added, waving her hand in the air like an eraser. "Not like us."

Old sheep meant Lucy and Ethel. Izzy bit her lip.

"But if you can face that hard reality, then I'm willing to try raising sheep for wool."

Could she? She didn't know how to feel about it, or maybe she just felt two conflicting emotions at the same time— excited and sad. In truth, she almost wanted to cry. But she was Amish now, this was her life. Caring for farm animals required hard choices. "I want to try, Amos. But maybe you could give me a heads-up when you take Lucy and Ethel away. I'd like to go see Jenny that day." Far, far away from the farm.

He smiled. "Fair enough."

"But . . . what about the yarn? I don't think it could hang in the farm stand. Humidity is bad for wool. And then there's the spinning. I could put the spinning wheel in my room—"

"Oh no you don't," Fern said. "Last thing I want in this house are tufts of wool flying everywhere."

"But where would I spin the wool into yarn?" And she hadn't even thought about where it could be dyed yet. That was a piece of this endeavor she had yet to figure out.

Amos and Fern had exchanged a pleased look. "We've already talked to Luke and Teddy about building you a store, close to the road, so buses don't have to come up the drive-way."

A store of her own? A place to belong? Oh my soul.

She tried to seal that moment in her mind for the rest of her life. She studied Fern's narrow face and intelligent eyes, with her gray hair peeping out from beneath her prayer cap. She took in Amos's kind brown eyes and bushy eyebrows, his chin framed with a gray beard. "How do I say thank-you for this? How do I even begin to say thank-you?"

Fern only laughed. "We'd better shear those wiggly wool-lies first, then see if you're still gung ho for a yarn shop."

But Izzy would be. She knew she would be. Her mind had started to spin with ideas. Her heart felt full to bursting, she was so overcome with happiness. It was like a door had opened, spilling light into a long dark hallway. Her future.

All those thoughts circled through her mind as she felt a push at her knees and nearly tumbled over. Lucy and Ethel! They wove around her legs and jolted her back to the pres-ent. She pushed them away—those two!—and watched Fern riffle through the mail down by the big mailbox. It occurred to her that it had been weeks since she'd last bothered to be the first to fetch the mail. No need. She knew exactly where Grace Miller was—still at the rehab clinic. Fourteen days now. David made it clear not to expect anything from her mother for a long while. Much needed to change, David said, and Izzy trusted him on that.

Maybe trust didn't have to be so difficult, after all. David had always acted in Izzy's best interests. If God was good like David Stoltzfus, then maybe she could leave Amos's failing heart up to him.

Oh my soul, she hoped so.

A dusting of snow covered Stoney Ridge in mid-November, the first snowfall of winter. Just a sugarcoating, beautiful to look at. Living in the barn was another story. Luke crossed the yard to the house, morning frost crackling beneath his boots, and stamped his feet at the kitchen door. He walked into the muggy warmth of the kitchen and went straight to the woodstove to warm his hands. He was surprised to find Amos up, alone in the kitchen, sipping coffee at the table. "Amos, the nights are getting mighty cold."

"I've been thinking the same thing."

Luke's eyes lit up. "So can I move into the house?"

"I'll ask Fern to put extra blankets on your cot. Maybe you could insulate the walls with hay, once winter really hits."

Once winter really hit? The night temperatures were already dipping below freezing.

"Can I use the kerosene heater down there?"

"And risk a fire around Bob? Never. A thousand times . . . no."

Luke sighed. "Amos, why can't I just stay in the house?" He pointed to the floor. "Down here. Near the stove."

Amos took another sip of coffee and set the mug down. "Now that I know you've got complicated feelings for Izzy, I can't allow it. Wouldn't be proper."

Luke groaned. He'd stepped into a trap.

That night, as Luke settled in for the night, he had to admit that it really wasn't too bad in the barn. Chilly but not as cold as it had been, now that he had extra quilts piled on him. Fern had left him a knitted woolen hat, too, and even though he felt silly in it, it made a difference. Now the only part of him that was still cold was his nose.

As he shifted and turned on the cot to find a comfortable spot, his mind envisioned another kind of list. A prayer list. He gave thanks to God for the changes he'd observed in Izzy over these last few weeks. Something was different. He could see it in her eyes. A wound had healed.

His thoughts traveled down the mental list. He thanked God for Fern and Amos Lapp, for David Stoltzfus, for their steady and powerful influence on him. For the delicate balance of kindness and firmness that they provided. Just enough pressure to keep moving forward, just enough kindness to give him grace on the journey. Amos had become the father he'd always longed for.

The greatest gift Amos gave Luke was to look beyond the present to see, and plan for, the future. Luke's prayer was that he would live up to—even somewhere close to—Amos's legacy. He yawned once, then twice, and drifted off to sleep.

During the night, from somewhere far away, he woke to a jumble of sounds. He rolled over on his back, confused, fuzzy with sleep, as the world slowly started coming back into focus. He could hear the faint yelps of a dog barking on a neighbor's farm, and the whistle of the cold wind. Then his eyes opened wide when he heard a familiar clip-clop-on-concrete sound. Into the tack room walked Bob the buggy horse. He stood over Luke's cot and let out a snort of hay-breath.

Oh no. No, no, no, no, no. He winced. The raccoon. It was back.

Read an Excerpt from Suzanne's Next

𝒟EACON'S ℱAMILY

NOVEL

STITCHES
IN TIME

$\mathcal{O}$NE

It took a lot to shock Luke Schrock. Generally, he was the one who did the shocking. So on the day that Bishop David Stoltzfus received whispered suggestions from each church member of Stoney Ridge to choose a deacon to replace Amos Lapp, it never once occurred to Luke that his name might be submitted. Never ever crossed his mind. Not once. Why would it? Luke was newly married, only twenty-five years old, and on his best days, he was just now starting to feel like a grown-up.

Yet someone had indeed whispered Luke's name to David as a choice to be deacon. Just *one* person. Who? Who would do such a thing, think such a thought? Surely, his wife, Izzy, wouldn't. When a man drew the lot to become a minister or deacon, it was a lifelong obligation. The poor wives of church ministers took the brunt of their husbands' responsibilities. Year after year, Luke had seen Amos called away from family gatherings for deacon business, and his wife Fern was left to manage alone. No, definitely not his Izzy.

Fern wouldn't have whispered his name, would she? No.

No way. She, more than anyone, knew that Luke wouldn't be any good at deaconing.

What about Fern's niece, Mollie? She was new to Stoney Ridge, stepping in as a much needed schoolteacher. Mollie loved to play practical jokes. Was she playing him for a fool? Sammy might know. His brother, he had a hunch, was sweet on Mollie.

Hank Lapp! It had to be him. He was sitting right in front of Luke with his wild and wispy white hair, blocking the view.

Luke leaned forward and gave Hank a poke in the ribs. "Did you give my name to David?"

Hank jerked like a fish on the line. "WHAT'S THAT, BOY?"

Luke sighed. Hank Lapp had one volume: loud. "Hank, don't say a word. Just nod or shake your head. Do not speak. Just let me know if you were the one who gave my name to David."

Hank turned around to look at Luke, one lazy eye trailing off to the side like it did. "SON, I DID NOT."

Heads turned. Lips pursed. Edith Lapp hushed them from across the room. Hank frowned at Luke and swiveled around to face the front.

Leaning forward, Luke put his hand on Hank's shoulder to whisper, "If you didn't, then who did?"

Hank batted Luke's hand away. "I DON'T HAVE the FOG-GIEST NOTION. But WHOEVER DID SHOULD HAVE HIS HEAD EXAMINED."

Luke heartily agreed. But that didn't help him in the slightest. He was trapped.

He shook off all those troubling thoughts. It really didn't

matter who had whispered his name to David. All that mattered was his complete confidence in God's great wisdom. Certainly, the Lord God knew better than to guide him to draw the lot. He relaxed and dropped his chin to his chest, praying for the poor soul who would open the hymnal and find the piece of paper that would drastically change his life. There were four other choices, all good picks. Any one of them would make a fine deacon.

One hymnal opened. No lot. Second hymnal opened. No lot.

Luke glanced across the barn and caught Izzy's panicked look. He shook his head slightly, to reassure her. Not a chance, he silently mouthed. Third hymnal opened. No lot.

Oh no. Oh Lord, please no. In case you need reminding, I am barely gaining some respectability. In fact, it's only because Izzy finally agreed to marry me that my reputation has improved a little among the church. Please, Lord, not me. Please don't make me do it.

David motioned to both Luke and Teddy Zook to step forward and claim their hymnals. *Lord, pardon my advice giving, but Teddy's the man you want.* Teddy Zook would be an outstanding deacon. In fact, he was the one Luke had nominated to David. Teddy Zook had a big heart, a great reservoir of patience, and an admirable tolerance for difficult people. Luke had none of those qualities.

He let Teddy reach out to pick a hymnal first, praying— pleading—all the while for him to grab the one with the piece of paper in it. Teddy picked up one hymnal, closed his eyes, and then put it down again. He picked up the other one. At that moment, Luke expected Teddy to open the hymnal and find that slim piece of paper, but no. Teddy didn't budge.

Holding the old book against his chest, he waited for Luke to pick up the last hymnal. David cleared his throat, a gentle nudge.

Luke's heart started pounding, so loudly he was sure everyone in the church could hear it. A drumbeat, an audible warning.

A barn swallow darted overhead and disappeared into the rafters. He'd never envied a bird before, but at this moment, he wished he could sprout wings and fly out through the hay door. His eyes shifted to the open barn door. Could he make a break for it? Run for his life? No. That was the old Luke. He was the new and improved Luke. A happily married Luke, who wouldn't dare embarrass his Izzy with such childish behavior. She told him once that she had married him because of his potential. What kind of potential was he showing now? A pathetic lack of potential, that's what kind.

He needed to man up. When he became baptized, he knew this day might come. He sucked in a deep breath, let it out. He should do this. With God's help, he could do this. But he did send one more silent, begging prayer upward. *Not me, Lord. Not me. Don't forget what I promised Amos, Lord, just before he passed. Amos gave me a big project. A huge undertaking. Not me, Lord. Choose Teddy.*

With a shaking hand, Luke reached out for the lone hymnal. He could sense the entire church held bated breath, waiting to see who had drawn the lot. Teddy gave him a solemn nod, and they both opened their hymnals at the same time.

Oh no.

Discussion Questions
for Book Clubs

1. Luke Schrock arrived in Stoney Ridge fresh out of rehab and soon slipped right back to his go-to behavior. "The first step in learning is unlearning," David Stoltzfus said. "It's the casting off of old habits." Have you found that to be true?

2. The benefits of honest confession is a major theme in this story. As David said, "Apologizing and confessing, Luke, it's for you." What about that additional aspect David tacked on—asking each victim how Luke's misdeeds affected him or her? What difference would that make in your life if someone not only apologized with sincerity, but wanted to hear, to truly listen to, how they hurt you? Flip that thought around. Is there someone who's waiting for a sincere apology from you?

3. Did your opinion about Luke change throughout the story? How so? Have you ever seen someone make a complete turnaround?

4. Too many doors opened too easily, Fern said, when a person was assessed on God-given good looks and not on character earned. It was a danger, not a gift, to be unusually attractive. A person didn't develop substance and resources to help them in life. Like a hothouse plant that couldn't survive in the outdoors. Beauty does not always benefit those who possess it. In what way did beauty harm Izzy? What about Luke? How did his good looks create problems for him?

5. The Plain community's lack of emphasis on a person's outer appearance felt like a relief to Izzy. What else appealed to her about the Amish life? Which of those qualities appeal to you, even in a novel?

6. After suffering great harm from her mother, then being raised in multiple foster care homes, Izzy encountered other people who extend grace to her—Amos, David, Fern. How did they positively affect Izzy's life?

7. What essential piece of the Amish life did Izzy overlook?

8. What were your thoughts as Luke challenged Izzy to consider that essential piece before she became baptized? Too much? Not enough?

9. "You block the pain," David said, "and you block everything." What are your thoughts about that remark?

10. Izzy had always sought—no, demanded—understanding from God, made it a condition between them. Maybe that was why she felt so blocked from God. For as long as she could remember, she'd been shaking her fists at God, demanding that he explain himself to her. How does Izzy's flash of insight resonate with you?

11. Fern Lapp and David Stoltzfus had something in common—they both had a tendency to share words of wisdom that influenced the course of others' lives. Have you had a similar person of influence in your life? How have their words affected you?

12. Who was your favorite character? Who was your least favorite?

13. If you were writing this novel, would you have kept Grace Mitchell Miller out of the story? Why or why not? Have you ever had someone keep circling back into your life, even though you wished they'd just . . . stay away? What purpose might there be in this relationship? (By the way, if you're interested in learning more about Grace, read *The Lesson*, book 3 in the Stoney Ridge Seasons series. And you'll read more of Grace's story in the next book in the Deacon's Family series.)

14. The gratitude Izzy felt to Amos, Fern, David, and the Amish church that embraced her was touching. Miracles do happen, she said. *Just look at me.* What about you? When have you seen a miracle unfold in your life? Or . . . if you're waiting for a miracle, what do you think Izzy would say to you as you wait?

15. Both Izzy and Luke had struggles with alcohol addiction, and both were given a chance to start again. Who do you know that is in need of another chance to change?

Acknowledgments

My first draft readers, Lindsey Ross and Tad Fisher, deserve a huge high five for reading this novel before it was, well, readable. In doing so, they provided feedback that helped shape and smooth this story. I don't think I've ever been more grateful for their "flyover" feedback.

Thank you to Ken Brickett, one of my favorite readers, for sharing a Quaker joke that his father used to tell him.

To my amazing Revellians—thank you, thank you, for all you do for me! Andrea Doering, Michele Misiak, Hannah Brinks, Cheryl Van Andel, Karen Steele, Barb Barnes, and many others. Each book gets your special touch.

A nod to the remarkable, all-encompassing Twelve Step Program of Alcoholics Anonymous. What a powerful template AA has given to those who want to live the life God meant them to live.

As always, my readers deserve a shout-out. Thank you for reading my books, and for letting me know too. I love hearing from you!

Finally, my heart is full of gratitude to God for giving me the opportunity to write. Sometimes, I feel like Izzy and have to pinch myself. Is this really happening? Am I really a published author? Miracles do happen! Just look at me.

Suzanne Woods Fisher is an award-winning, bestselling author of more than two dozen novels, including *Phoebe's Light*, *Minding the Light*, the Amish Beginnings series, The Bishop's Family series, and The Inn at Eagle Hill series, as well as nonfiction books about the Amish, including *Amish Peace* and *The Heart of the Amish*. She lives in California. Learn more at www.suzannewoodsfisher.com and follow Suzanne on Twitter @suzannewfisher and Facebook @Suzanne WoodsFisherAuthor.

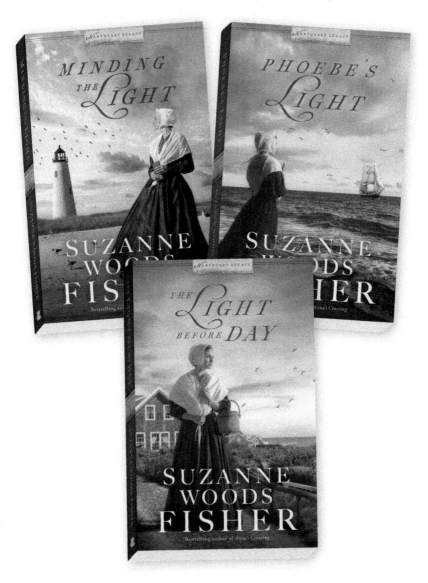

IMMERSE YOURSELF IN THESE HEARTWARMING—AND SURPRISING—TALES OF *young love, forgiveness,* AND *healing.*

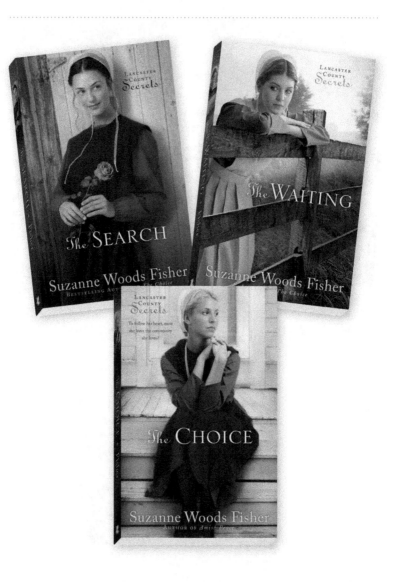

WELCOME TO A PLACE OF UNCONDITIONAL LOVE AND UNEXPECTED BLESSINGS

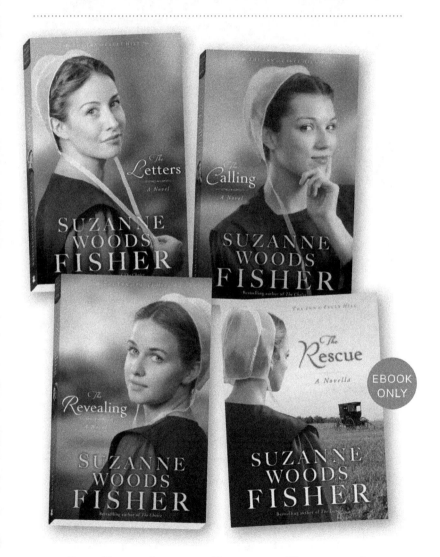

THE INN at EAGLE HILL

MEET SUZANNE
www.SuzanneWoodsFisher.com

Visit
AmishWisdom.com

for More Recipes, Blog Posts, and Information about the Amish.

Also, sign up to receive an
AMISH PROVERB
delivered daily right to your inbox!